BEATRIX LEHMANN

(1903–1979) was born at Bourne End, Buckinghamshire, the third child of R. C. Lehmann, and sister of Rosamond and John Lehmann. She was educated at home and then trained at RADA, making her professional debut in 1924 at the Lyric, Hammersmith, in *The Way of the World*. In the following two years she twice understudied Tallulah Bankhead in long West End runs and went on to gain important experience in *avant garde* theatre with Peter Godfrey at the Gate. But it was in 1929 that Beatrix Lehmann first made her mark: as the fanatical Susie in Sean O'Casey's, *The Silver Tassie*. This led to notable roles in the 1930s, including parts in J. B. Priestley's *Eden End* and *They Walk Alone*. During this period she spent some time in Berlin with her great friend Christopher Isherwood, who dedicated *Good-bye to Berlin* to her.

In 1945 she was the President of Equity, followed (in 1946) by a brief period as director-producer of the Arts Council Midland Theatre Company in Coventry. In 1947 she was invited to Stratford-upon-Avon where she played Portia and Viola, and the Nurse in Peter Brook's production of *Romeo and Juliet*. In a career spanning fifty years, Beatrix Lehmann became known as one of the most strangely individual actresses of her generation, renowned for her ability to create a sinister or brooding impression with little apparent effort. This particular quality also pervades her two novels, *But Wisdom Lingers* and *Rumour of Heaven*, published in 1932 and 1934 respectively.

Whilst Beatrix Lehmann ranked as a tragedienne, she could also turn herself to comedy and is remembered for her role as the landlady in Ben Travers' *A Cuckoo in the Nest*, which she played in 1964 after five years absence from the stage. In later years she also acted in films and on television, working steadily through her seventies until failing health made it impossible. Beatrix Lehmann became ill after opening to excellent reviews in T. S. Eliot's *Family Reunion* and died in London at the age of seventy-six.

RUMOUR
of
HEAVEN

Beatrix Lehmann

WITH A NEW INTRODUCTION BY

GILLIAN TINDALL

PENGUIN BOOKS – VIRAGO PRESS

PENGUIN BOOKS
Viking Penguin Inc., 40 West 23rd Street,
New York, New York 10010, U.S.A.
Penguin Books Ltd, Harmondsworth,
Middlesex, England
Penguin Books Australia Ltd, Ringwood,
Victoria, Australia
Penguin Books Canada Limited, 2801 John Street,
Markham, Ontario, Canada L3R 1B4
Penguin Books (N.Z.) Ltd, 182–190 Wairau Road,
Auckland 10, New Zealand

First published in Great Britain by Methuen & Co. Ltd. 1934
First published in the United States of America by William Morrow and
Company 1934
This edition first published in Great Britain by Virago Press Limited 1987
Published in Penguin Books 1987

Printed in Great Britain
by Cox and Wyman, Reading.

TO
ELSA LANCHESTER LAUGHTON

CONTENTS

INTRODUCTION

BEATRIX LEHMANN, the sister of Rosamond and John Lehmann, died in 1979 after a long and successful career as an actress. It is for this that she is principally remembered. But in that gifted, competitive, literary family—Rosamond one of the best known women writers of her generation, John a writer too and a distinguished editor, while their father R. C. Lehmann was an editor and contributor to *Punch*—it was perhaps natural that Beatrix should turn her mind towards writing also. In the early 1930s, when Rosamond was reaching the first zenith of her popularity, Beatrix published two novels, *But Wisdom Lingers* and *Rumour of Heaven*. The latter book appeared in 1934, two years after Rosamond's *Invitation to the Waltz* and two years before *The Weather in the Streets*. This sequence places it squarely and inevitably in competition with Rosamond's acclaimed works, and it must be admitted right away that no justifiable comparison can be made. Beatrix, though certainly not without talent, was not primarily a writer, and seems indeed to have come to this conclusion herself, for after *Rumour of Heaven* she published no more. It is perhaps not unfair, in this context, to see a fleeting reference to an obscure novel such as *Rumour of Heaven* in Rosamond Lehmann's own great novel about sisterly relations, *The Echoing*

Grove—particularly in view of the fact that, when depicting the younger sister in that book, the author apparently had the physical characteristics of her own younger sister in mind.*

> Dinah ... went to live on her own in a cheap room in Pimlico, wrote a subdued, not very interesting or well-written novel, semi-fantastic, about a deaf girl and a blind man, got it published.

If this seems an over-harsh judgement, it might also be added that, some ten years after Beatrix's effort, Rosamond herself was to publish a novel, *The Ballad and the Source*, which, while not actually semi-fantastic, is in parts poetically unrealistic, and which—like *Rumour of Heaven*—takes as its basic situation a family of children whose mother has gone mad. What hidden element in the Lehmann background should cause both sisters, separately and at different periods, to light on this theme is probably now irrecoverable. (It certainly could not have been Mrs R. C. Lehmann, by all accounts a redoutably down-to-earth figure.) I would not wish to pursue comparison, speculation or identification too far, but merely signal that the literary links between Rosamond and Beatrix Lehmann, while apparently tenuous, nevertheless seem to have been both deep and complex.

There is also the further, more obvious but more superficial link that, by the 1930s, both sisters were

*Gillian Tindall, *Rosamond Lehmann, an Appreciation*, Chatto & Windus, 1985.

moving to some extent in the same literary-artistic circles—a territory described by Rosamond in *The Weather in the Streets* as 'Mayfair Bohemia'. Three characters in *Rumour of Heaven*—Paul, Tony and Theodora—have walked straight out of Mayfair Bohemia, and it must be said that, however timeless and non-metropolitan *Rumour of Heaven* sets out to be, its preoccupations and themes are overwhelmingly those of post-First World War intellectuals. Few novelists, in any period, transcend their own times so effectively as to make their books still intensely readable and relevant fifty years on, and it would be unreasonable to expect Beatrix Lehmann to be one of them. We thus have the curious situation that while Rosamond's best books, written at the same time and patently 'of' their time, yet seem as fresh and true today as when they were first published, Beatrix's read as if they were written an eternity ago, in an era now as remote from us in its preoccupations and perceptions as, say the late Victorian era was from the Lehmann sisters. It is thus, I suggest, that *Rumour of Heaven* should be approached; not as a satisfactory delineation of any truth about life as we perceive truth today, but as an interesting curiosity and period piece. Only then can its qualities, its intensity, its occasional emotional force and its vivid descriptions, be appreciated at their proper worth.

The novel starts with a sustained flashback, an evocation of the (already) lost pre-First World War world in which William Peacock married his dancer and produced three children. There is a powerful fairytale element in this opening which creates its own standard of reality—and unreason. The reader believes in the enchanting but vulnerable world-for-two that the Peacocks create, and in Miranda's mounting strangeness: her wild-creature attempts to conceal her children from the world, her intermittent conviction that 'we are not well hidden' even in the country retreat her husband has established for them all. There is an awful convincingness (never quite equalled later in the novel) about Miranda's forays round the countryside with her brood and the midnight climax when she is found attempting to stuff the screaming youngest child into a rabbit hole. The picture of her mania is deadly and complete:

As that summer had blossomed and overblown, Miranda, like a swallow on the wing, had flashed from sight. She had suddenly become a great philosopher and laughed quite immoderately at everything that happened ('Come wet, come fine,' as Mrs Humble put it). Peal upon peal of happy laughter echoed through the house at night. A lock grated, a cry soared up, breaking into trills of mirth as the nimble dancer's feet came scampering, pursued, always pursued, down the staircase. Mrs Humble, as cunning as a fox, would lock the drawers that housed the cutlery, empty the kettle on the glowing coals and make fast all outer doors. If a child were playing near Mrs Humble stood over it, spreading her apron in a starched wall that muffled the sound of fairy laughter.

When they took Miranda away ... [she] leant out of the

carriage window, and was dragged swiftly back as the horses started, but a second later her head and shoulders had appeared again as perkily as a cuckoo in a clock, and she blew kisses to the house, to the walnut tree, and to William, bowed and broken, by the garden wall.

When the next section opens a good many years— and, it appears, the War—have passed; Miranda has died, incarcerated; William is a mourning recluse; the country retreat (Prince's Acre) is unchanged and so is the indispensable Mrs Humble, but the children are now big. However it gradually becomes apparent that the two younger ones, Hector and Viola, are both defective in unspecified ways, one mentally and the other physically. It is left unclear whether this is the result of their mad mother's mistreatment of them, and the poetic vagueness which surrounds this and other practical aspects of their lives sits rather oddly in a context which is otherwise 'modern' in the self-conscious 1920s and 30s use of the term. Their rural seclusion is invaded by Paul, the principal emissary from Mayfair Bohemia, who rents the classic primitive country cottage nearby in order to escape from the world and write—that equally classic advertisement of moral intent. Paul is presented with an intermittently sardonic eye: he is actually on the run from a failing marriage, or at any rate a coolly independent wife, he yearns to do good to Tony, the latest of a selection of protégés and spongers who haunt his life, he is neurotic and pathetic—yet at the same time the reader can't help feeling that Paul's own nervy, hyper-romantic view of his neighbours at Prince's Acre is invading the texture of the novel and impugning its authenticity.

But Paul himself is a significant and true figure, and in a sense the heart of the book lies in him, for he is a survivor of the War, haunted by the horrors through which he has lived and by the memory of one dead friend in particular, the poet Roger whose biography he means to write. It is almost impossible to over-estimate the long-term effect that the slaughter of the First World War had on British society and hence on the British literary consciousness; *Rumour of Heaven* is simply in the mainstream of its time in being impregnated with the sense of a recent cataclysmic event as yet barely assimilated. (So indeed was Rosamond's celebrated *Dusty Answer*, published a few years earlier.) Paul is the archetypal shattered survivor, laden with survivor-guilt, his life now dominated and deformed by the need to make some grand gesture towards his particular dead:

> He would rather forget; but how now could he destroy that gigantic symbol that he had created? A vulgar, ornate monument to a friendship that had once been a simple, unobtrusive, and tender thing. He was growing to hate that ghost.

The extent of the psychological damage to Paul only gradually becomes apparent—as when, half-way through the book, wandering around at night, he becomes momentarily convinced that he is back again in the trenches, and runs in blind terror from the voices that assail his ears:

When Paul said that his nerves were shot to pieces he only spoke the truth, but what he could not understand was that a person with a shattered nervous system was not acceptable as a mate or companion to people of more equable temperaments and undamaged susceptibilities . . . He and the world had suffered a sea change, not into something rich but certainly into something strange.

Only later again, indeed towards the end of the book, does the off-stage wife, Theodora, appear, explaining much that has not hitherto been clear about Paul. She spirits him off to a more satisfactorily integrated existence in London—and, almost incidentally, finds patrons of art to take the camp Tony off their hands. A rich, free lady *de l'époque*, by Evelyn Waugh out of Ursula Bloom, she is perhaps the weakest element in the book, and yet she does provide the necessary mechanism to bring to a close a story that has been threatening to lose its way in the very nature of the insoluble situations it postulates:

Theodora, in a grey-blue diaphanous *négligé*, was lying on a sofa standing at the foot of the bed and a supper-tray was on the table beside her. Light spilled softly from behind parchment shades, and she lay half in lilac shadow and half in amber light, her dark head turned on the pile of cushions and her sleepy, veiled eyes scrutinizing Tony as he stood with head on one side and his hands folded in front of him at the door.

How are the world of Theodora and Paul and the picturesquely mouldering backwater of Prince's Acre ever to be drawn together into one fictional scheme?

The answer lies in the persona of Max Ralston, a Conradian character who appears in a small boat down in the watery countryside and proves to be the author of a book about a secret island that has long fascinated the lonely William. Peacock takes it for granted that this South Sea Island actually exists (as Max himself maintains) while Paul takes it equally for granted that the whole book is a clever literary hoax. In spite of an eventual, implausible, yet haunting explanation from Max, the readers themselves are uncertain that the island is real: its significance lies in the intersection point it provides between William's sad obsession with finding the ultimate hidden place—('We are not well hidden')—and Paul's need for healing*:

> Quite a few men [Max] had seen just after the War had that bewildered look, as if their minds and actions had no connection—a pathetic effort to 'join in' and play a game that had not been explained to them; going through the actions, trundling along with everybody else; but they lived in another world. In dreams he had seen these stunned, disconnected souls and bodies flocking to his standard to be transported to the island to be healed and comforted ... But they, curiously enough, were the greatest unbelievers of all.

The search for the South Sea Island, or at any rate a satisfactory Mediterranean analogue, was in itself a cliché of the inter-war period, not only of literature but of life. One of the more oblique results of the War, at

---

*A semi-tropical island as a healing place appears in Rosamond Lehmann's after-thought novel *A Seagrape Tree*.

any rate among the class with the leisure and a little money for travel, was a new disgust with England and with northern Europe in general, a desire to repudiate its weather, its food, its Protestant ethic. The Good, Free life was perceived to be located on some distant shore *in the sun*, where social and sexual taboos were less pressing than at home. Somerset Maugham's *The Moon and Sixpence*, published in 1919, set a mood for a whole generation. It is easy to laugh at this now as the origin of the gross mass-tourism of our own era: in the 1920s and 30s the dream was potent and shining-new, not just with hedonism but with moral force. Like the Utopian dreams of other eras, it had overtones of political idealism on the one hand and a back-to-Nature repudiation of all man-made political systems on the other. It is vaguely envisaged by Max Ralston and William Peacock that some Community should be set up on the island but also, in a more general way, it is clear that an exodus to this distant shore is seen as some sort of re-joining the cycle of Nature after many fallow years. The swallows that are building their nests at Prince's Acre early in the story proper, make a heavily symbolic reappearance near the end, as they gather to fly off:

> Away, away, all together—a last turn over the top of the woods, a dive across the river, and there, beneath them, was a chequered landscape. Prince's Acre did not look screened or separate from a bird's-eye view. From that height it was simply an indistinguishable part of the rolling, autumn country.

One more dizzy whirl around the old chimney-stack, one more English gnat, and then—forward! Southward! Southward!

The longest section of the novel is called 'Spring and Seed-time', the next 'Summer Lightening'. The pathetic fallacy imbues the writing, weather and scenery forming one with the characters' own actions. At best, the images are clear, delicate, well-observed:

> The sea has chewed at the coast pastures until they have become a network of dikes and marshes only visited, in the late summer heat, by a few wild ponies strayed from the gnat-infested glades of the forest.

In less happy moments, the description and the general tone come perilously close to that triumphant satire of the same period, Stella Gibbons' *Cold Comfort Farm*, with Clare Peacock in the role of Elphine.

Nevertheless this uneven novel has its moments of sharp delineation, even of original perception. We are shown Paul on a picnic, talking loudly of the beauties of the landscape—behaving indeed a little like Mr Mybug in *Cold Comfort Farm*!:

> They all looked obediently when he cried: 'See those beeches, like the flying buttresses of a cathedral! Oh, the sublime architecture of Nature!' They tried to see as he saw out of an uncomfortable feeling that courtesy was needed, but they felt depressed because of the passing thought, a vague suspicion, that Paul saw nothing.

Or here, belatedly, is Tony described:

Tony had no friends. Occasionally he attached himself to people—watched them with amusement and pleasure, enjoyed their lives quite impersonally, but never got involved or really interested. He quite liked everybody— impartially. He understood them in a way; particularly women—he sympathized with women and knew, better than they did themselves, how women felt about men. But it all passed and left no mark, no yearning or regret.

Elsewhere, in describing the 'might-have-been' rooms that the Peacocks had planned for their children, had life (and the children) turned out differently, the author captures again, fleetingly, the nostalgic, exotic, dream-feeling with which the book opens. Clare likes to steal away to a barn where, under the rafters, is 'the ghost of a room' for her, full of discarded and despoiled objects: 'Miranda's ballet frocks sprang upwards like frosted cabbage leaves when the lid of the trunk had been lifted. Such a musty, bitter-sweet smell lay in the folds of bright garments.'

Best of all, perhaps, are the moments—there are several of them—when we come upon the crippled and imperious Viola, the youngest child, continually reading and re-reading *Wuthering Heights* with passionate identification, her tears raising blisters on the pages, oblivious to other people's dreams:

'The colour of the water inshore,' said Max, gulping down the last mouthful of cold rice-pudding, 'is like mother o' pearl ... There's a haze round the hills sometimes in the evening that looks like smoke; purple, cloudy—looks like part of the sky if you see it when you're coming in from the sea. The only thing one small bit like it is that glowing bloom that hovers over heathered moors in the evening . . .'

Viola pushed back her empty plate and looked up.

'Have you ever been on the moors of the West Riding of Yorkshire?' she asked loudly.

'Yes,' Max answered, turning his head sharply in her direction. 'Yes, indeed I have. Have you?'

'I'm staying there at present,' said Viola carelessly, drawing her book towards her.

The literary genesis of most novels is complex, and the more inexperienced or unsure the author, the more evident the patchwork tends to be. One might guess that Viola and her favourite book represent a scrap of Beatrix Lehmann's own bookish youth—though it is also a fact that she was acting in a play about the Brontës the year before *Rumour of Heaven* was published. Paradoxically, this straightforward stitching-in of *Wuthering Heights*, complete with quotations, works to the advantage of *Rumour of Heaven* in a way a more covert plagarism would not. In such passages, the novel transcends its derivative and confused story-mechanisms and attains an originality and an authenticity that any writer might envy.

Gillian Tindall, London, 1986

PART I
THE DANCER'S CHILDREN

CHAPTER I

QUEEN VICTORIA was on the throne of England when William Peacock married Miranda Mirova.

Miranda, at eighteen, was famous in all the greater European capitals, and in later years old people, snorting critically at the enthusiasm of the younger generation for the Russian Ballet of the nineteen-twenties, murmured dreamily: 'Ah, but *you* never saw The Mirova.' Other memories might fade, but those who had once seen The Mirova dance in the brief years of her success never, never forgot her.

If wisdom were measured by years, William and Miranda were scarcely eligible for the responsibilities of marriage and the exalted position in intellectual London society that they held. Famous men of letters at that time were chiefly bearded veterans, so that William's brilliant criticisms of current letters caused a considerable sensation. For William was twenty, and a week of abstinence from the razor would not show more than a golden down upon his childish cheek. In those days he wore Byronic collars and a black velvet jacket with wine-coloured frogs, and his hair grew in a thatch. At evening parties in his Bayswater house he gave readings to select groups, chiefly female, and his voice (Oh, Willie Peacock's wild-wood notes!) drew tears or sprinkled laughter, according to the theme.

On Sundays in Hyde Park Miranda's basket carriage

3

and cream ponies were the smartest to be seen. Elderly gentlemen took off their hats and envious women stood on chairs to see the lovely creature pass. Women asked each other eagerly: 'What is The Mirova wearing this year?' And the dancer's name was given to styles of hairdressing, shoes, and capes, and even a new design of a pony carriage was called 'La Corbeille Mirova'.

William was given the editorship of a literary quarterly, but when Miranda had to go to fulfil engagements abroad the sub-editor reigned supreme, for, to William, life apart from Miranda was no life at all. In London, Paris, Berlin, Vienna, St. Petersburg, when Miranda Mirova was billed to dance William sat in a box near the stage, his eyes misty with wonder and adoration.

And so they lived for several happy, dream-like years. And then Clare was born, and Miranda never danced again. It was not because her body had suffered from the advent of the baby, for Miranda never lost her breath-taking beauty of form and face; but she no longer wished to dance. And what was stranger still, she might never have been a dancer nor worn a pair of ballet shoes for all the reference she made to her former glory. She developed an aversion to crowds and noise so that William soon ceased to take her to the theatre, and the gay parties in the Bayswater house were discontinued. The ponies and the carriage were sold, and Miranda, ecstatically happy with her baby, seldom left the house.

At first William had disapproved of this incarceration and had taken her for walks in the Park at dusk when they could not be recognized in the fading light. But a carriage bowling past, a dog barking, or any sudden sound would startle Miranda, and if by some evil chance William had not been holding her fast by the arm, she would speed away, fleet-footed as a deer, and with flying coat-tails he would set off in pursuit, along the grassy bank of the Serpentine, up and down the steps, and around the nightmare magnificence of the new Albert Memorial, only to catch up with her when she was exhausted. One such evening when she crouched whimpering and panting for breath in her fashionable furs on the steps of the Memorial, William asked insistently: 'Miranda, what are you afraid of?' She huddled lower and hid her face in her gloved hands.

'Miranda,' he insisted, 'there is nothing to be afraid of when I am always with you.'

She had raised her head, and taking his face between her hands, she gazed at him, wide-eyed, for a moment before whispering softly: 'It is not for myself only. We are not well hidden. We are not well hidden.' And struggling to her feet she would have run off again if he had not spread his arm and cloak above her like a protecting wing and led her home.

To the friends who called to inquire after Miranda William would say she was a little melancholy, and gaze up at the sky as if the English climate were to blame for her sad mood.

Doctors were consulted, and after such incomprehensible phrases as: 'A little effort upon the part of the patient', or 'Self-control during these dark moments', had been murmured into William's anxious ears, he resolved to ask for no further aid.

5

The visits of the doctors had upset Miranda terribly, and for many days afterwards she insisted that William and Clare and Mrs. Humble (Miranda's dresser and maid) should sit with her in a room with doors locked and windows barred. Often in the night she would wake, and William, who had become a light sleeper, would start up and place his arm round her as she sat trembling upon the edge of the bed.

'Hush,' she would whisper close to his ear. 'I hear them, William.'

William bowed his head and strained to hear some foreign sound, something other than the soft tick of the clock on the stairs or the faint, faint rumble of a passing cab.

'Can't you hear?' she would whisper anxiously.

'There's nothing, dearest.'

'There is, there is. Why can't you hear what I do?'

And, looking at her horrified eyes and parted lips, William knew that there was some sound that his less sensitive hearing could never catch.

'Lie down, dearest. You're safe with me.'

Her hand pressed the words back on his lips.

'Hush, hush. Don't make a noise or they'll creep past when I can't hear them.'

Sometimes she would steal softly down the passage with William holding a candle and open the door of the room where the baby in its cot slept beside Mrs. Humble. Miranda moved as lightly as a bird, peering over the high railing of the cot, flitting to the window and trying the catch and back to William at the door.

6

'Safe, all safe,' she would whisper, and follow him quietly back to bed to fall into peaceful sleep.

There were long periods, however, when, except for her abnormal liking for seclusion, Miranda seemed unchanged, and her greatest joy was to care for her baby. Mrs. Humble did all the work of the house, and the two servants that left after Clare's birth were never replaced. Mrs. Humble's title of 'Mrs.' was a courtesy title like that held by cooks and actresses of a past century. She was of a rigid, acid virginity, and her cockney voice cut like the whine of a rusty saw. Miranda filled her horizon, and because of this love anything belonging to Miranda (such as William or Clare) had virtue in her eyes and she cared for them all; vigorous, bad-tempered, and impersonal, thrusting herself between her charges and the outer world.

When Clare was a year old, Hector was born, and William, seeing the joy in Miranda's eyes, decided that motherhood might conquer all the fears. The moments of darkness were certainly more rare, but when they came they were of a terrible intensity. In broad daylight the curtains of every window in the house would be drawn to give Miranda the illusion of sealed safety which she cried for, or she would stay in bed for days at a time saying that her poor feet wanted to run away without her. She would stroke her feet and murmur over them, hushing them as though they were babies, and then tuck them away under her night-gown in a sudden terror, and Mrs. Humble would be ordered to pile the pillows upon them.

She developed a dragging walk and would trail heavily around the house, stopping every now and again to

7

look behind her, puzzled and irritated, searching for the invisible chains that impeded her progress.

When Clare first began to totter unaided about the house Miranda would watch fascinated, and several times she would suddenly break from her own slow, weighted progress and take a few running steps or pirouette. It was after Viola came to reign in the family that Miranda developed a dislike of the four walls of the house. Outdoors the streets and people terrified her, but indoors she cried for light and air. William was in despair, and even Mrs. Humble displayed a certain anxiety.

Clare was the only one of her three children who remembered Miranda, and in later years she could recall her mother's face and a dozen incidents as far back as her third year as though she had seen Miranda but the moment before. There was a certain extravagance in Miranda's movements and gestures that remained in the mind. Her face, her voice, and many of the things she said meant so much more than did the average person's face and voice. Clare always felt that in the time she had spent with her mother she had been on the verge of some great discovery.

The early years of her childhood had been anything but unhappy, for the atmosphere of the house was one of warm, tender affection. If anxieties and passing sadnesses were shared by every member of the household, so were the joys. Nobody had ever thought to treat Miranda as a 'case', so that Clare was never aware of fear even when the house was shuttered and Mrs. Humble and William stole about on tiptoe.

It was not until the end of the last year the family spent in London, shortly after Viola's birth, that Clare noticed a change in William's attitude.

Usually, in the evening, William and Miranda took turns in reading aloud or telling stories to Clare until it was her bedtime, but there had been some complications following Viola's birth, and the doctor had been obliged to call more than once. Miranda had never cared for doctors, and consequently the peaceful evening programme had been interrupted. Clare had not seen her mother for several days, and the bedroom door was closed fast against her. She spent hours playing silently with the other children—a strangely quiet and solemn trio—on the floor of Mrs. Humble's room. Sometimes in the evening William would come for Clare and wrapping her in a quilt would carry her downstairs to sit on his knee whilst he ate his solitary dinner. They seldom spoke, and Clare memorized the look of the dining-room on those silent evenings so that she never forgot it. The unmoving flames of the four candles on the table, the surface of the damask cloth, as shiny as fallen snow, bright silver reflecting many colours in miniature, and the glowing heart in the centre of the port decanter lay before her, and beyond, over the edge of the world, great shadows and impenetrable darkness. Her father's arm was round her, the quilt was tucked snugly under her legs, but she was not happy, for the silence that had once been so safe and so peaceful was quivering with taut nerves; eyes, somewhere, were staring, ears straining to catch some far distant sound. Clare was terribly alone.

9

On one such evening, with no preliminary bang or scuffle, the door had opened suddenly as if a gale had burst upon it and an unclothed figure had leapt to the centre of the table to dance a nimble measure, without so much as upsetting a salt-spoon, before that startled audience of two.

And after that came Prince's Acre.

In the early days of their courtship William and Miranda planned that one day when they had made a great deal of money they would retire, with a large family, to some country scene. A solid house with wide wings and a stable surmounted by a belfry and a moon-faced clock. Rose gardens and orchards and a park with elm-trees and a rookery. Young horses in pastures in summer with the sunlight dappling their coats. Log fires in winter on the hearths. Tall rooms walled with books. Mellow wines, and produce from the home farm. Maids in print frocks to dust and polish at Mrs. Humble's bidding. And several guest rooms with sheets turned down upon ever-welcoming beds.

William's spirit faltered when, after long search for some really hidden spot, he saw the dust, the weeds, the deserted decrepitude of Prince's Acre. But Miranda had seen something more, for she hid in corners, pressed herself crying against the peeling walls, and would not leave. And so they stayed and for a time all fear left her.

In a knickerbocker suit, high boots, and a gentlemanly hat adorned with a pheasant's tail feather, she coasted down the track to the river on a bicycle. All through that spring and summer she ran about the deserted place in a state of wild excitement. She was never tired and never sad; running, pedalling, climbing all over Prince's Acre from sun-up to sun-down, a spirit released from prison and darkness. It was all William could do to persuade her to eat and sleep enough to keep herself alive, but he was comforted by the sight of her flushed cheeks and sparkling eyes from which the shadows seemed to be finally banished.

The children ran or crawled, bare-limbed in the grass. Clare learnt to swim, dog-fashion, splashingly, in the creek beside the hazel copse. Miranda took her children everywhere with her, and they were fascinated by this entrancing adult who seemed so near them in age and understanding.

Viola's first steps were retarded because Miranda never walked when she could run and rather than leave the baby at home she carried her or stuffed all three children into the pram and careered across the broken ground of fields and lanes. Viola sat regally in the pram, her tiny head nodding on her frail neck, and Clare and Hector, their legs dangling between the flying wheels screamed with hysterical mirth.

That summer passed with new sights, new sounds and scents, until the first winter nights with wind and rain and oppressive darkness descended, and Clare lay shuddering in her bed, unable to deafen her ears to Miranda's wailing voice and the patient tread of William's feet as he paced the house all night through with his beloved.

And then clearer than all the rest came a night when Clare heard a patter in the passage, softer than the scurry of a mouse; a candle flickered wanly and her mother's face bent above her. 'Come, darlings, come all of you; we are not well hidden.'

She peeled back the warm bed-clothes and lifted Clare to the floor, then Hector from his neighbouring cot. She stroked their soft cheeks and smoothed their hair with an agitated hand, and gathered the sleeping Viola into her arms.

'Hush,' she had whispered, cautioning them anxiously. 'Step softly, they follow and we are not well hidden."

Down the narrow stair . . . through the unbolted door.

Their sleepy eyes widened and gazed questioningly at her as the frosty air pricked their flesh. They gathered closer to her in the awful darkness and followed trembling, dragged onward by her dynamic urgency. The borders of their white night-gowns brushed a dark path over the dewy grass as they followed to the wood. Viola began to whimper, and as her cries increased their mother started to run and Clare and Hector, grasping the long folds of her flying gown, stumbled after, bruising their bare feet until pain and terror became one and broke in mounting cries from their throats.

William awoke, Mrs. Humble awoke; a lantern swung like a will o' the wisp across the misty fields; hither and thither until it was drawn swiftly forward by Viola's vociferated reluctance to be crammed alive into a rabbit hole and Clare's screams as she struggled to restrain Miranda's frenzied hands.

A babble of voices rose confusedly, the light darted over a tapestry of withered bracken and far above, nearly piercing the sky, gaunt trees leapt upward like flying witches and swung away into darkness.

And then, after a blankness, Clare felt the warmth of blankets around her once more and she lay staring at the pale square of the window safe and solid in the wall and heard Viola's hiccoughing sobs dying away, away down long corridors of sleep.

And so that winter had passed and with it went the children's sheltered nursery life. No more gay excursions with Miranda, or visits to the drawing-room before bed-time to blow a magic breath on William's watch. Except for occasional feverish onslaughts from Mrs. Humble with soapy rags, dry boots, spoonfuls of medicine and orders to go to bed at continually varying hours, the three infants lived the life of wild animals and they became as shy and timid.

Clare, at five years old, was the self-appointed nursery maid. She helped the younger two with tapes and buttons, spoons and forks, and the various obstacles to comfort and health of the young and inexpert. She pushed the pram-ridden Viola about in all kinds of weather, and Hector, on spindly legs, assisted from a lower elevation.

They spent whole days in the woods when spring was approaching until the squirrels, rabbits, pheasants, and pigeons became accustomed to the silent band.

When Clare remembered that time she saw a picture of people perpetually listening. She would ask Mrs. Humble some question and getting no reply she would peer above the kitchen table and see a still hand holding a spoon or fork poised above a dish, and a half-turned face with wide eyes. She would find her father in the passage at dusk, his head bent against the panel of a closed door. At night, Mrs. Humble slept in a bed drawn across the doorway of the night nursery, and on the washstand trembled the flame of a night-light pale inside a china bell; and Clare, often wakeful, knew that the old house, with every creaking board and tattered strip of wallpaper still with attention, was listening. Outside in darkness the tall grasses were rigid, the trees, huddled in shadows, bent forward and the sky came lower, listening—all listening. And Clare, straining wondering ears in the silence, heard only the quiet heart-beat of Prince's Acre pulsing in unison with her own.

As that summer had blossomed and overblown, Miranda, like a swallow on the wing, had flashed from sight. She had suddenly become a great philosopher and laughed quite immoderately at everything that happened ('Come wet, come fine,' as Mrs. Humble put it). Peal upon peal of happy laughter echoed through the house at night. A lock grated, a cry soared up, up, breaking into trills of mirth as the nimble dancer's feet came scampering, pursued, always pursued, down the staircase. Mrs. Humble, as cunning as a fox, would lock the drawers that housed the cutlery, empty the kettle on the glowing coals and make fast all outer doors. If a child was playing near Mrs. Humble stood over it, spreading her apron in a starched wall that muffled the sound of fairy laughter.

When they took Miranda away (Mrs. Humble and an old Santa Claus tricked out in the inter-seasonal mufti of top-hat, frock-coat, and watch-chain) she had laughed with flashing teeth, her light eyes sparkling and her hands

14

fluttering like flames. Clare, hiding behind the front-door, watched the strange procession. Laughing and chattering to her bodyguard Miranda leant out of the carriage window, and was dragged swiftly back as the horses started, but a second later her head and shoulders had appeared again as perkily as a cuckoo in a clock, and she blew kisses to the house, to the walnut tree, and to William, bowed and broken, by the garden wall.

Feeling as if a hole were exposed in her breast, Clare ran for comfort to her kind and found Viola in the yard cutting a tooth on a well-picked mutton bone, and developing a wolfish gleam in the eyes during the process.

Not long after this, William, who now seldom emerged from his study, was away from Prince's Acre for several days. Returning late one windy night, he locked himself into the silent house until a need to share his burden of sorrow made him take a candle and climb the stairs to the children's bedroom. Mrs. Humble needed no longer to guard the door, and she now slept in a room of her own. William tiptoed past the sleeping Viola and Hector to Clare, who lay regarding him from her pillow with bright, welcoming eyes. Neither of them spoke as William lifted her from her warm bed and wrapped her in the quilt. He had meant to speak to her, but when she was on his knee and his arm was round her, they both remembered in a perfect unity of thought another occasion when they had sat thus. For a long time they remained cheek to cheek, silent and very close. The candle fluttered in the draught like a dancer seen a long way off, and Clare, wise beyond her years, knew that Miranda was dead.

CHAPTER II

THE winter always seemed longer at Prince's Acre than in any other part of England. Low skies, and rain falling week after week, month after month. The woods along the boggy margin of the river estuary could not uphold the leaden, rain-charged clouds that tore like worn-out canvas on the tree-tops and hung in scarcely visible wisps blown to the texture of fairy gossamer amongst the lichen-encrusted branches.

The first promise of spring came when the wind, flapping, howling, and driving the sheets of rain, quietened its violence and blew softly, bringing a cloudy Scotch mist that veiled one's face in moisture. Even then a sudden gale along the Channel would withdraw the first promise of the changing season and clasp the countryside a little longer in a barren and icy embrace.

The early spring tides in the estuary flooded the marshes, leaving on their retreat a curving trail of seaweed, drift-wood, and broken reeds rotting in yellow foam-clots along the river-path, the path that all through the summer months would be high and dry, the black mud sun-baked and trampled hard with a fine upper-coat of dust to powder the shoes of picnic parties.

The frost, the rain, and the wind battled over the rotting corpse of the countryside, and one wondered what life could ever spring again from the putrefaction. The sea brought a sharp, salty taste, and in more sheltered corners the air was heavy with the smell of mud and rotten wood. In the orchards the old fruit-trees, hardly able to put forth one leaf, furred over with silvery lichen and moss, looked like submarine plants disclosed by the retreat of a sea.

No sign, no promise, until—sometimes in the first week of April—in a sheltered corner a pale gleam of colour appeared. A strongly sprouting pussy-willow; catkins on the hazel-hedge, chameleon-like, merging themselves in the misty pastel of their background. A sudden sea of primroses breaking through the bracken and flattened brambles, spraying over the moss and sodden wads of beech leaves. On the lip of the ditch, overflowing with its moving burden of rain and spring-water, stood a half-opened blossom on a short stem, so blue that it seemed to break the grey stillness with a sound—a note of music in the dead world.

The birds had some inside knowledge of the resurrection, for in the driving rain they sang full-throated—obstinate optimists with instinctive logic who knew, despite all signs to the contrary, the inevitable sequence of the seasons.

A red squirrel rippled, a warm shadow, across an aerial railway, paused on a barren swaying branch, his balancing tail curved upwards and watched with bright, impersonal gaze the sparkling fall of raindrops to the lane below.

When the weather was beating up for a storm, and the wind moaned through the branches of the walnut-tree, the seagulls came flocking on the wings of the storm to stand sullen and plaintive in the ploughed fields farther inland. Often the cries of the fleeing sea-gulls could be heard before the wind raised its voice, and Clare ran to drive her chickens into the safety of the barn.

There was always at least one pair of boots baking on the rack above the kitchen range, the leather stiff and greyish from incessant soakings; and on the clothes line under the cracked ceiling, like the draggled banners of a conquered army, hung a steamy row of socks and stockings and sometimes a dripping shirt, neck downwards, with the sleeves dropping in mute appeal towards the floor.

The gutters, like streams in spate, overflowed the water-butt and made a miniature lake beside the back door, where little flat-leaved water plants, the fruit of some mysterious seeding, floated in healthy content.

But then a fine summer in England is at its finest over Prince's Acre, for the place is exaggerated in all things. Meadows are greener, the woods denser and the brambles more fruitful—even the thorns seem sharper and glow a rich blood-red on their snaky stems. Rare birds nest unmolested in the silent glades, and the pheasants, strayed from neighbouring preserves, strut beneath the tunnelled undergrowth.

The barren orchards, skeleton memorials of another and fruitful age, have a peculiar character of their own, and many of the trees support the strangling embraces of rambler roses, so that in July when other fruit trees labour with the first swellings of their fruit the Prince's Acre species foam and spout white, pink, and red blossom and fill the air with perfume.

The place takes its title from the old farm-house that stands on the low hill above the river, and the name embraces a dishevelled garden, some fields, a hazel copse, an orchard with a duckless pond, an obsolete ship-building yard, and the remains of a jetty and a pier and, along the broad grass track sloping upward from the river a half-dozen cottages muffled up with ramblers and creeper and roofed with mossy tiles upon which meadow grasses sometimes take root and ruffle in the wind blowing round the battered chimneys.

Prince's Acre is vaguely included in some parish, although, at some time in history when wooden ships had been built and launched down the estuary to be fitted and rigged at some larger port, it must have been a prosperous place and a famous name. But the origin of the name has faded from memory, and the one royal acre has swelled to many more—a triangular piece of country on one side of which the sea rolls up the Solent from the English Channel; on the second side the river flows gently, to and fro with tide and tide; and on the third and northern base-line, bordered by a forest of beech trees, lies all of the rest of England. No crumbling tombstone in a neighbouring churchyard marks the grave of the first lord of Prince's Acre. Forgotten and unblossoming in the dust of faded centuries, the roots of that ancient growth are for ever buried.

Timbered ships have been replaced by ships of steel, and the estuary has silted up into a narrow and dangerous outlet only fit for small sailing vessels and craft drawing little water. The sea has chewed at the coast pastures until they have become a network of dikes and marshes only visited, in late summer heat, by a few wild ponies strayed from the gnat-infested glades of the forest.

The track along the river is a right of way from the marshes through the woods to the nearest village. The orchard and a cottage that it shelters were bought long before the Peacock's advent by Mr. Kay, a farmer who owned a large property farther inland. But after one passing season had shown him that the trees were past their fruit-bearing prime he forgot his morsel of distant land and the cottage remained untenanted and rabbits burrowed amongst the roots of apple- and cherry-trees.

The farm-lands had been tilled, once upon a time, by generation after generation of peasant stock until the male line becoming extinct the place went up for auction and was purchased by a gentleman farmer with lung trouble. For two or three years good crops wilted on the wrong soil (the process being intensified and the *débâcle* accelerated by patent chemicals, manures, and methods learnt from books). Pedigree cattle imported from the high Cotswolds had taken unkindly to the marshes and the dikes and the young man with the faulty lung had spent many a fine harvest afternoon lying under his new Canadian reaper searching for the fault that prevented him from reaping the stunted crop that he had sown. He left for a more kindly clime and Prince's Acre was back in the market.

The old house and garden overflowed with silence, dust, strange weeds, and wild creatures. A glint of sunlight, a spatter of rainfall, a passing of wings from light to darkness, a reflection of sky and a shadow of cloud; a stillness hollowed into chaos and a dream undreamt was Prince's Acre until (in the year nineteen hundred and ten, to be precise) William Peacock with his wife and family came to rest there.

And yet how can one describe this plot of English countryside?

Though one continue to describe it, foot by foot; pastures, orchards, forest, and marshes, it will only seem like some other small, unfrequented country place which you, or you, may know and treasure secretly as your own —a place to go to write a book, to spend a honeymoon, or heal a wounded heart.

Indeed, looking at it from the point of view of earth and sky, weather and vegetation, it is just such a place as you do know of. A triangular piece of country lost between sea-marshes and forest somewhere on the South Coast of England. But it is marked on no map, and it is of no importance to you or I who have other havens as solitary and beautiful. There are places like it where rivers flow past sedgy banks and over sandbars to the Channel. Where screens of beech and hazel shadow deep pastures and old orchards. But first to Miranda, and then to one called Roger, came something else out of the earth and sky of Prince's Acre, something that lay like a light fog upon a mirror's surface, so that reflections were dim and the very harshness of reality and ordinary things became softened and transformed. In their minds perhaps there was a map of Prince's Acre, but they have both gone, and though the breath of their ecstasy still fogs the mirror we can only question their secret through those they left behind.

The World War brought but few changes to Prince's Acre. Mr. Vaux of 'The Load of Hay' (the lop-sided public-house that guarded the entrance to the forest where the rutty lane became a decorous highway) was remembered by his King and country. He was plucked for a short while from this careless and unprofitable business of dispensing inferior beer to the handful of local clients. He returned embittered with his contact with the outside world having left a leg behind him. The aluminium limb with which he had been provided by a grateful nation was discarded for an ash stump fashioned from a local tree.

At that time four of the cottages lost their masters and the discouraged families packed up and went adventuring inland, and their homes, left empty, with the passing of wind and storm became uninhabitable.

The other cottage-dwellers found casual-labour 'over at Kay's' and with the dawn they plodded away, over the rim of silence, and with the twilight they stole home again.

William was exempted from serving on account of his eyesight, but Mrs. Humble took advantage of that time of stress to make one of her periodical announcements that she was leaving. Rearing Miranda's children was a 'thankless task', she said. And: 'The country needs its women and I'm going where I'm happreciated.'

Leaning out of the window on still, thundery afternoons she snorted like an old war-horse scenting battle

22

and swore that she heard the guns in France. But her patriotism never carried her away from Prince's Acre.

.   .   .   .   .

Those years of wind and rain, frost and sun, had painted a deeper colour over the roof of Prince's Acre. The cracks in the beams had widened, and in summer the creepers muffled the windows and swallows kept house beneath the eaves.

Mrs. Humble, who had stayed on, often said:

'I don't know what possess me to bury meself in this god-forsaken 'ole.'

It was not in her nature to admit that her heart was filled with pity, love, and a haunting memory of one who had been to her as sacred as the Queen of Heaven. But unceasingly, when Viola was not so well as usual, when Hector disappeared for days, when Clare bought chickens and was out in every kind of weather, Mrs. Humble trumpeted: 'I don't know what possess me to bury meself in this god-forsaken 'ole.'

Every care and kindness was flavoured by acid remarks in fear that any member of the family might discover that she was 'soft'. When Viola had an attack in the middle of the night and lay gasping for breath Mrs. Humble appeared from her attic fastness long before Clare had had time to call for her and, clad in pink flannelette from chin to heel, lifted the panting child, and as she administered the soothing drops she muttered: 'Your days 'uld be numbered if it weren't for me; not that you'll see a ripe owld age hin spite.'

23

'*Ordinary* children can drive yer wild, but when it comes to an 'ole pack of *hex*-traordinary ones then I arsk meself.'

What she asked herself was not known. She stayed, she grumbled, and she was loved, and she was ignored.

Once William had overheard some desperate plaint and he said:

'But Humble, dear, you must go. We mustn't stand in your way; she wouldn't have liked it, I know.'

And Mrs. Humble whipped her apron over her head and slammed the kitchen door upon her bursting grief.

And so year after year, buried in that solitary place, Mrs. Humble cooked and scolded and the three children preserved their strangely ethereal charm on cold bacon, batter puddings, and such vegetables as the garden yielded.

Life at Prince's Acre ran like the works in a clock that only ticked for a day. Every morning the clock had to be rewound—the wheels turned obediently and busily until the lamps were lit when ever more slowly swung the pendulum until all was silent and a day at Prince's Acre was over. Clare's hand was the one that wound the clock. She lay awake at night in her quiet world and rested from her daily labour of sheltering her brother and sister. When she thought of them, and they were nearly all the time secure in the back of her mind, she knew that they were safe and the world in the triangle which she had made her own was peopled by their frail spirits. But if upon rare occasions some foreign and passing thought possessed her mind she would remember

them again with a spasm of terror. Where had they
wandered in that moment of darkness? What horror
might they not have suffered whilst they were not well
hidden?

Before she slept at night she would raise herself and
gaze down the beam of candle-light to where Viola's
hair sprouted upward in a pale bush from the pillow
which buried her head; and as the flame was blown out
her anxious ears would be reassured by the soft creak
of bed-springs in the room next door as Hector turned
in his sleep. They were there, they were real, warm and
breathing, and if they were real then so was this world
of hers and everything was well. According to Mrs.
Humble, Hector had developed into the most 'hextra-
ordinary' of the whole 'peculiar' bunch. The word
developed might be a slight exaggeration if it were being
used of the ordinary healthy schoolboy. Physically, Hector
had outstripped his years perhaps. He was an abnormally
tall child, and his hair, like the dusty feathers on a sparrow,
grew from dark to fair in a down along his cheekbones.
With other eyes and a well-fitting collar he might have
been likened to an early portrait of the Prince Consort.
But of worldly knowledge and learning Hector had none.
His talents lay in other fields. It was because of him that
in the garden, even in December, there bloomed some
flowers. He planted by the pennyworth irrespective of
the directions on the packet; but he had a way with plants
and small shy animals and if it is true that Miranda had
once charmed hearts from out of steely bosoms with her
dancing, her son, with the same talent, could have made a

25

garden in a desert and charmed the birds out of the trees.

William had taught Clare to read and write and she passed on her learning to Hector and Viola. By the time Hector was twelve he was able to stumble slowly—spelling out the longer words—through the beloved pages of Gilbert White's *Natural History of Selborne*.

Viola had learnt quickly and reading was to her as necessary and simple as breathing and she spent the better part of every day (under the walnut-tree in warm weather, or on the couch in the living-room in cold) deaf to the world around her, deep in the pages of a book picked from William's library through which she was steadily ploughing her way, beginning with the first volume on the top shelf on the north wall. There were two thousand books in William's small study, ranged in shelves from floor to ceiling, stacked in dusty corners, overflowing chairs and tables, and Mrs. Humble sent to replace a volume and bring back the next would mutter: 'You won't never see the hend of the shelf you won't.' ''Er 'Ighness,' Mrs. Humble called Viola, for she had a regal and respect-commanding personality, and her brother and sister, ignoring the missing aspirates, shortened it to 'H.H.' She was the only one amongst those busy people who laboured not at all, for she had been denied her full quota of life; half was warm flesh and blood and half was cold shadow, so that her lack of strength enforced upon her a life of luxurious and queenly ease. Even Mrs. Humble was a little awed by the imperious presence of this child, and she wept regularly on New Year's Day when Her Highness entered the kitchen and shaking her by the hand very graciously wished her a Happy New Year.

If William had ever had any thought of returning to London and a life that had been so full of promise it could only have been a very small and swiftly passing thought. All his hopes and ambitions died a sudden death when Miranda was no longer with him, and the last years of her life had set his feet upon a path from which he had neither the will nor the power to turn. After the first agony had ceased a little he may, for one brief moment, have raised his head in exile and wondered why he remained. Perhaps he feared the struggle, perhaps his gentle, thoughtful eyes had fallen upon his children; but in the end he, like Mrs. Humble, had stayed on. His household never disturbed him. He had taken some pains with the foundations of Clare's rudimentary education, but being at heart a sensitive person with no hint of cruelty in his nature he had made no attempt to do the same for his son. However, when he was severely reprimanded he did his best to conform to methods used by other parents.

It had been the fault of the Vicar of the parish. Bicycling fussily from the neighbouring village that gentleman had come to Prince's Acre one afternoon to investigate a rumour of 'heathen doings' at the farm. The rutty lane unseated him, the duck pond splashed green slime round the bicycle-clips on his trousers, but armed with right and fired with Christianity he reached the sacred quiet of William's study. The result of this invasion had been disastrous. A governess had been imported for Clare and Viola, and Hector, manacled to the Vicar by the latter's God-fearing hand, had been sent to a preparatory school. The governess, a nervous woman with a methodical and unimaginative mind, had left suddenly at the end of three days during which Mrs. Humble had refused either to cook, sweep, or speak; and Hector was labelled 'Empty' (figuratively speaking) and returned to the bosom of his family a quarter of the way through his first term. The shock of this disturbance was felt for some time. Viola ran a temperature and was so imperious that she was quite insupportable, and as for Hector, Mrs. Humble despaired of ever breaking him into house-living again. He spent days and nights in the woods, ran for miles at any sudden sound (such as the tinkle of a bicycle bell) and trembled like a young horse when he was spoken to. He even climbed to the ridge-pole of the roof and sat clasping the chimney in a feverish embrace. But Clare understood her Hector and she once more awakened his interest in her method of arranging twigs and pebbles in the letters of the alphabet. Viola's fever evaporated and she resumed her happy perusal of Darwin's *Origin of Species* at the place where she had been obliged to leave it when an outraged governess had snatched it from her. A spider with an exceptionally malevolent countenance spun an intricate web across the door of William's study. The dust settled once more protectively upon Prince's Acre.

William's exemption from military service during the War had made a great change in him. Perhaps some

long-hidden desire for self-destruction without infringing
the law of his country or causing undue pain to his family
had awakened in him; or perhaps it was only the outcome
of some muddled poetic fancy that he would answer the
call to arms, but his failure distressed William a good
deal and during that period of wholesale destruction of
youth he lost for ever his young man's bearing. His hair,
still long and waving, was grey, his flesh shrunk upon his
bones, and his walk became an old man's springless
shuffle. And now, at forty, he had the appearance of a
saintly monk who had spent a life in fasting and prayer.
Sometimes he would emerge from his study and meander
vaguely in the kitchen-garden with a spade or a barrow-
load of manure; but if it hadn't been for Clare's watchful
eyes the asparagus would have grown into miniature fir-
trees and the lettuces 'bolted' three feet high without
the larder ever being stocked by her absent-minded parent.
William's short-sighted eyes yearning towards far-flung
horizons gazed upon stranger visions.

He had become obsessed by a fantasy of tropical
forests where great trees rising to fantastic heights mingled
with the stars, and exotic blossoms with human faces
were caught and imprisoned in tangled vines. The
distant sound of breaking surf surged like an orchestra,
and every now and again, down long-shadowed glades,
he saw the sea and a long line of breakers rolling in and
rustling up a dazzling strand. He read avidly all that
he could find dealing with tropical forests, desert islands,
lost tribes, or uncharted seas. He made copious notes
upon tropical flora and fauna—he wrote enough to fill

a dozen volumes. His work had no definite purpose, but without this dream of exotic, rich, and static life he could not have existed. So little did it have to do with reality or an ordinary tourist's desire to travel and behold the wonders of the earth that an advertisement in the paper announcing the departure of some liner to the waters of the Amazon or the South Seas barely attracted his attention. His vision was of a place never inhabited or seen by man, of a beauty greater than beauty, and of a peace deeper than peace. He had his spaces of melancholy when the vision would not come, and he sadly considered that the age of romance was dead and the tracts of the earth from pole to pole were all discovered. Poor humanity, it was not well hidden.

He had always been supremely unpractical, and his brain, once brilliantly equipped with abstract ideas and theoretical reasonings, was now entangled in a web of fantasy that seemed a little disproportionate in a person who was no longer slipping through the brief, undamaging phases common to imaginative and extreme youth. But, let it be remembered, William was cut off from the living and he might have done worse had he (as many would have in his circumstances) spent his time, and dulled his senses, by table-tapping, spirit-writing, and unsatisfactory conversations with Miranda across the void.

CHAPTER III

IN the summer of 1917 Roger, a stranger, came to Prince's Acre. On leave from the front for a week he had left London to walk alone across the chequered counties. He had a still face which formed a façade for people to look upon without realizing that behind that broad, peaceful brow lay a miniature world in torment.

Roger was not born to be a soldier.

He walked, searching for some small space of peace outside the rocking world where his spirit might, for one life-restoring moment, close its eyes in safety. Lying in bed at some quiet inn at night he knew not that his body lay relaxed and motionless between uncrumpled sheets and that moonlight flowed across his closed eyelids. For him there was no unconscious passing from minute to minute and from hour to hour. There was a pursuer that always overtook him, and he must be ever ready to wrestle and keep his soul from being torn from his exhausted body like a reluctant root. From the depths of nightmare his tired hand would rise and slowly fall; but a century might pass in that one second before he woke to find his fingers tangled loosely in a flaccid grasp upon the bedclothes.

And then on the sixth day he stepped over the edge of the world into the quiet pool of Prince's Acre, and for a time there was a singing in his ears before his tortured senses fluttered to rest in the sudden hush. Out of the layered shade of the forest he had come, his flesh chilly from its shroud; past the fly-blown windows of 'The Load of Hay', his feet shuffling mechanically along the rutted lane tunnelled over by hazel branches and starred by scented dog-roses; sputtering through the duck pond that at one place submerged the lane, skirting the edge of Mr. Kay's forgotten orchard till he reached the low wall of the garden of Prince's Acre. Trembling, his cold hands cupped over the sun-warmed stone, his knees sagged a little until his thighs pressed against the wall; the silence lapped and rippled up, up over his bent head, and flowed through him until he was filled and still.

The young green and russet leaves of a walnut-tree flecked broken patterns of shadow on his cheek, and slowly, from that deep shaft of silence, tiny sounds detached themselves and the monotonous murmur of bees, the clear, many-noted whistling of a thrush, and a brief flurry of wind through the tasselled grass dissolved and became a part of the silence.

And Roger, submerging, gave himself to the air until it became a solid thing receiving his imprint and holding his image, finer than vapour, thinner than cobweb, invisible and indestructible.

How long he leaned against the wall he could not tell, for time, as a succession of seconds, minutes, hours, no longer existed. Like an unending strand of elastic drawn out from two invisible points it stretched out and out, never ceasing to elongate itself across space. But bit by bit his outward eye reflected, imprisoned, and took note of concrete objects.

In front of him lay a small garden surrounded on three sides by the wall against which he leant. Along its sides rambled a profusion of budding columbines, delphiniums, pinks, pansies, golden-rod, and poppies all tangled and entwined with wild convolvulus and nettles. In the centre was a carpet of deep moss that still showed signs of fresher green where grass had made a lawn. A small garden; the branches of the walnut-tree, spread broken shade across half of it. Straight in front of him on the farther side of the moss carpet was a long, one storied farm-house, a double row of sun-dazzled windows netted by tendrils of creeper and wisteria. To the left a yard; a decayed barn, a mouldering haystack, scattered and shapeless. Beyond the right-hand curve of the wall the ground evidently sloped away so that the foreground was invisible, but in the distance the river curled along the woods that, beyond its farther bank, merged from green to blue, to a misty confusion with the sky. The whole place looked deserted but enchanted in its remoteness, and it seemed to stir and ripple slightly in fluid colours caught in a net of gold gossamer.

Something began to stir, to unfold in the heart and brain of the boy leaning by the wall. A wonder, a mystery detaching itself like the opening petals of a night-blooming lily. Words came silently, music followed after muted—it spouted, rippled out, and flowed through him. And then as he stood folded in quiet ecstasy he saw three creatures on the top of the wall on his right. One after the other, like cats they dropped into the tumbled flowers. A lanky boy with pointed shoulders

33

and ears and the strangest eyes as transparent as sea-water: and two girls; a sturdy child with a defiant poise, and a frailer one with not much more substance than a puff of thistle-down. They parted the flowers that were taller than themselves and were about to scamper on some mysterious errand across the lawn when, all together, they saw Roger. The boy and the smallest girl turned and fled and leapt to the top of the wall, he helping her after him, and with a faint cry they dropped from sight. The third stood her ground bravely for a moment, as if covering the retreat of her companions, and then she stepped slowly backwards, keeping Roger in view until the delphiniums parted round her and swinging gently back hid her from his sight. Peaceful once more Prince's Acre shimmered in its net of gold.

'Some part of me must leave this place,' thought Roger; 'an empty shell must go to be broken and scattered, but in some way I am for ever here, buried in this softer shroud where I have had my vision.'

At evening his dark shadow broke from the wall, turned from where the sun had stained the sky as the rich day bled to death, and entered the dark gateway of the trees. Down the long road glimmering in advancing dusk till, when he came through the barrier of the wood, star-spangled night claimed the sky, mist filled and over-flowed the deep fields and the fragrance of mown hay and flowering bean-fields lay lightly on the air. On, on went his mechanically moving feet until their even fall, the only sound in a sleeping world, became the steady tramp of a million marching men. In the cool palms of his hands he still felt the rough, warm pressure of the wall round Prince's Acre.

. . . . .

But several years were to pass before those others, Paul, Tony, and Max, were to find their different ways, by devious paths, to that same spot from which Miranda had set forth so gaily and Roger so calmly to face their fates. The mortal shape of the last two might have faded from mortal eyes, but who can tell what invisible fabric they may not have left behind to weave its pattern and make this story?

CHAPTER I

THE April day of Clare's seventeenth birthday was fine—really fine—with that translucent clearness that startles one physically; a pause between breath and breath; that still sunshine between rain and rain.

At half-past six she had opened her eyes upon a cold dawn, grey as a shadow cast by the moon; but there was a different flavour to the air and a new note in the voices of the birds which showed that the first real day of Spring was unfolding.

The bedroom that she now shared with Viola was, like all the rooms on that floor, directly under the peak of the roof, and the ceiling sloped down to an angle in the wall that was on a level with her pillow. The window was only thigh-high when one stood up, so that to look at the view—the garden and the topmost branches of Mr. Kay's orchard—one had either to kneel on the floor or to go to bed. Squinting down her nose and along her chest Clare looked into the opaque grey square of the open window. The parted curtains hung like drooping ghosts, colourless and drenched with dew. In full sunlight they would become solid objects of thick green cretonne emblazoned with red and purple birds.

In the neighbouring bed Viola, a little afflicted by her adenoids, snored peacefully in a gentle and unprovocative key. She never stirred until long after Clare had gone about her business, and then she would open her eyes with a look of surprise as if she were going to exclaim upon some strange phenomenon, but just as suddenly changing her mind she would bury her face in the pillow again and sleep deeply for another ten minutes.

Clare kicked back the bedclothes and pattered to the mantelpiece to peer into the face of the clock. It was always half-past six. She woke punctually every morning as the two hands ticked on to the six. She shivered as she washed in cold water and dressed, and then shuffling her bare feet into a pair of muddy shoes she tiptoed out of the room, the untied laces tinkling over the bare boards. Her dog, Sherbet, was waiting in the passage and he rose from his square of private carpet (the only one in the house) and stretched himself first on his front paws and then on his hind paws. He opened his jaws in a wide yawn that ended in a plaintive 'yow', sneezed, shook himself, and trotted after Clare down the stairs.

Advancing directly towards the beholder Sherbet was a bull-terrier of unquestionable lineage, but retreating in an opposite direction his stout white quarters displayed a maze of black spots and patches that commemorated an ancestor's dalliance in Dalmatia. His mother had strayed, much distressed, a few years back, into the yard of Prince's Acre and Clare had made a bed for her in the barn where she was safely delivered of five mottled pups. She brought them up to years, or rather, months, of discretion amd then vanished never to return. Her legacy was a sore embarrassment to Mrs. Humble so that Clare was obliged to find homes for all but Sherbet. Four of the cottages along the green drive to the river were protected now by a bull-terrier or a dalmatian (according to the angle of approach). Some were spotted fore, and some were spotted aft, but nature had not seen fit to clothe even one wholly in virgin white or complete from tip to stern in plummy spots, thereby denying Prince's Acre the possession of two perfect breeds.

Clare and Sherbet found Mrs. Humble already about, opening doors and windows and raking ashes in the fire-place of the sitting-room. Clare exchanged her shoes for a pair of boots and putting on a coat stepped out into the yard with Sherbet at her heels. A cock crew in the dis-tance and another, more faintly, answered it. Strips of light were widening in the sky and a salty smell came softly across the wet field. Clare opened the door of the barn where the hens were roosting—grey, shapeless bundles on the broken racks and mangers. One made a sleepy clucking sound and flopped to the ground. As Clare climbed the fence into the paddock she saw it step-ping cautiously into the yard as if it were very particular about not getting its feet wet.

In the hazel-copse beyond the paddock birds were stirring among the branches, twittering feebly and occa-sionally hopping to another tree and trying a little hesitat-ing song. Here, in the shelter of an old wood-shed, lived Charming, the veteran feathery-footed horse. He was Mr. Kay's property, but as he was past his prime and usefulness he lived in William's pasture where he payed for his lodging by cropping the grass and keeping it from growing to a height that would have demanded a scythe and an expert to wield it.

As Clare pulled open the creaking door Sherbet squatted on his haunches to watch a performance which he knew was inevitable in the day's work. Charming, prostrate in the straw, gazed upon the intruder with a wild and bloodshot eye which belied his gentle nature.

'Up, boy!' shouted Clare. Obediently, Charming heaved and managed to get his legs bent under him.

'Up, boy!' she shouted again, holding his head with a steadying hand. A volcanic heave and Charming was on his feet. Clare seized each feathered hoof in turn and pulled the stiff leg to its fullest extent. It was a labour of love, for without this daily limbering Charming would never have got his rheumatic joints to carry him about the paddock.

Tramping back up the green hill Clare saw that the sun had risen in a clear sky and the last veils of night had melted.

Hector was in the yard stirring a pail full of steaming chicken meal with a wooden spoon. He gripped the pail between the insides of his feet and stirred fiercely. Clare perched on the fence and watched him sympathetically.

'Many happy returns,' he said without glancing up, and added, 'I heard the cuckoo.'

'Fine growing weather,' said Clare, sniffing the air. 'Shall we send for some pansies?'

'Twopence a pot,' Hector answered thoughtfully and then seizing the pail he swung off to the troughs with a flock of hens bustling round his feet.

'Brekfus'! screamed Mrs. Humble from the house, and Clare went indoors and hung up her coat. Two steps at a time she ran up the stairs and poking her head round

the bedroom door whistled a piercing note. Viola rose
from the pillows, raised her eyebrows, parted her lips,
and then collapsed once more into sound sleep.

A little later Viola joined her brother and sister at the
breakfast table in the sitting-room. As she took her place
Mrs. Humble attracted her attention by a sharp cough
and pointed to the calendar which hung on the wall
behind Clare's head. Viola peered at the date and tried
to think. . . . Somebody had got a birthday because
Humble always went on in this way on anniversaries.
'Many happy returns of the day,' said Viola, glancing
from Hector to Clare to see which of them accepted the
wish. Clare smiled and Viola repeated the greeting more
loudly and with greater warmth. Birthdays would never
have been noticed at all if it hadn't been for Mrs. Humble's
reminders in the form of nudges and coughs and an
immensely doughy cake with a pallid veil of icing over
its crusty surface. 'The Lord knows why I should remind
'em of what's better forgot,' she would sometimes mutter
to the kitchen range. 'All born under the full moon as
hanybody could see with their heyes shut.'

'H.H., I heard the cuckoo,' said Hector.

'Good,' answered Viola, graciously accepting the hunk
of bread he offered impaled on a knife.

'I think the warm weather has come to stay; I shall sit
out in the garden.'

Mrs. Humble reared above the coffee cups at the end
of the table.

'If one of yer so much as dares to cast yer woollen
combinations before May is hout . . .'

43

Clare leant forward and patted her chair.

'Sit down, Humble, dear, your coffee's getting cold.'

'There's going to be visitors in these parts,' said Mrs. Humble settling like a ruffled chicken. 'Last night has I was putting the hempty bottle in the 'edge for the milkman what do I see but a van houtside of Mr. Kay's hempty cottage and two young fellers carrying in a bath, a full-length henamel bath, and there was packing-cases and hall sorts.'

Clare stared at her with a startled expression and Viola said: 'Ha, gentry,' between mouthfuls of bread and butter. Hector had drunk his coffee scalding hot and was on his way to the door.

'You'll 'ave to mend yer ways when there's strangers about,' Mrs. Humble called after him. 'No more gallivanting in the horchard stark naked in yer night-shirt hevery time yer 'ear the cottagers' cats caterwauling hafter yer precious nightingales.'

But Hector was out of earshot, running swiftly to the woods. In spite of years of endless reverses Mrs. Humble never tired of preaching a code of conduct which she deemed normal in the best brought up family. She turned to Clare:

'Run hup and see if yer father wants 'is brekfus sent hup to 'im.'

.   .   .   .   .

William waved away a form that spoke to him of strange incomprehensible things, but he smiled to lessen the impatience of his gesture, for the form bore a likeness to his daughter Clare of whom he was very fond. He was not aware that he lay in his bed, that the morning sunshine slanted across the counterpane, and that the third of the candles that he had burnt throughout the past night was still alight and guttering on the table beside him.

Beneath the shelter of a vine with leaves as big as soup plates William gazed beyond the jewelled spangle of surf breaking on the coral reef to the silken bosom of a sail and a dark prow cleaving the water at the entrance of the lagoon never before seen by man.

William was deeply moved. All night he had been reading a book that had only lately been published and established itself as a best seller. He had first seen it advertised in his Sunday paper and some criticisms headed 'Civilization Condemned' and 'Real Estate in Eden' attracted his notice. The reviewers wrote of the book as a fantasy, an amusing, symbolical treatise, an imaginary creation of a new world . . . but one and all rather resentfully pointed out that the writer of the book over-emphasized the truth of the subject whilst it was only too plain that here was a leg-pull in the grand manner and that Mr. Ralston's only fault was in pretending that such a superb fantasy could be anything but fiction.

In studying these reviews and their description of the book in question William found himself becoming so excited, and yet so anxious, that for some weeks he was unable to send for it. Fantasies, symbols, and witty satires were not for William, whose longing had now so far outstripped the bounds of possibility that he no longer derived any satisfaction from a portfolio of Gaugain reproductions and the lyric passages of Hudson's *Green Mansions*. He dreamed that he had read the book—*Come With Me*—and that it was true. A new land, a perfect land, 'undiscovered by man and beast and consequently unspotted by sin' (as a review had quoted). Then he dreamed again and it was all a cruel joke, an obscene lie, and the fear of disappointment kept him from sending for the book. But in the end curiosity got the better of him and *Come with Me* with its magical photographs of sea and land lay between his hands.

He began to read at bedtime and at midnight he had paused, swayed between disbelief and ecstatic, unquestioning acceptance.

He had the physical sensation of being carried away and overwhelmed by the writer's infectious enthusiasm. There were descriptions of many of the little known islands of the Pacific Ocean, strange visions leapt from every page, but they all, in the first part of the book, had the stamp of truth. Then, suddenly, came this other vision, this other island beside which its predecessors were like pieces of cheap glass beside a flawless diamond. William hesitated, shivering, like a bather on the margin of an icy stream. He closed the book, opened it again, breathed deeply in an effort to control the fluttering of his pulse and then he took the plunge, the stream whirled him away to follow Max Ralston to the last chapter.

The shabby walls of the bedroom were gone, the darkness of the damp night gave place to sunshine and clear views as William stood on the deck of the little schooner driven through storm and tempest to the quiet shores of an earthly paradise.

He read it all, and turned back the pages to read again, and hear, and see, as Max Ralston had heard and seen.

The course of the currents was so bewildering and the atmosphere so curious that nobody but Max Ralston with his unerring instinct for locality (even in a waste of water) would ever be able to find the island. He made charts and took soundings and revisited the island during different seasons only to discover that it possessed the pleasantest weather at all times of the year and that things planted at any time yielded, in the least possible time, a crop of abnormal proportions and quality.

William lingered lovingly over the passages describing the sweetness of the climate that made all things grow in fantastic abundance. Of course it was an equatorial region where vegetation enjoyed a very rapid maturity and, by its consequently rapid decay, enriched the earth for new growth. But on this island the state of things was even more satisfactory. The seed of some known fruit planted in that soil germinated at a speed that could be seen by the eye if one watched for only a few hours, and the fruit that was eventually yielded had altered its character into something hitherto unknown and indescribably delectable.

A trader amongst the Solomons being given a specimen of the produce to taste became instantaneously intoxicated and offered to go into partnership to grow and export the new varieties. He had suggested that trade be carried on secretly and no other person shown the difficult passage to the island until enough money had been amassed to lease the island from the British Government who would undoubtedly establish a claim as the discovery had been made by a subject flying the Union Jack. Max Ralston refused the offer and explained his scheme of a self-supporting community of pioneers of a new golden age; upon which the trader had stolen the charts which were only recovered after a brisk battle. The trader had been removed to hospital and Max Ralston sailed for England bearing his tidings of great joy.

William's fingers itched for the trader's throat and he groaned with relief when he read that Max Ralston was safely across the Atlantic. And then he turned once more to the preface, the preface that the reviewers had enjoyed almost more than any other part of what they referred to as an 'entertaining make-believe'. But William thought the sentiments were admirable, for here it was stated that all proceeds of the book would go towards stocks of grain, farm, and building implements and the purchase of such domestic animals as made life pleasanter and, in the beginning of the winter, the author was setting out for his island to live for ever and ever in a climate where man, if he lived according to the dictates of the highest impulses of his spirit, would never grow old. Any person discontented with civilization and desirous of accompanying him and never returning should write, c/o of the Publishers, making a full and honest statement of their reasons for application and their letters would be dealt with in strictest confidence.

Reluctantly William detached his mind from peaceful

prospects of streams, lily laden, flowing to the sea; live coral swaying in rosy terraces beneath the waves; and an advancing ship bearing the happy pilgrims into the last safe harbour left on earth. He turned to the frontispiece of the book and gazed for a long time at the photograph of Max Ralston's schooner, and then he sighed and leant back upon his pillow. For a moment, his fingers stirring delicately, touched the dewy petals of orchids, stroked over fine sand and then he felt the roughness of the blanket; his eyes took in the glimpse of treetops and cloud-flecked sky framed in the window, and the sound of rattling crockery below stairs suddenly filled his ears.

'Oh, Miranda,' he thought, 'if this had only happened years ago we might all have been saved.'

Out in the garden William heard Clare call to her brother and sister and as her voice faded away a look of resignation settled upon his face. It was too late. He must guard the little space of known safety he had found for his unfortunate children and bid farewell to this unknown land where they might not be so happy and where he could not go without them. Then swiftly came the wish to write to Max Ralston, even though the letter might contain but two words: 'I believe.'

4

CHAPTER II

M R. KAY had let his cottage: 'Rosemary' it was called, after Mrs. Kay, who had died of dropsy following twenty years of over-indulgence at 'The Load of Hay'. The tenant had shared the bill for repairs as well as adding many modern improvements. There was no gas or electricity within a radius of ten miles, but a bath was cemented into the scullery floor and the plumber from the nearest village had contrived a fanciful web of pipes through and around the new kitchen boiler. Ridiculous waste of money Mr. Kay thought it, the one time he rattled through the wood from his farm to behold the alterations. What was gained by fixing a pipe and fixing a bath when you could get all the washing and all the warmth you wanted in a large tin pan set before a glowing kitchen range? But the tenant was not bringing his wife with him and, of course, filling the saucer on Saturday night was a female occupation.

But there was no end to the fuss and bother which seemed exaggerated considering that the rent of the cottage was only ten shillings a week.

The tenant had a car and as it was an expensive car it could neither be driven down the spring-cracking lane nor garaged beneath the shelter of an apple-tree as was Mr. Kay's honest Ford. Mr. Vaux offered a shed behind 'The Load of Hay' and it was accepted on condition that a new lock was fixed to the door and that a few rolls of rabbit wire, an old wheel-barrow and Mr. Vaux's aluminium leg (all articles that might scratch the glossy surface on the irreproachable coachwork) should be removed.

The tenant had a small motor yacht. Would the Harbour Master arrange for a safe mooring in the river? Mr. Kay didn't think that there was such a person as a Harbour Master; one of the cottagers lit the lamp at the end of the decrepit pier to keep occasional water traffic from running into it and he also kept the gate locked so that venturesome trippers should not break their legs on the broken boards. The tenant was displeased with this unsatisfactory state of affairs, for he was a person who liked pigeon-holes, filing systems, and up-to-date railway guides and telephone directories.

The tenant had a delicate friend who needed fresh vegetables and certified milk. . . . The wonder of it all was that such a person should contemplate living at 'Rosemary'.

But Paul Millard had a very good reason. So good was it that it ceased to be a reason and became a mission.

.   .   .   .   .

One late afternoon in the April of Clare Peacock's seventeenth year a very young man of almost celestial beauty was sitting on a kitchen chair in the back yard at 'Rosemary'. He was painting another kitchen chair bright green. Around him stood other specimens of his handiwork: a cupboard, a tallboy, and a wooden screen, all painted green or blue and decorated with unfinished patterns of fruit and flowers and ponderous-limbed nude figures.

In the parlour of 'Rosemary' was an older man whose countenance, if it had ever had celestial light, was now marred by a look that seemed to be composed of a mixture of superciliousness and self-disgust. Possibly the arch-angel, after losing caste in Heaven, had a face rather like Paul Millard's. He was nailing up a bookcase and a lock of his dark hair falling over his frowning brow consider-ably obscured his vision.

Tony in the yard, smoothing long green strokes on the bars of the chair, could see his friend's inefficient efforts through the open window.

'Wear a hair net.' He stretched his arms and yawned.

'Getting too dark to see out here.' Tony had a fluting tenor voice and an over-careful enunciation.

Paul sauntered out nursing a hammered thumb and leant against the door. He screwed up his eyes and peered at the sky flushed by the sinking sun. One fire-white star trembled above the orchard, and beyond in the hazel-hedge a bird was trilling up and down a scale of three notes.

'What a place! Roger was right, it *is* peace in chaos. It made him write that one perfect poem—the only one that didn't have the War as its inspiration. Peace, beauty, contemplation; and he wrote it under fire . . . three days later he was dead.'

Tony grunted. He dreaded the dramatic note in Paul's voice when he mentioned Roger. As the latest victim of Paul's philanthropy Tony hoped to get through the summer by grunting (often a sympathetic sound) every time Paul spoke of Roger, for Tony was delicate, impecunious, and willing to suffer a great deal for a bed and good meals. Others had failed: a pianist, an ungrateful little Polish beast, who, Paul said, would play to Theodora for nothing but expected Paul to pay or arrange concerts for him if he wished to hear him. 'I'd done a lot for him,' Paul would explain pathetically. 'He didn't know a soul, and I introduced him to all the right people, and,' he would add darkly, 'I'd have done a lot more if he hadn't been so ungrateful.' There had been the young Italian painter who had lived on the fat of the land in Paul's London flat: Paul's newest and dearest friend for three months, and he had painted a portrait of Theodora that he sold for fifty guineas to an unknown admirer of hers. Snatched it away from under Paul's nose when he would willingly have paid him a little something for it if he hadn't thought all along it was to be a gift in return for free meals. At these times Paul would remember Roger, the only one who had repaid kindness with kindness and friendship with friendship.

Tony, who had never known Roger, often wondered what kind of person he had been . . . either a saint of patience and utterly selfless or else quite impervious to jarring relationships.

But then, let it be remembered, Paul had changed a good deal since the War—since Roger died. There was a portrait of him, painted ten years ago, and it was a beautiful face; calm, sensitive, a visionary brooding over the world from a cloudy height. There was none of that introspective, disappointed heaviness in the eyes in those days. And so one had to take it for granted that he had once been capable of perfect friendship and continue to wonder (for people of Theodora's age could not always make the War an excuse for so much change) why he had lost the capacity. He still yearned for the fellowship of sympathy, but he created such a tangle of reservations and rules that spontaneity was made impossible. It was a method of bribery and corruption. . . . 'You do something for me and I'll do something for you.' And then with his fist held to the victim's nose (figuratively speaking) he called him 'friend'. And such unlikely people that he chose. Adopting young hopefuls in memory of Roger; giving much materially and expecting spiritual return. It was as if the mysterious fount from which spring love, sympathy, and unquestioning tolerance had quite dried up in Paul and he still hoped to win friendship by the offer of money and all worldly things. When these relationships failed, as they always did, nobody could be more bitterly bruised and pained than Paul, for it only served to show him to himself as a person who had lost some power of mind or heart, and the disclosure made him unmerciful in pouring abuse upon the heads of persons who had taken advantage of him.

And so the memory of Roger became an exaggerated thing that was fast obliterating the reality in Paul's mind, and failing a human victim he blamed God. To Roger he had given the best of his mind and all his friendship, and an unjust God had slain Roger who had taken with him to his unmarked grave all that Paul had given him.

Tony glanced up cautiously and saw that Paul was
still brooding upon death and corruption, for with unseeing eyes turned to the western sky he murmured:
'Dead, dead,' and then added briskly as some sound
caught his attention:

> 'The nightingale since set of sun
> Her throbbing music had not done.'

He paused dramatically, sighed and closed his eyes.
Tony contemplated the seat of the chair.

A pierced heart encircled with a wreath of deadly
nightshade should decorate that seat, he thought, and
bent to mix red and blue paint.

Tony had failed to ask for the author of the lines
quoted and Paul drew himself up with an expression of
noble resignation upon his face.

'I shall go and find a farm; your milk has not arrived,'
he said, stretching his arm through the window for his
coat.

'Don't worry, I'd just as soon drink whisky.'

But Paul had wandered off hitching his thin shoulders
into his perfectly tailored coat.

Paul's clothes showed a studied country carelessness.
Tony wore flannel trousers, baggy and worn at the knees,
that were too big for him; they had obviously once
belonged to somebody of broad stature; and his shantung
shirt had been dyed dark green. Tony, in the country,
affected a semi-humorous fancy dress; made-overs, odds
and ends of borrowings from friends male and female—
on a sunny day he sported a floppy straw hat encircled

by a wreath of velvet pansies. But Paul was the victim of his clothes, they utterly submerged his personality in their correctness and their perfection. He had once told his wife, Theodora, that he was at his best in a top-hat, and she had later discovered that because of this he was in equally good spirits at a funeral or at a wedding. Everything he wore or used invested him in a curious semblance of inefficiency and lifelessness. His tennis flannels and his two latest-pattern rackets were far and away superior to his game, and his peaked cap and double-breasted blue yachting jacket made one suspect, in a way impossible of analysis, that he did not know the port from the starboard. It was one of the many petty reasons that made Theodora sometimes seek a life apart from Paul's.

'It is so common of the poor old boy,' she would say, trying vainly to explain to some intimate friend why Paul was impossible. 'And yet he's not a bit common really, he's over-bred in a Jewish sort of way, and of course he's always harping on that as if it were some supreme martyrdom. But you can't divorce a man in this country because his clothes exasperate you or because he makes a Jewish mother (the most beautiful woman that ever walked, my dear!) a reason for suffering unknown wrongs. Thank God he doesn't ride; if I ever saw him in breeches I'd commit adultery in public.'

For Theodora, upon occasions in smart hunting countries, was also seen at her best in a top-hat.

Through the orchard where the branches scarcely showed a bud of green and the slim, crooked trunks

56

lent confidentially to the lane Paul stepped with a fastidiousness that betokened a consciousness of good shoe-leather. At the duck-pond he paused to watch three swallows curving and dipping from shadow to fading light.

> Birth means dying,
> As wings and wind mean flying. . . .

He stopped abruptly, there was nobody near to mark the aptness of the line, but he remained leaning on the wall of Prince's Acre lost for some time in a train of melancholy thoughts.

Beautiful this place might be in a remote, unearthly way, but mixed with this recognition was a feeling of anxiety and discomfort. At the best, that is to say in a large, well-staffed house, Paul did not like country life. He had suffered it often for Theodora's sake, but he seldom spent more than week-ends away from London. He found that it was easier to work in London, and his books of criticisms and his literary biographies had all been written in a room that neither by its height from the street nor by its double-windows was sealed from the noise of traffic speeding down Piccadilly. Crowds made him feel safe, and noise lulled him into peaceful slumbers; the few blue days and the many grey days of a big city were his joy. But he liked to think, and he insisted that others should know, that he was at home in all atmospheres. Throwing out his chest and extending a dramatic arm he would cry to woods and fields: 'How can anybody want to live in a town!' Theodora loved the country. She didn't say much about it, but she always looked more

57

beautiful there. Roger had loved it. That perfect poem showed the depth of his love, and it had been written about this place where, Roger had said, 'something happened to me'.

A bat came flitting down the lane and did a banking turn round Paul's unconscious head. He was remembering Roger's face in the dim light of that filthy, stinking dug-out. . . . He was just back from a week's leave. . . . He had bent over the table, scribbling the outline of a map on the back of an old envelope. 'Here's the main road . . . there's a big town.' (He had printed its name carefully.) 'And another big town . . . and then a village. You walk and walk (if you're me) or you drive and drive (if you're you) till you come to the forest.' (A black fuzz had been scribbled on the envelope.) 'Here's a pub, don't know its name, but its got a crooked hat and a dirty face . . . if you're you, you'll have to get out and walk there because there's no more road, but if you're lucky it will be no effort—you'll float through the air.' Roger had laughed as he pushed the envelope across to Paul. 'You go and float around there some day my lad, you'll like it. I wouldn't like anybody else to find it, but I leave it to you in my will, just in case I predecease you.'

Paul remembered that all this had rather bored him and he had inquired of London and theatres and people.

'Search me,' Roger had answered with a shout of laughter and bending, silhouetted in the dim doorway, he had called 'Good night,' and gone.

The bat nearly struck Paul in the face and he ducked his head. He always felt a bit sick when he remembered

Roger calling 'good night', for he hadn't answered him. Annoyed and upset about something . . . probably minded not hearing about London. Anyway he hadn't answered and he could never forgive himself (Oh, to live that one minute over again!) for Roger had been killed that 'good night'. Again and again, at the strangest moments—sometimes when he was happiest, at a party, in the midst of work, when his whole brain was concentrated on some pleasant task, or just before he fell asleep—the hours of that departed night were lived again. Those long, long hours of waiting, every cry stabbing the darkness holding some ghoulish likeness to Roger's voice. . . . Listening, waiting, hope dying slowly, in agony. . . . The murmuring of the old soldier crouched at his side . . . the bitter comfort of his rough advice. . . . The empty, shattered dawn. . . .

There had been a great many poems, all war poems, written on leaves and in hospital the first time Roger had been hit; but the one found amongst his kit, the only one actually written under fire, was a poem of the country, this country, and it was a peaceful lyric of melting loveliness. They were going to publish his poems now, and Paul, of course, was asked to do the editing and write a life. It had got to be done anyway, but it ought to be done in the place Roger had spoken of—the place where you float through the air.

'I wish there'd been a decent habitation,' thought Paul, leaning on the wall.

He shivered and looked around him. It had grown nearly dark whilst he lingered; outlines were blurred and mist was rising. He was a little exasperated with himself for the romantic, sentimental emotion that had caused him to announce that Roger's life should be written at Prince's Acre. He had taken a good deal of trouble; following that silly, inaccurate map, discovering the name of the place and then in a very passion of sentiment taking the lease of that cottage. The exasperation was doubled by the fact that he could not admit that he didn't want to be romantic in Roger's terrestrial paradise, writing about Roger who was dead. . . . Did he want to write about Roger at all?

Of course Roger had been one in a million, one in a life-time, never to be found again; but he'd talked about Roger until his real character had become confused truth and fiction; and he'd hurled Roger at people until there was nothing of Roger left.

Remember him, remember him; photographically, yes, there was a picture of the stocky, big-headed, calm young man who had been his friend. But where was the stabbing, blinding pain, the devastating sense of loss that that picture had once called up? For so long after his death the gulf had been bridged by a longing for his company, a longing that sometimes made him live again —the miracle of resurrection was performed by one whose misery and longing were too great to be borne without some sign. . . . But now—a picture, a loyal effort to recapture even that unhappy emotion of deprivation and (as he flung up his head impatiently) Paul saw the fiery star piercing the lacy ceiling of a walnut-tree.

Theodora must guess (for she sometimes had peculiar

intuitions about him) that he couldn't write about Roger
—not about that ghost, transformed into a thing that
haunted now, a symbol, a pathetic memorial to be endlessly exhibited to unsympathetic people: this was Roger.
This was Paul—you see now what he once was?

He would rather forget; but how now could he destroy
that gigantic symbol that he had created? A vulgar,
ornate monument to a friendship that had once been a
simple, unobtrusive, and tender thing. He was growing
to hate that ghost.

> I have a friend in ghostland—
> Early found, ah me, how early lost!—

Paul smiled, feeling better. He never quite reached the
farthest depth of melancholy nowadays; remembering
some happily pointed lines always saved him. It wrapped
the whole emotion up in a neat parcel that could be dis-
patched at once. Good old Christina . . . it must be
the country scenes that made her poetry come so trippingly
on his tongue. What was the last verse of that fragment?

> If I wake he hunts me like a nightmare:
> I feel my hair stand up, my body creep:
> Without light I see a blasting sight there,
> See a secret I must keep.

That wasn't so fortunate. Paul wished he hadn't attempted that verse and he frowned into the shadows and
suddenly noticed the long, dark shape of a house looming
before him. To the left was a barn and an irregular
outline that might be a haystack. Funny, he hadn't
noticed it before. He could have sworn it hadn't been

there a minute ago. . . . Suddenly spirited up from nowhere to remind him that he was out to buy a pint of milk. No light shone from the front windows and so he circled the garden wall in search of the back door, and there, on the farther side of the house, beside a rainwater-butt, was a door, wide open, and two windows filled with lamp-light. He knocked and stood waiting on the step looking at the dipping field and the misty line of marsh and woods underlined by a pale glint of water where the river ran. There were no answer to his repeated knocking and no sign of life in the dark tunnel of the passage, so he stepped to the nearest window and pressed his face against the pane. In one instant he felt as though he had been whirled through space into another life. There was something peculiarly foreign about the room and its occupants sitting there so quietly; poised and still, as if they composed a pattern of a picture rather than of a live reality. Paul had the impression that the whole thing might fade from sight at any moment, leaving him peering into the dark window of an empty, unlit room.

A ship's lantern hung from the low ceiling on a chain and illumined the faces of two girls and a boy who were gathered around a big table set with tea-things. The boy was on the farther side of the table, crouched on a chair and staring straight through the window at Paul without a flicker of expression on his pale face. Beside him in an arm-chair was a child bending over an enormous leather-bound book. She looked deformed, so bent was she over the page, her fair hair falling over her hunched shoulders and her tiny old-young face close to the page.

At the other end of the table, her shoulder turned to the watcher at the window and her dark head bent over some sewing, was another girl. Her hands were still on the sewing. They all seemed to be waiting and listening. Slowly the dark head turned to the window where Paul's forehead was pressed against the pane and he saw her lips part in a soft exclamation. She turned and said something to the boy who nodded once and continued to stare straight before him. Paul drew back quickly and prepared for flight when out of the shadows he saw advancing a little old woman in black and carrying in each hand a pail of water.

'Good evening,' he said. 'Have you got any milk?'

'Ain't got no cows,' she answered coming to a standstill before him.

Paul felt comforted by the familiar accent of the London streets.

'I *could* let you 'ave 'arf a pint. We've more'n we can use to-night or to-morrer morning.'

'If you can really spare it,' he said politely, and stood aside to let her pass into the house.

'Come along in,' she called over her shoulder, and he followed her down the dark passage to the doorway of the lamp-lit room.

'Gent wants 'arf a pint 'o milk,' said the old woman to the three silent creatures who turned to stare at Paul.

'I'm frightfully sorry to disturb you. I don't know my way about this part of the world, and I thought this might be a dairy farm,' he explained.

The strange, pale-haired girl placed a thin finger on

63

the page to mark her place in the book and nodded at him and said in a startlingly loud, powerful voice:

'We understand. You may sit down.'

Paul collapsed into a battered chair by the door and began to feel that he was a servant waiting to be interviewed about a situation. They all stared at him, and he found the silence quite acutely painful. Paul had no mean reputation for charm of manner and grace of speech. At ill-assorted parties he could weld discordant elements into a smooth, well-ordered harmony—even Theodora admitted his social assets. Under the battery of these watchful eyes he writhed inwardly as he sat tongue-tied by the door.

The old woman, bearing a blue jug, came bustling back from the adjoining room. Paul, like a hound unleashed, sprang to his feet and started to fumble in his pocket for change.

'Oh, no!' exclaimed the child with the book, and the dark girl blushed the colour of a peony.

'But you must let me pay for it,' he begged.

The dark girl rose and came to his side.

'We'd much rather not,' she said in a tone that made him feel she was asking a great favour.

'I'm frightfully grateful,' he murmured backing out of the room and clutching the jug. He had an uncomfortable sensation that though nobody had touched him he was being hustled out of the room—his absence was so urgently required that it was almost a physical sensation of invisible fingers pushing and prodding against his chest.

64

'Don't cher forget to bring back that there jug,' shouted the old woman.

The dark girl was by his side, silent and insistent, courteously showing him off the premises.

'Please don't bother, I know my way,' he said.

She made no reply and it was now almost too dark, with the swift-running nightfall of early spring, for him to see her face. But he was very much aware of her and of the electric urgency with which she was speeding him upon his way. He was troubled by the need to classify her and her companions and by so doing calm the little ruffle of annoyance this encounter had caused him. It was impossible to put them down and dismiss them as an ordinary farmer's family or servants. That pale crippled child with the deep voice and cultured accent. The half-wit boy with the old-fashioned side-whiskers sprouting in their first down upon his cheek; the colourless eyes that stared unwinking without a trace of insolence. And this girl stepping lightly by his side. . . . The face that she had lifted to him in the lamp-light had been the face of a child, smooth of cheek and with clear dark eyes above which her eyebrows arched upward like the wings of a bird about to take flight. It was instinctive in him to take in the lines of any woman's figure on the instant that his eyes fell upon her: the curves of breast and thigh, the length of throat and limbs. It was a coldly critical glance that left him in a moment with a well-balanced verdict—solemnly ignoring, or coolly satisfied. In spite of an ill-fitting cotton frock he had noticed this girl's body beneath the clumsy material, and the ripe,

5

animal grace with which she moved. She had come to him in the room with a movement that had a curious and quite unconscious abandon. He had drawn back when, without touching him, she had seemed to press against him and the recoil had been one of excitement and it had bewildered him. It was then that he had felt her antagonism thrusting him out.

As they circled the house he spoke again :

'I've taken Kay's cottage; do you know it?'

'Oh, yes, I've lived here a great many years,' she answered, her hushed, musical voice taking a tone of gentle reproach.

At the broken gate leading to the lane she stopped and murmuring a hurried 'good night' she left him before he could speak. As he turned homeward he heard the pat-pat of her feet running rapidly across the yard, the distant bang of a slammed door, and then silence.

Paul trudged along in the dark and began at once to form a plan of campaign in which this girl's mysterious antagonism should be changed to a more normal reaction of liking. He couldn't bear to be disliked; it mattered terribly, always. He would go to extraordinary lengths to persuade quite unimportant people to react in his favour. Presents, invitations, compliments showered upon some person whose slight disregard of him had made him feel a blast of hostility was being directed against him. Even Theodora, who once upon a time had loved him quite unreservedly, had moments of cold dislike that had to be dispelled with gifts and praise of her looks out of all proportion to her merits. The pity of it was that that

method no longer worked with Theodora. She used hard
words and murmured of 'bribery' and 'kept women' and
'lack of understanding'. It made him, in her presence,
shrug his shoulders and say bitter things, hurling at her
(every word perfectly remembered) phrases of tenderness,
love, and even sacred, passionate things (which should
never have been repeated) which she had once told him
in the early days of their marriage. But then Theodora
was incomprehensible; sometimes tender with a cherish-
ing sweetness as if her heart were breaking for him and
then suddenly exasperated, dissatisfied, shrinking from
him and, after a burst of bitter quarrelling, away for
months, refusing to see him.

But this girl at the farm had no reason, no right, to
dislike him at first sight. To pin a person down with an
arrow of hate the minute you met him—no, that couldn't
be. He'd take the jug back . . . he'd see her again . . .
often, they were neighbours. . . . Love thy neighbour!
Grasping the milk jug, stumbling on the ruts, he reached
the orchard where he cannoned into an apple-tree and a
little milk was spilt.

.   .   .   .   .

Tony had carried the half-painted furniture into the
parlour and it was grouped untidily in the middle of the
floor. He lay on an old sofa by the open window, his
thin limbs so uncomfortably arranged that he looked like
a jointless rag doll discarded by a careless owner. A
candle was lit, a book lay open, but with head
twisted sideways, leg twined round leg and one arm

67

trailing to the floor Tony slept in perfect peace and comfort.

Sometimes at parties ladies going to retrieve their evening-cloaks would discover beneath the heaps of ermine, brocade and velvet, this contortionist figure slumbering peacefully. He would smile when roused, straighten his tie and smooth his hair and murmuring: 'Oh, what a lovely sleep!' he would straightway close his eyes again unless ejected into the night air and obliged to seek his own less comfortable couch. The only vitality that he expended was in the bursts of creative frenzy that at rare intervals caused him to paint. At other times he lay in shade or sun upon other people's sofas, beds, and lawns, a semi-moribund, but not un-decorative figure. But there were strange rumours about Tony; a story of a twenty-mile walk (when all others had fallen by the wayside) in August upon a burning road in Greece; and the report of an eye-witness who had beheld this frail creature dive from Westminster pier one night because his old clothes were 'only fit for the wash-tub'.

Paul had seen some canvases in the disorderly studio where Tony lodged when not adopted, and he had decided, as was his way, that this genius should have his course steered by an able hand and his destiny hewn in grand proportions if all rules and regulations were observed. And so it had fallen to Tony's lot to squire the knight in search of Eldorado.

Theodora had taken herself off in a huff to the shores of the Mediterranean, and Paul, grass-widowed for the twentieth time in the three years of his married life, had to have company and the companion would benefit if he fulfilled his simple obligations of being sympathetic, attentive, grateful, and, of course, companionable. Tony had had a qualm that the Lord might not provide for the coming year so that the unexpected offer of a roof and leisure in which to fill a few canvases seemed enough of an inducement. Paul was all right, particularly if one slept the better part of every day and stored up energy enough to cope sympathetically and patiently with a person who missed his wife without admitting it, lost his temper without reason, and expected saint-like tolerance on the excuse that his nerves had been all shot to pieces in the War and that the world was not the place it used to be.

Paul would provide and, everything working according to plan, Paul, also, would reward.

Stranded on his sofa amidst a welter of furniture, packing-cases, canvases, and bundles of blankets, Tony slumbered on unaware of chaos around him and gave the appearance of one who had lived in the room for years, the victim of a slovenly housekeeper. The shadows heaped in the corners and the light from the candle-flame rippled a quivering yellow petal to and fro across the low ceiling. The draught through the open window blew a scent of cool earth and ripening grass round Tony's unconscious head. A branch cracked in the orchard, a passing wind lifted the fresh leaves of the creeper and let them fall again and reassemble with a soft patter against the wall.

Tony untwined a leg, lifted a trailing hand to an easier position on his chest and opened his unclouded eyes. He sniffed the air, smiled, yawned, and no thought disturbed his cradled mind until Paul, like the first man appearing in Eden, destroyed a world created perfectly before humanity had been planted there to mar its beauty and destroy the harmony of all unthinking things.

'I've had an adventure,' said Paul, putting down the jug and fingering the mantelpiece for a cigarette.

'No danger I hope,' murmured Tony, smiling at the ceiling where the shadow of Paul's head bending over the candle-flame spread and then contracted in a fascinating semblance of a huge umbrella being opened and closed.

'I looked through the window of a house that sprang up before me on enchanted ground and saw an elf, a gnome, and a fairy sitting by a table loaded with honey-dew and forbidden fruit.' He paused in the fabrication of nonsense and chuckled as he remembered a gigantic cottage loaf, a hacked plum cake and a homely brown tea-pot.

'I turned to run and there, at my elbow, stood a witch who said in cockney: "Ain't got no cows." She spirited me into the house and the gnome turned out to be Queen Victoria resurrected and incog. She said: "We understand. You may sit down." The elf was over-grown and a bit batty and he didn't speak. The fairy tried to bring herself to my level and led me safely out of the hallowed circle; but just as I was about to shake her hand she was snapped back into the house as if she'd been fastened to the table leg by a length of elastic. And then I found myself wandering in the lane with a blue milk jug in my hand.'

'Perhaps we'd better not drink the milk,' said Tony. 'We might come over queer or grow cloven hooves.'

'The fairy would make a very presentable human being,' Paul murmured thoughtfully.

'That was probably the family of Peacock that live up the lane at a farm called Prince's Acre.' Tony was sleepy but rather smug.

'How do you know?' asked Paul suspiciously.

'I exchanged amenities with the landlord of "The Load of Hay" this morning while you were putting the car away.'

'You're an inveterate gossip.'

'I delight in it, it's my only emotional outlet. Mr. Vaux (pronounced with the accent on the x he'd have us know) told me that Mr. Peacock was a literary gent and that his wife was a dancer and she was odd, and then more than odd until death during detention spared Vaux's eyes the unfortunate sight of her dancing naked by moonlight outside his respectable pub.'

'Vaux appears to have a light and breezy manner of relating tragedy.' Paul was thinking hard. . . . 'Peacock. . . . Literary gent. . . . Where, when had he heard that name?'

'Yes,' said Tony, closing his eyes again. 'He's a fellow with an evil eye and a malicious tongue and I delight in him.' He twined one leg around the other and his breathing became deep and regular.

For an hour Paul banged furniture about in his cottage by the light of a candle.

'Peacock? Literary gent?' he muttered once or twice and then let out an oath as his hands stuck to the paint on one of Tony's chairs.

'Waste of paint on these twopenny-ha'penny chairs, and nothing to sit down on——' he began, but mumbled to silence as his eye fell upon the corpse-like figure on the sofa. An effigy on a tomb. An effigy—the chiselled order of whose limbs had been cruelly disrupted by some vandal hand.

Frowning and dishevelled Paul struggled with a packing-case of books.

Nothing would get done till the invaluable Jackson came up the river in the morning with the *Theodora*. . . . He ought to have arranged for Jackson to get here a day earlier. . . . The place was unlivable. . . . The car needed washing. . . . Tony was no bloody use—a half-man. . . . Roger could turn his hand to anything . . . that breed was exterminated . . . Jackson could wrench off this lid with a hammer . . . must have a book though; no chance of sleep in this eerie hovel. . . .

Paul wrenched off a slat of the lid with his hands.

'I'm hungry,' said Tony, opening eyes of innocence. Oh, lovely place. . . . Sleepy, then hungry; no time, no feverish rushing. . . . Flow on deep tide of bliss. . . .

'No—cook—until—to-morrow,' Paul gasped, wrestling with another slat.

'We shall have to dine on fish-paste and cocoa, like actresses.' Tony wandered into the tiny kitchen and sang in a mock falsetto voice as he rooted amongst a pile of parcels.

'When summer comes again. . . .' He trilled as he lit the oil-stove.

'Where are the biscuits? All right, I've found them. . . . And the tumty-tum are tumty . . . What about that milk? Think the cow was a changeling?'

Paul grunted as he dug amongst the books and ignored the singing and the questions.

'It will really be much the worse for us if the beast was deranged like the rest of Mr. Peacock's property. . . .'

'*Got* it!' shouted Paul as he bent over a book.

'*A Study of Ten Victorian Poets* by William Peacock,' he read aloud, bending to the candle.

Tony in the dark kitchen shrugged his shoulders. Facts, facts. Paul always wanted an explanation for everything. What's what? Who's who? Pin them down, label them neatly. Tear down veils. Dispel fogs. Heave a brick into every quiet pool. What a man it was for leaving its mark on everything.

'There'll be a metal road, a cinema and a drinking fountain (presented by) in this place before he's done,' thought Tony.

'I've got him, Tony!'

'Bet you have,' Tony whispered into the cocoa tin.

'Used to be editor of *The Quarterly Review* . . . wrote some good stuff too. Haven't seen anything of his for years.' Paul's voice sank to a murmur, and Tony could hear the pages of a book fluttering.

'Did Vaux say those were his children?'

'Yes, three of 'em, all dippy.'

73

'Poor chap. . . .'

More murmuring. Tony turned his head and listened.

'Expect that's the reason he's buried in this hole . . .' then raising his voice:

'The dark girl is all right: she's a beauty.'

'*One* ripe plum,' said Tony to the cocoa tin, and added more loudly:

'What dark girl?'

There was no reply to the question, and when Tony went back into the parlour with a loaded tray he found Paul standing by the window gazing at the star-spattered sky.

'A sort of infant prodigy of that time,' said Paul turning. 'Almost a contemporary of ours—Roger's and mine.'

'Who? Have some cocoa, half Bournville half translated cow, nothing like it. . . .'

'Peacock. They use his stuff for the English tripos.' Paul perched on the arm of the sofa and let his cocoa grow cold.

'Tony, I'd rather meet that man than any I can think of. . . . Same job as mine. Wonder what he'd think of Roger's stuff?' Paul smoothed an excited hand through his hair. 'He'll be interested in the poem written about this place. . . . Probably wouldn't mind if I asked his opinion about the editing——' Paul stopped speaking suddenly. A shadow approached. Writing about Roger. . . .

'Wonder why he dug in here . . . active brain like that——'

'Probably turned necromancer. Stews up bats' brains and toads' legs. Might——' Tony bit gently on his too nimble tongue. He had nearly suggested an application for a love potion.

Paul was lost in a dream of a literary colony—the simple life and interchange of sparkling intellectual conversation. The Lake Poets . . . (Some of the modern men were planting a banner in retirement in the South of France . . .) But here . . . himself; William Peacock; a few others would soon settle . . . those empty cottages by the river. Herd 'em altogether—a careful selection of jewels—and then see them sparkle with a light that would penetrate to all the dusty corners of uncultured England.

Paul's face was illumined by an inner radiance that smoothed every furrow and lit his dark eyes with an almost fanatical gleam. Solitude of any kind was unbearable to him, but the greatest pain of all was intellectual solitude. His was not a creative brain, fed by inner fires whatever his circumstances or surroundings. It was from the brains of others that he took fire. His work and his inherited wealth had brought him in contact with most of the mental giants of his day, but he grieved that the standard (set by himself and Roger) had been lowered. There were no leaders and no longer any willing to be led. Rossetti, William Morris—all that circle had no heirs. All fallen with the petals of their holy lilies and faded with the celestial light of their visions.

The musical winds across the lakes blew around the heedless, empty heads of American tourists at Grasmere, and their heavy shadows fell across Dr. Johnson's throne in London. . . .

There *was* a place called Bloomsbury. . . . Paul was not at ease in London, West Central.

He did not know that what he really mourned for (passing over all the present richness) was his youth and the ecstatic adventuring down paths that he had discovered with Roger in the awakening of their intellects in Cambridge days. Never could he turn back the page and look again at that new-found land; it had been beheld, crossed and left behind and the present landscape had a different aspect—it no longer invited a wayfarer of thirty-two years to answer its mysterious challenge to seek and find. Paul, from a little eminence that he had reached, had a bird's-eye view of what lay before him and it did not stir him to adventure farther.

Roger had often talked in those heady, golden days before the War of all that they would do. . . . He hadn't much liked the idea of well-ordered groups and societies.

'Wild animals turn savage in captivity—smell a bit too,' he had said.

'We'll all shake down and do our stuff. It's bound to be a muddle at the start, but you can't organize an unknown quantity; its too personal. The strong ones find their own level. I've nothing to give yet; lots of dreams, but no reality—but I'm not impatient.'

Roger had been patient and a shovelful of clay upon those dreaming eyes had been his reward.

Paul leant wearily against the window-frame. The

happy mood was gone—swept away by the memory of waste and destruction.

The serenity of the spring night was over everything, indifferent and heartless, stretched above the quick and the dead. A quiet night like this brought back the nightmare so vividly. Another season rolling by, the world swinging on peopled by stupid, destructive humanity closing doors, fastening windows against the screams of agony, wrapping themselves in fold upon fold of callous silence. This place standing serene and unheedful in a world destroyed.

Paul clenched his fists in a declaration of enmity against all peace and serenity, oblivious of the fact that he was ranging himself upon the side of the destroyer.

He turned and looked at the untidy room; books and wrapping paper scattered everywhere. He had brought an enormous amount of property with him in the hope of recreating the atmosphere of his London life; books around the walls like people of the right sort—you put out a hand and touched them at the moment of your need. But they were only books after all, read and re-read, dusty and dead. If only there were a few real people. . . . He suddenly thought of William Peacock and as the book and the writer became identified in his mind he bent over the packing-case and extracted a book called *Come with Me*. Here was another that mattered. He dusted the mantelpiece with his handkerchief and set Peacock and Ralston, shoulder to shoulder, against the clock.

77

Two loud bangs on the ceiling made him jump and swear under his breath.

.   .   .   .   .

Tony retiring to bed had dropped his shoes on the floor. Attired in the tattered remnants of somebody's champagne-coloured silk pyjamas he wedged his shoulders into the narrow window and leaned out to sniff and feel the night.

Oh, heavenly place! Like a cool hand smoothing his brow and cheek, caressing his body. . . . The ecstasy was too great to be borne standing. Tony went to bed under an unsorted pile of blankets and sheets.

CHAPTER III

As she trudged up the hill from Charming's shed Clare noticed that without colour or glory a pale sun had risen and a thin drizzle of rain had begun to fall. It was a wan day with no definite beginning and, probably, no definite end—a slow sliding from darkness to light and back again to darkness. That one clear trumpet call of Spring, blowing over the countryside for the weeks succeeding her birthday, had faded into the golden evening of the previous day. Winter had not quite finished with the land. A trail of frosty fingers before dawn and a heavy darkness at nightfall. But the air felt purer— purged of the scent of mud and decay, and on the hazel hedge in the lane the buds were frothing into green.

The recent warmth had drawn sweet smells from the earth and now, on this grey morning, they blew all the more pungently through the damp air, a cool, familiar draught curling the straying tendrils of her hair and making her nostrils quiver as she breathed deeply. It was these colourless days when nose and ears were stimulated more than the eyes that made her heart-beats quicken and filled her with an almost holy worship of her home.

So often in the most unlikely weather in early spring when such a scent was wafted full of promise she would get an overwhelming sensation of a hot summer day. For one instant the barren earth flowered prematurely;

the grass felt rich and thick beneath her feet; banked colours of flowers in Hector's garden swam before her eyes in still golden air and the drowsy murmur of bees and the cawing of rooks flapping indolently in green tree-tops drowned the whisper of the present rain.

In autumn too, a clear and unexpected whistle of some bird would turn back the page, and the ghost of the last spring would pass again.

This visionary juggling with past and future seasons gave her the happy feeling of being unchained by time. Unspoken fears for Viola or for Hector were set at rest. They would be always there. The little flame in Viola's face would never flutter down and the fear that lurked at times in the clear depths of Hector's eyes could never swim to the surface, for the next year could be the year before with them all secure and ageless.

If Clare could have been asked what counted most in her life she would have found it impossible to explain that ever-present almost sensual pain that pierced her bosom—a longing to protect, to shelter, and to love all helpless creatures.

There had been moments, watching a shadow pass on a beloved face, when that sweet pain had become a sharp agony, a sword turning in a wound, and horror rushing on her battered her and engulfed her spirit. But the shadow passed; a bird cried 'Spring' amongst the falling leaves or the bare earth blossomed in its richest beauty.

Last night some inexplicable terror had possessed her when she saw the tortured mask pressed to the window. That sudden leap of fear standing erect and quivering within one that is felt when a bell rings sharply in a silent night or a cry pierces a lonely scene. Like a bird on its nest, freezing its very heart-beat for fear of discovery by some passer-by, she had not dared to move until the pressing and mysterious terror gave her courage to expel the stranger.

A silly, silly fancy she told herself as toiling up the paddock she saw the tall chimney of Prince's Acre dark and solid in the rainy mist. A few more plodding steps and the weather-stained roof appeared, the eaves and then the windows of her home.

Hector was in the barn feeding the chickens and he looked up as she passed and called in his curious muted treble:

'If the rain stops I'll paint the old scow; I've found the paint.'

'A good idea,' she shouted back encouragingly. 'The poor hulk won't blister so badly as she did last year.'

Hector came after her into the yard, running in his long-legged shambling way. The spring smells excited him and he tried to communicate to the one person in the world who understood him the sudden burst of dizzy rhythm that was beating in his mind. When he spoke his lips hardly moved; all sound was centred somewhere in the middle of his throat, emerging without effort in a fluid, bubbling jumble of soft sound. It made him look rather like a ventriloquist's doll.

'There may be some nests on the marshes, Clare. We could row down when the paint drys. . . .'

He paused and stood listening, his head thrown back and his pale eyes turned up under their lids.

'There's that cuckoo again,' he whispered.

Clare turned on the step and shook the raindrops from her hair. She saw Hector planted like a gawky sapling in the yard, and Charming plodding over the grass as if he were drawing a cart-load of bricks behind him.

By holding her breath and twitching back the muscles of her ears she could just hear the staccato notes of the distant bird. . . . Then Hector started forward again in a shambling run; Charming leaned over the paddock rail and blew loudly down his nose while his eyes rolled hopefully towards the pail swinging in Hector's hand. Mrs. Humble screeched from the house. 'Yer father's maundering in the lane, Clare; go and tell 'im 'is brekfus is ready and get the milk while yer howt there.'

Clare sighed as she went off across the yard again. It was not an unhappy sigh, only a light breath expended into the ruffle of sound and movement that had disturbed the mirrored surface of the picture whilst the cuckoo called.

She saw her father walking slowly up the lane towards 'The Load of Hay', and when she whistled he turned and called out something about the postman.

'He'll be here in a minute,' she called back and went down the lane to the duck-pond where the milkman left the bottle every morning in the grassy bank.

Standing beside the bottle for Prince's Acre was another, and as Clare bent down she glanced across the orchard to the little cottage. The door was closed, but the windows were open and the fresh curtains blew out for a moment, fluttered and collapsed again. It had the compact, blind appearance of a house in the early morning when all the inmates are asleep.

Clare walked back thoughtfully with the milk bottle nursed in the crook of her elbow.

.   .   .   .   .

Viola looked out of her bedroom window and sniffed the air. She ignored the thin rain, the grey sky and damp air. It mattered not what the eye saw, for her keen nose told her that spring had at last come to stay. Viola dressed and cast a clout—her woollen combinations were exchanged for a vest of lighter weight and her sober attire of dark blue serge and black wool was freshened by a pair of white cotton stockings donned so that they wrinkled in careless bracelets round her ankles.

Mrs. Humble purchased all their clothes; choosing from catalogues and allowing for growth of stature during long service. Clare took in seams and put back buttons; but Viola was not particular, for royalty is seldom well dressed.

The performance of robing herself in the morning took a considerable time and a vast amount of energy; but she insisted that nobody should help her. Sometimes Mrs. Humble moved by a pity that was unrecognizable under a display of impatience and exasperation attempted to dress the languid, breathless child; but Viola, with head held high, returned to bed obstinately clasping her bundle of garments.

83

'Humble, you take too much upon yourself,' she would say.

She rested for a moment by the window after the labour of fastening buttons had been performed. The vest and the bridal hose as a declaration of independence were enough to wear anybody out.

She saw her father wandering hatless in the lane. The distance lent him youthfulness and his carriage, as always, was aristocratic in the extreme. Viola gazed at him thoughtfully until he was no longer her father but that well-bred youth with 'great blue eyes and even forehead'. It was Edgar Linton wandering in the lane, and the lane was not the bosky southern thoroughfare of usual but a windswept track across the high moor of the north.

Viola's eyes dilated as she saw another figure, 'taller and twice as broad across the shoulders. . . .'

'Heathcliff,' she murmured, closing her eyes with fear and longing.

She went down to breakfast, clasping an old leatherbound book against her chest, and was so talkative and animated that she was compelled to retire to the sofa for the remainder of the morning.

Surprised by her sister's flow of colourful and dramatic conversation Clare glanced at the book reposing beside Viola's coffee cup. For some weeks now Clare's ears had become attuned to a spate of pure Scots pouring from Viola's lips so that she was interested that morning to see that The Waverley Novels were finished and her sister was now moved by the spirit of *Ellis Bell*.

.   .   .   .   .

William took out his watch a dozen times as he walked slowly up and down the lane. It was half-past eight and the postman's red bicycle had not yet emerged from the woods.

William had read Max Ralston's book, *Come With Me*, three more times since he had written, in early April, to the author to declare his belief. There had been no reply and as the need to hear more of this perfect land increased so did the nightmare doubts. Perhaps, after all, the critics were right. . . . A bright young man had written a satire on civilization and a fantasy of a perfect world. . . .

That climate, those streams and trees; the flowers and fruit and colours undreamed of. The music on the soft sea-winds that peeled off the burden of age as if it were the skin of a chrysalis. . . . The atmosphere of celestial peace and content that would make every man love his neighbour as himself. No lusts, no crimes or fevers of discontent. . . .

William felt that if it were all a smart hoax he would take to his bed and never stir again. With the now hot, now cold anxiety of a lover parted from his lass, William haunted the lane every morning to watch for the red bicycle.

He raised his head and saw Mercury spin gaily from the dark wood.

The postman dismounted and came down the lane, a packet of letters in his hand. Nearer and nearer he came, the rain glistening on his macintosh. He tipped the peak of his hat as he passed Mr. Peacock of Prince's Acre and went on to leave his packet for the new tenant at Kay's cottage.

.   .   .   .   .

When the postman rattled on the door Paul had hoped that Jackson had arrived. He took the letters and threw them disgustedly on the table. The place was a sight. He'd lost his shaving brush. The kitchen boiler had not been lit. He'd been cold in the night and had had to go into Tony's room to snatch two blankets off his selfish friend.

He passed a hand over his rough chin and went across the orchard to look for the milk in the odd place where the man from Kay's had said he'd leave it.

As he jumped down into the lane he saw the disconsolate form of an elderly man standing in the ditch with hands locked and head bowed in prayerful resignation.

'Have you any idea where they hide the milk?' Paul inquired as he searched the hedge.

William raised his sad eyes and shook his head.

'My daughter Clare——' he began, waving vaguely towards Prince's Acre.

Paul stood up sharply and looked at the man again. At first he had thought him old and nondescript, but now he noticed the scholarly brow, the thin nose like a bleached bone and the wide sensitive mouth and, over all, a ghost-like semblance of extreme youth.

'You must be William Peacock,' said Paul smiling. 'My name is Paul Millard, I'm a neighbour of yours now. I've read your books and . . .' His voice trailed off as he saw the vague look on William's face.

'You *are* William Peacock, aren't you?'

'A—yes,' said William, and then added more firmly. 'Yes, I am.' And he turned slowly away and went up the lane through the gate to Prince's Acre.

Paul was a very sensitive person and he actually blushed as he kicked angrily at the grass, searching for that damned milk hidden by the blasted milkman.

CHAPTER IV

THE rain had ceased by the afternoon, but the sun still shone so wanly in the grey sky that one could stare straight at it without frowning or blinking. Hector went down to the river with a pot of vivid green paint and an old, moulting brush.

His little dinghy was lying, drawn up on the dry mud under the pier, bottom uppermost.

Hector splashed daubs of paint on the cracked and peeling sides.

So occupied was he that he didn't see a young man come down the green drive past the cottages. He was burdened with a box, a canvas, and a tripod.

Tony liked working in a bad light and he had decided to paint the pale curve of the estuary curling between the yellow reedy banks to the sea. At the same time he could watch for Jackson and the *Theodora*. He felt the need of a hot meal and a little order—anything to stop Paul banging round that pleasant hen-coop in such a disagreeable fashion.

Tony dropped his accoutrements and shook the locked gate. There would be a much better view at the end of the pier if only. . . . He peered down the bank and saw a man painting a boat on the mud under the pier.

'Harbour Master,' said Tony politely. 'Have you got a key to this gate?'

Hector looked up startled, and shook his head.

'Isn't there a key?'

Hector shook his head again and gathering up his pot and brush he prepared for flight.

Tony grunted and set his tripod on the bank. Standing sideways on to the canvas, his box of paints (full of a muddle of tubes and brushes and bits of broken palette) held to his stomach, and with one leg twined around the other upon which he balanced himself Tony set to work quite happily. Hector crept cautiously up the bank and would have shambled away up the field if he hadn't looked over his shoulder and seen what the stranger was about.

He saw the brush slide swiftly across the white surface of the blank page leaving behind it a faint grey line . . . then another, and another, a curious outline of a shape.

The stranger paused, fumbled in a box, ducked his head, and then, whizz! Right across the page flickered a vivid blue weal.

Hector squatted on his heels at a safe distance and watched. Something was appearing on that blank, white surface, something as formless as the rhythm in Hector's mind; but seeing it growing thus made him feel quite sick with excitement.

Tony, glancing once casually over his shoulder, saw that the long-legged youth was watching him and, though he got no reply, he conversed lazily as he worked.

'Get many people here in the summer, Harbour Master?' Another shuddering blue streak flowed across the canvas.

'Don't suppose the average tripper finds much to bring him out here . . . um?'

Tony screwed up one eye and rubbed the tip of his nose with the back of his hand.

'Now, in Greece—(know Greece?)—the older the ruins and the more remote the places . . . up in the mountains sometimes . . . tourists, tourists all the way . . . Ma and Pop and Junior . . . "stoodents" photographing one another leaning against pillars. But tourists don't *look*, Harbour Master, do they?'

Hector was enchanted. This careless, one-sided conversation was no more than a soft musical accompaniment to the colours flowing on to the page as the brush stroked and streaked in the wizard hand. It was all mixed up with a sensation of fear—fascinated, breathless fear only just controlled.

When Tony hopped a step backwards Hector retreated too; and as Tony hopped forward again and bent to peer at his canvas Hector drew nearer than he had been before.

'Now the trouble with tourists,' said Tony, his nose nearly touching the paint, 'is that they go to a place to say they've been there . . . eat a hard-boiled egg on some one's grave and leave the shell there . . . A treble voice near Tony's elbow said:

'A white ship!'

Tony turned quickly, but the uncouth creature was squatting motionless on his haunches with his mouth hanging open and his idiot eyes staring straight in front of him. As Tony eyed him suspiciously the voice spoke again:

'A white ship with sea-gulls round her.' And the voice

came right out of the creature's face; not a muscle moved round his lips.

'Like one of those chaps that chuck their voices about in music-halls,' thought Tony as he turned his head towards the river and saw the neat prow of the *Theodora* ruffling through the silver water.

He laid down his box and brushes and said severely: 'Now, Harbour Master, you'll have to find the key. That's Mr. Millard's boat and he's got a mooring here. It's my first hot meal for two days too, so you must forgive me if I appear insistent.'

Tony rubbed his hands on the seat of his trousers and smiled at Hector so charmingly that the smile took instant flight and settled upon Hector's face.

'You come on up to the cottage with me and tell Mr. Millard what arrangements you've made. His man sleeps aboard but he'll be buzzing to and fro and he'll have to bring the dinghy in somewhere.'

Trembling a little, Hector found himself following the godlike person up the grass path past the cottages. On three of the doorsteps sat three white dogs, two spotted with plummy black upon their muzzles and breasts; the third was sitting on his spots. They bore one another an undeniable likeness.

Tony pointed to them and burst out laughing.

'Make you think you'd had a drop too much; seeing treble, eh, Harbour Master?'

Hector caught the laugh this time and had difficulty in stopping, but he nearly choked with terror when Tony, with a wicked look from under long, curling lashes, put out his hand and ran it lightly down Hector's sleeve.

'You're a man after my own heart, Harbour Master,' he said with a puckish grin.

As they went trailing across the orchard Tony hailed the cottage:

'Ahoy there! The *Theodora's* coming up the river.'

Paul came through the door.

'God is merciful,' he said, yawning.

'Brought the Harbour Master——' Tony began when Paul cut him short by saying to the hesitating figure beside him:

'I haven't returned that jug yet, but I will.'

Tony stared and then shrugged his shoulders.

'We all make mistakes.' He smiled at his companion. 'Saw you planted out under the pier pottering with a boat and thought you must be the fellow that rules the waves.' Then turning to Paul: 'Jackson can't get through that gate, it's locked.'

'He'll climb it. Let's all have some tea, we don't have to wash the cups now. Come in, Mr. Peacock.'

'Yes, come in Neptune,' said Tony with a wicked laugh and a wink at Hector with whom he thought he shared a private joke.

Hector stood balancing on his toes, longing to fly, chained to the earth with terror, and then as he caught Tony's long-lashed, flickering glance he found that his truant feet were moving and he passed across the threshold of the cottage.

When Tony closed the door Hector wanted to scream,

but he could only edge to the window and seat himself on a chair as near the fresh air as possible. His pale face in profile against the open window was like a cameo in a frame.

Paul gave him a puzzled look and said something quite gently. He was always kind to sick people and children.

But Hector could only hear a confused murmur and he refused to turn his head to look at the prison that had closed around him. Silently he cried out for help.

.   .   .   .   .

Clare had gone down to the river to look for Hector and she had seen the paint-pot abandoned on the mud beside the old scow, and above it, on the bank, a tripod and a smeared canvas. A large motor-launch was chugging evenly up the estuary; it turned in a wide circle as she watched it and a flock of sea-gulls cried and dipped above its wake. Sudden panic seized her and she ran up the hill calling her brother's name. By the duck-pond she paused a moment and then some intuition made her scramble up the bank into the orchard.

'Hector, Hector,' she called, peering through the trees.

'Somebody's lost a dog,' said Paul and he saw a quiver flow across the face by the window.

Clare bending under a mossy branch saw the pale, tortured profile framed in the cottage window.

'Come on, my dear, come on,' she called softly.

Hector rose to his feet with difficulty, stole to the door, fumbled at the latch with the weak movements of a sleep-walker, and, opening the door a very little, he slipped through and began to run.

Paul and Tony stared through the window and saw the brother and sister, hand in hand, disappearing through the orchard.

'Well I'm damned,' said Paul.

Tony gave a sudden screech.

'I believe in all the gods, here's Jackson! Oh, holy man, oh, blessed vision!'

CHAPTER V

MAY that year was a soft-footed, secret month. Every morning, cool and pale with uncertain sunlight, had some fresh wonder to disclose in the garden. Under cover of the night a patch of cloudy blue or sprinkled white appeared in the warmer corners, as if a mysterious nocturnal visitor of careless habits had let some bright objects fall in passing. One heavy rainfall and a stronger burst of sunlight following it loaded the syringa and the lilac bushes by the back door with a swaying burden of blossoms. A heavy branch clustered with blunt, purple spear-heads swung into the open window of the kitchen. 'You take your cheeky face out o' 'ere,' said Mrs. Humble, dusting the sill and releasing a shower of raindrops over herself as she thrust at the wayward branch.

Hector had planted out his pansy plants, but their black and rusty faces were still sheathed in tender green when the forget-me-nots were a mist of blue and the tulips unfolded waxy pink cups in the border. The bluebells were out in the beech woods and the light beneath the branches was as transparent as green water.

The trees and flowering shrubs predominated over the more reluctant flowers of early summer, and the birds were bustling and vociferous as they busied themselves with profiting by the growing shelters. Flirting, building, squabbling, and trilling from sun-up to sun-down.

'It's my straw! It's my straw!' chirruped the sparrow, always too argumentative to go directly about his business.

'I found it first,' called an iridescent and hostile starling. And Hector watched him sail across the hazel hedge with a long grass floating from his beak.

The swifts settled in the dusty lane at twilight, fluttered a short distance, and flopped down again as though wounded. And then, as an anxious hand stretched out to them, they rose, cleaving the air like the flash of a dark knife-blade, and were gone. Hector crouched over White's *Selborne* and read out under his breath:

'Now is the only time to ascertain the short-winged summer birds: for, when the leaf is out, there is no making any remarks on such a restless tribe; and, when once the young begin to appear, it is all confusion; there is no distinction of genus, species, or sex.'

'That was late April in Selborne,' thought Hector. He must hurry, the year was ahead of him for the first time. What was he about? Seeing nothing, hearing nothing, no remarks to make on the 'restless tribe'. He closed the book and started at a jog-trot for the woods.

'It is all confusion,' he repeated over and over again as he ran.

Slower and slower moved his feet until he stopped, faced about, and saw the figure of a man beside the pier, a tiny square of white canvas and, beyond, the silver snake curving to the sea.

'Confusion, confusion,' muttered Hector, the words

96

pumping in sobs from his labouring breast as he ran, more swiftly now, towards the river.

.   .   .   .

As she crossed the yard Clare saw her brother's figure leaping across the tufted grass in the paddock. She shaded her eyes and watched him settle on the river's edge beside a man who turned to greet him.

Viola was sitting under the walnut-tree, *Wuthering Heights* lying face downward on her lap and her limpid gaze fixed on the glimpse of Mr. Kay's cottage hiding amongst the orchard trees.

'Where they go I must follow,' thought Clare, going on more slowly to the barn. Sherbet lolloped at her heels, a mound of earth upon his nose and his eyes half-closed by nettle stings.

There was a loft under the leaking roof at one end of the barn where unwanted and outcast furniture and boxes were stored. A ladder rested against the open trap-door, but for many years now nobody but Clare ever climbed up into the room beneath the rafters.

She heaved Sherbet's large bulk up on to the ladder and encouraged him to mount by making throaty, wordless sounds.

Left at the bottom of the ladder, with his mistress out of sight above, Sherbet would have moaned ceaselessly so that Mrs. Humble would be attracted to the spot to make unwanted inquiries and a general disturbance. Mrs. Humble was neither of an age nor build to scramble up the ladder, but she could shake it.

97

'Whatcher doing up there?' she had shrieked the one and only time Sherbet had been left below.

'Nothing,' Clare had answered from the cobwebs and the gloom.

'Well, you come on down. There ain't a blessed thing up there for you to go poking and prying into.'

Clare had descended so meekly that Mrs. Humble had not imagined that she would ever return to gaze upon the shabby, bursting trunks that were stacked in a corner of the loft all powdered over with white dust.

Hector had the wide world of out of doors, and Viola asked no better than the familiar shelter of her home, where she could watch her family around her; but Clare had always wanted some secret place of her own where she could dream and think her most private thoughts, away from the constant round of responsibility and shared existence. One cloud upon her face would call forth a remark from the far too observant Mrs. Humble, so that, much against his will, Sherbet became a climber of ladders and a sharer of sad solitudes.

He hesitated on the bottom rungs, his mournful white face turned over his shoulder, and then, a victim of the canine passion which says, 'Where you go I will follow,' he ascended on cautious paws with Clare's steadying hand upon his collar.

In the house that never was to be, planned by Miranda and William, the children of the house would have had their own rooms. For the Viola of the might-have-been a tiny boudoir, albums, pressed flowers, photographs framed in fragile sea-shells and, perhaps, a harp.

For Hector a mixture of sport and study would have furnished an airy, white-distempered attic. Books, ranging from the crude romances and adventures of boyhood reading to the well-bound poets and the classic prose of past centuries. On the walls a brace of foils, a fencing mask and the hollow fists of boxing gloves dangling from a hook.

There is no telling where fancy might not have led Clare had life been just a little different and more over-looked. Under the dusty rafters of the barn was the ghost of the room for Clare.

There was an old sofa with a broken back and hanging tatters of faded silk. In the seat was a large hole where a squirrel had slept a comfortable winter deep in the wads of horsehair. Beside this reposed a long mirror with a surface so yellowed and defaced that it no longer caught the reflection of a face; a change of light would be marked in a dull gleam upon some less damaged portion of the glass, but no more. A bicycle of antique pattern lay against the wall; a long-handled carriage whip with tarnished silver bands; a battledore and an unfledged shuttlecock. Dangling on frayed ribbons from a beam was a row of old ballet-shoes made for feet half the size of Clare's. The trunks in the corner had been dusted, and one, made of wicker, displayed the name 'Mirova' on its bursting side; and all were open and their maws foamed with overflowing treasures. Yellowed ruffles of tarlatan that time and repeated packing had not quelled. Miranda's ballet frocks sprang upwards like frosted cabbage leaves when the lid of the trunk had been lifted.

99

Such a musty, bitter-sweet smell lay in the folds of bright
garments folded under the tarlatan. The moth had played
havoc with the fur trimmings and the embroideries.
There were piles of music scores, and programmes, and
photographs. Clare had placed one of the latter on a
table against the wall, and it showed in time-mellowed
tints the picture of a young lady from whose tiny waist
sprang the brisk billows of a long, old-fashioned ballet
frock. She held a rose under her nose; her feet were
wonderfully pointed and, in spite of the dimness of the
photograph, one remarked the strangeness of the eyes
that peeped half-roguishly, half-appealingly over the rose.

There were photographs of uniformed gentlemen of
imposing mien, and across the medals on their chests
were scrawled royal names. Clare had arranged them in
stacks according to their looks: handsome; not so handsome; downright plain. There were books ranged in
a neat and dusted pile against the wall—books of small
literary importance, the pale reflection of a time that had
faded and names that had not survived. 'To the Queen
of Hearts', 'To the Spirit of the Dance', were some of the
inscriptions on tattered flyleaves; and there were many
more scrawled in languages Clare did not understand.
She read them, all those written in English, so that the
outcasts from William's library of greater and more
lasting works found a rebirth in the shadows of the
loft.

Sherbet lay in a corner with his eyes closed and one
ear twitching uneasily under the attentions of a fly. With
every movement of Clare's his heart leapt with hope of

release from this tedious imprisonment, but he continued to feign sleep. He knew well it was better to meet disappointment half-way, for there were many uncertain and tantalizing pauses in the dull performance.

Clare dusted her crippled furniture and shook out bright garments and folded them again. It was so seldom that she climbed up here, and always in her absence a million tiny unseen creatures had shaken down a film of fine white dust and had woven cobwebs amongst her treasures.

Those duties once performed, she curled up on the sofa with her heels under her and her arms folded and prepared to deal with her worries. She had so little experience of life beyond the quiet familiar round at Prince's Acre that she never compared her lot with that of other people. Except for a passing greeting to a labourer returning to his cottage in the evening, to a woman on a doorstep, or a tradesman calling at the farm, she knew nobody outside of her own family. She read and thought deeply, she had instinct and uncanny perception, and therefore she knew that another mode of life and very different people existed, but she was not conscious of a longing for change or a conflict of choice. Viola, Hector, and her father were the realities in her world and it was a world created apart to give them shelter. That they could not have existed in another setting was accepted by her as an undeniable fact. That even tenor and that unchanging sweet mood of peace for which she was partly responsible was the means by which she kept herself surrounded by those dear, dependent people.

She could not wish for anything different, for in another life she would have been alone, denuded and unfruitful as a withered branch. The Vicar had once brought tidings and a bitter taste of how the rest of the world lived, and that strange encounter had nearly cost Viola her life, Hector his reason, and her father his hard-won peace of mind. Anyway, that is how Clare reasoned on her fate, and probably at the time of that first disturbance she had not known which way to turn in her despair at that glimpse of destruction and had at last, in some deep chamber of her mind, resolved to wrap her world and its inmates in fold upon fold of dreams.

But now she had blundered; in some way her guardian-ship had been lax, and at some time between light and darkness, or between sleep and waking, a foreign element had invaded her dream, and it refused to be expelled. Viola, like a rabbit held frozen and hypnotized by the eyes of a snake, sat hour after hour in the garden with her peaked face turned to the orchard. At night she woke screaming, and not until Clare had rocked her in her arms and spoken soothingly did her eyes clear, and with the recognition of where she lay and who sat beside her Viola would smile a swift, bewildered smile and fall back into the deep sleep of utter exhaustion.

Hector flew hither and thither in a sort of desperate, unorganized hurry. It was as if his body were inhabited by active machinery that nobody knew how to control or drive. Wheels and pistons whirled and flayed, they battered him and drove him to and fro without purpose.

A few days past Clare had seen him cross the garden

with a box of seedlings. He had knelt by the border and as his hands reached for the trowel they stopped and became rigid, as if he had suddenly been attacked by paralysing pain. For a moment he had knelt there petrified and then leaping to his feet and leaving his task undone, he made off to the woods; shambling, jogging, leaping tufts, until once more that machinery had twirled him round on the very borders of his goal and sent him careering in an opposite direction.

Clare huddled on the sofa, and pressing her hands against her breast felt the sword turn in the wound.

'Let me see clearly, oh, let me see clearly,' she whispered, and the prayer, offered to no god or person in particular, was answered by a low growl from the corner where Sherbet lay.

A sound had caught his sensitive hearing and his pink-rimmed eyes were open and fixed. The door of the barn below had creaked softly on its hinges and the head of the ladder protruding through the open trap shuddered as somebody began to ascend. Another growl rumbled in Sherbet's throat and Clare turned her head swiftly towards the ladder.

Two brown hands clasped the topmost rung, and then the head and shoulders of a man came into view. He stood on the ladder, half in and half out of the loft, and gazed at Clare with an expression of great friendliness lighting up a pair of dazzlingly blue eyes and a face so sun-tanned that if it hadn't been for a mop of straw-coloured hair one would have thought him an Indian.

'Phew,' he gasped, 'it's hot.'

103

Clare's heart was beating very fast, and she still held her hands against her breast, but the first flurry of alarm was stilled as the stranger smiled. Like the intermittent rays of the sun on a cloudy day the smile flickered warmly over Clare, and she smiled dreamily back. She was so wrapped round in visions that the intruder seemed to have little reality, and when Sherbet growled again uneasily she whispered without turning her head: 'Hush, hush, my dear.'

'I'd like to come up a bit farther, but my pack is stuck in the trap. . . . Think you could give me a hand?'

Clare uncurled her legs and crossed the floor to the truncated man. She bent and pulled at the rucksack strapped on his back until it was clear of the opening and he swung himself into the loft with easy, cat-like movements.

'God bless you,' he said. 'Couldn't make a soul hear when I called at the house. This is Prince's Acre, isn't it?'

Clare nodded and retreated to her sofa. The stranger followed her and deposited himself at her side. Sherbet stalked across to sniff the man's outstretched legs.

'Been walking for miles, so I thought I'd rest in the barn until somebody came along. Heard this old sinner grumbling, so I thought there might be somebody up aloft.'

He tickled Sherbet vigorously on the spine, so that he was obliged to stand on three legs and scratch his undercarriage with the fourth.

'Did you want to see any one in particular?' asked

Clare, staring in amazement at the pleasant creature stretched beside her. He seemed so completely at home: legs extended, hands locked behind his rough, sunburnt head, and on his face an expression of childlike happiness and good-fellowship.

'Yes,' he answered, smiling straight into her eyes. 'I've come to see my friend William Peacock.'

'My father . . .' whispered Clare.

'Delighted,' said the extraordinary man looking as if he meant it with all his heart. 'My name's Ralston.'

.   .   .   .   .

When Clare opened the study door William was sitting by his writing-table with a blank sheet of paper before him. For days now he had been trying to start some work; anything to fill the void, to take the place of a faded dream and occupy his dreary round in a grey world.

'Father,' she whispered, 'there's a Mr. Ralston here; he wants to see you.'

Before she closed the door and tiptoed away she saw her father rise to his feet, steady himself a moment by the table edge, and then advance with hands outstretched to meet Max Ralston.

CHAPTER VI

MAX leant against the study mantelpiece and talked to William. Every now and again he took a turn across the room, from wall to wall, and in and out of the piles of books. He spoke excitedly with a nervous, almost exaggerated sincerity. A more critical observer than William might have wondered why this young giant put so much strained vitality into his conversation.

'It's heaven on earth! It shall not be exploited by the bloody capitalists!' he cried, and pinned William down with a smile so winning that it could not but dazzle and enchant the observer. His fingers strayed from his belt to his pockets, a few coins were jingled and then out shot the hands; a fist hammered on a palm, an arm flew out in an all-embracing gesture, and then, as Max stopped talking for a moment, he rumpled his faded green-gold mop and filled the dangerous pause by chuckling quietly to himself.

There was something sympathetically childlike about this man: his enthusiasm, his half-rueful agitation, and his innocent longing to be liked, to be believed, to be approved. His story was fantastic, and as he emphasized and over-emphasized its truth any ordinary beholder might have been tempted to scoff (but a kindly, humorous scoffing of the kind directed at a nice child who recounts a dream as having passed in reality).

But William only saw a figure radiant in a nimbus of

light and heard a voice that was melodious as a chime of bells.

The Max that Clare had seen was a man of over six feet in height, clad in a blue jersey belted at the waist and a pair of trousers of the kind that can be bought for very little off the peg at any seaport. He had a splendid head, rough and gold-crowned, but looking a little colourless in contrast to the glowing tan on his face. His eyes were icy blue and netted by fine wrinkles at the corners—the eyes of a person who gazes, against sun and wind, to far horizons. Sometimes as he talked the ice would melt and a warm violet shade would creep into the depth of his eyes, giving him a dreamy look.

He was made in such grand proportions, square-shouldered, firm-loined, and long of limb, that it seemed impossible that such a massive edifice could ever lie down or relax in sleep.

If you shook hands with him you ran a risk of permanent mutilation of the fingers; and a friendly pat on the back from that brown palm was enough to fell you to the dust.

But in spite of over-building, over-colouring, and general over-emphasis of character and person, after the first gasp of surprise you liked Max—you almost loved him.

'I've got the money now, sir,' he said to William. 'Enough for the journey and enough for housing fifty people. But I haven't even started to think of making purchases—nobody to make 'em for. The only reason the book sold so well was because people thought it was all a funny eyewash. . . . The letters I've had—witty, some of 'em, and some good bits of writing from people who thought they were entering into the spirit of the thing. Men who want to get away from wives, from mothers-in-law and the income tax; women who are tired of society and want to go native in grass skirts— they ask the price of a round-trip and want to know if there is surf-bathing, sharks; or only angels invisible playing harps. Some of 'em just send invitations for parties—to meet Mr. Thingumyjig who wrote *Watchamadoodle*. . . . But they *all* think it's a good joke, and I believe they'd freeze stone cold if they imagined for a moment that it was true.'

Max scratched his poll and chuckled.

'There was one that sounded genuine—a chap who begged me to take him with me, wanted to start at once— but the police got him before I did, and *he'll* never come back from where he's gone. Somebody suggested that I should plant the Union Jack and grow bigger and better oranges or something or other for the home market.' Max paused in a scramble over the books and smiled at the enchanted William.

'Funny, isn't it, sir? No romance left—not an honest adventurer left alive. And what is so amazing is that with all the misery and the suffering, and the grumbling and the wailing, they *don't want to give it up*. Just as well though, I realize that now.' He sighed, and the sound was like the blast of a north-easterly gale. 'The wrong uns would go—the Government would send convicts to colonize, and the Church would send a few missionaries to pray over 'em; and then other nations would want to prove a claim and there'd be another bust up.'

'You're the only believer, and you say you can't go. . . .' Max looked suddenly dejected and he sat down and nearly broke the sofa springs.

'Wouldn't the family come along too?' He was quite wistful, and he eyed William shyly as if he were asking for a sixpence to buy sweets.

William blinked and twisted on his chair.

'They are not very strong,' he said with a great effort.

'The climate would put 'em right in no time,' Max answered in an eager whisper. 'You've taken my word for the truth up till now, and I know——' William looked so distressed that Max stopped abruptly and was silent—not even a chuckle or a sigh.

'My second daughter,' said William, averting his face from the sympathetic eyes of the kindly giant, 'has been an invalid since—since—childhood, and a journey of even a few miles would prove fatal to her. And my son—my son——' His lip trembled and he hunched forward in his chair. 'And—I couldn't leave them. . . . No, Mr. Ralston; my dream has come true and I thank you.'

'I don't leave until the end of the year,' said Max gruffly, 'so if you can reconsider you know where to find me.'

He suddenly sprang to his feet and set everything creaking and quivering.

'I'm going though, no doubt of that.' He threw back his lion's head and gave a shout of laughter. 'I'll come back in a hundred years' time and try it on another generation.'

His voice was even more emphatic than before, his gestures more dramatic, and his spirits wilder.

'Where did you learn to write so well?' William asked, for in the brief emotional struggle that he had suffered his vision had a little cleared and he was able to see Max in a truer light.

'Oh, I had quite a good education,' said Max with a twinkle in the corner of his eye. 'English private school and a German university . . . skipped off to sea when I was seventeen. I'd learnt a bit and I wanted to *see* a bit more. There was nothing to keep me—no home or people; no definite nationality. . . . I was on the island when war broke out, didn't know a thing about it until the Germans copped me sailing through the China Sea. They said I was English and I said I was German, but I spent three years behind a barbed-wire fence. . . . Began writing the book then and tried it on my fellow-prisoners . . . they thought I was crackers . . . called me Mr. Crusoe. . . . But I never saw any fighting.'

'I'm glad,' murmured William earnestly.

'My mother's name was Ralston,' said Max abruptly. 'Never met my father; she wouldn't tell me his name, but she called me Max, so I expect I've got Central European roots—a waiter or a grand duke.'

'A poet or a hero,' William whispered dreamily.

'She died years ago, when I was seventeen. Strange woman—good works and funny hats.' Max grinned, for the brief description had immediately conjured up a clear picture of his eccentric parent. But William only saw a basket loaded with soups and firewood and bandages, and an incongruous, plumed and beribboned confection floating in the air unclaimed and untenanted.

William, looking at Max with new eyes, was beginning to be troubled with more human problems.

'My boy, you're far, far too young to retire from the world—even to that perfect land. You've got everything before you—life has only just begun for you.' He straightened in his chair. '*You* mustn't live alone . . . it wouldn't be—it wouldn't be—natural.'

As long as William had been an entranced listener, absorbing and accepting in unquestioning beatitude the fantastic colour and form of the picture painted, Max had seemed to expand and glow and fill the room with unconquerable vitality. But at last William had realized the curious contradiction in the young man. The eager pioneer, the natural leader of men and builder of Empires, one whose influence and personality would be felt and tested and not found wanting in times of crisis—the stuff of which national heroes are made. And yet, with life but half-experienced, and apparently no burden of care or unbearable sorrow upon his broad shoulders, he was about to depart, self-banished, from off the face of the civilized earth which should be no more than a playground for such as he.

'You say that romance is dead and no honest adventurer remains.' William went on, speaking slowly and with care, as one unused to dealing with such problems. 'Perhaps you are right. The covered wagons rolled westward across the New World many, many years ago. The bloom was rubbed from the innocence and beauty of the South Seas before even I was born. Aeroplanes can cross the uninhabitable regions of desert and jungle. Man has made his map of the world complete and has settled down for ever . . . he knows the texture of the universe and, because it is useless now, men are born without the spirit that animated their pioneering forefathers. The adventure that you offer would seem like suicide to the youth of to-day—self-burial and an unknown quantity. The old spirit of adventurous curiosity has been sublimated into a desire for experiences of the brain and fingers in this mechanized age. Amongst all the useless misery in the world there is not one, excepting those possessed of a suicidal tendency, who would exchange the known for the unknown. Youth should not turn its back upon life until life is finished—extinguished. For myself it would be different. . . .'

William sat silent for a moment with his eyes wide and fixed upon something newly realized that was raised before him.

'My dream of an undiscovered land,' he continued in a voice that was barely audible, 'was not conjured up by a spirit that panted for adventure, that longed to blaze a trail, to found an empire—I was dreaming of—of life after death, of a place where I might dwell for ever—a happy ghost.'

As William spoke Max had seemed to lose a little of his immense breadth and stature. His face grew a little paler until one thought that bright flame burning within him must have dimmed a little until it scarcely glowed at all.

'I know, I know,' he murmured, unconsciously taking William's soft tone. 'I planned it differently. . . .' He sighed—quite a normal, small sigh of one lightly expended breath.

'I did think they would follow me—in their thousands. All the young, powerful, eager people who cannot find room to spread their wings in this over-crowded civilization. But you are right, there are other customs now and different uses for the descendants of Vikings and pioneers. . . . But that only makes it the more evident that there is no place for me in civilization. It is I who am different, out of tune—*I'm* the freak. I belong to another world and I'd better go to it before—before'— he bent his head into his hands and struggled to express himself—'before I burn up.' He suddenly laughed and threw back his head.

'You can see the prehistoric horse in a museum. It once had a cloven hoof—centuries of civilization and domesticity welded that hoof. Well, I suppose I'm a throw-back, a horse with a useless cloven hoof.'

Max's light began to glow more brightly; his giant proportions, lit up again, returned.

'They usually destroy freaks at birth, don't they?' He struck himself mightily on the chest.

'Well, this one escaped.' He took a turn around the room and his eyes shone wildly.

'This place is a reality, sir. It's my religion, the only thing that matters to me. I've dreamt its history for the next hundred years. I could no more forget it, call it a day, than I could cut my own throat. The beauty of its spirit is so pure and strong that even in the noisiest, dirtiest, and most polluted parts of London I can feel it, hear it, taste it. Those who will not follow me are denying truth, beauty, purity—they deny their God!'

William once more hovered in pearly light outside the world; his eyes dim with dreams of trees and flowers and seas celestial. He was scarcely troubled by a roar from Max.

'I know how to live alone!'

.　　　.　　　.　　　.　　　.

The sun was sinking and the river had turned to gold. Tony packed up his painting materials and let Hector carry them home for him.

Paul was out in the *Theodora* with Jackson—gone to Cowes for the day. Paul couldn't settle to anything, he was fidgety, irritable and apparently consumed with nervous energy which he could put to no constructive purpose.

Tony was mildly sorry for him, but thankful that his before-dinner nap would not be disturbed this day. He didn't get nearly enough sleep at night now. Paul woke him from the deepest and most perfect oblivion by dashing out of the cottage in the small, grey hours of morning. When the front door of the cottage was left open the wind tripped in and set everything banging and creaking. Tony would leap from his bed, forgetting where he was and the habitual cause of the disturbance. His sleep was always so deep that it wiped out everything— memory, circumstances, and environment. A bang, a flutter, and a rushing round his bedroom door made him clutch the tattered bosom of the champagne-coloured pyjamas. 'Burglars!' he thought. Then: 'The end of the world!' The last veil of slumber melted as he saw the open window and branches traced against a grey sky. He rose, he leant over the sill and saw the restless figure cross the orchard and disappear up the lane. At first he thought: 'The old dog's got an assignation,' but Paul would come wandering back five minutes later and thread in and out the ghostly trees for an hour or more as if he were weaving a pattern. . . .

Now Tony woke in alarm as usual, his heart beating as nervously as any old maid's, but he would finally mutter, 'Insomnia, again,' and without bothering to go to the window he would turn over, beat the pillow, and wrap a deafening cover of bedclothes over his head.

But Paul was away for the whole day. Hector knew it, for he went all the way to the cottage door—a thing he would never do when that other one was at home.

'Come in a moment, Neptune. I need you,' said Tony as Hector deposited the tripod and the canvas against the door.

The look in Tony's eyes, not his words, drew Hector into the cottage.

'Sit down, Nep—over there by the window. . . . Go on, it's all right; no bogies. . . . Now sit—not on the floor, Nep; on the chair—that's it. Just enough light . . . won't keep you a moment . . . might never get another chance. . . . Paul away and you in the hen-coop.'

While he spoke Tony had lifted a cupboard door, unscrewed from its hinges, and carried it to a low stool in front of the quivering, obedient Hector, and he squatted with the door propped on his knees. His pencil traced an outline on the central panel, which was painted in soft, watery green and blue. His head was bent and his hand moved and then paused as he glanced up and gazed piercingly, eyes cold and narrowed, at the pale, motionless face six inches from his nose.

Hector tried to moisten his lips . . . his tongue stuck to his palate . . . his eyes fluttered . . . a creeping faintness chilled him. . . . He was losing something—it was being taken from him. Out of the corner of one eye he saw a skeleton face growing on the door. . . . It flowed from him. . . . It covered the panel of the door. . . . He would never get it back. . . . But no sacrifice was too great.

'The colour can go on any day,' murmured Tony, bent over his work.

'Who shall we put on the other door? Good Queen Vic? Um? I can lug it down to the wall and take a squint at her sitting under the tree to-morrow. . . . Then I'll have you both. . . . Thanks, Nep, you can fly now. . . . Go on—the operation's over.'

Hector couldn't move. He sat encased in ice.

'Go on, funny face. . . . Trot!'

Hector rose on trembling legs—they still answered to the word of command. He trotted.

.   .   .   .   .

Viola nestled in her basket chair under the walnut-tree. It was getting cold.

It must be nearly supper time. . . . Hector and the other one had crossed the orchard several minutes ago—nobody else.

She bent her head over her book for the hundredth time.

'. . . Mr. Heathcliff, *you* have *nobody* to love you; and, however miserable you make us, we shall still have the revenge of thinking that your cruelty arises from your greater misery. You *are* miserable, are you not? Lonely like the devil, and envious, like him? *Nobody* loves you—*nobody* will cry for you when you die! I wouldn't be you!'

Two large tears fell upon the page and raised crinkled blisters.

Somebody was coming along the lane! Viola raised herself in her chair to see above the wall. She saw Hector trotting along with his head down. It was cold . . . too dark to read any more. . . .

'Hector, will you take me in?'

He scrambled on to the wall and jumped the flower-bed. Viola gathered up her book and rug and took her brother's proffered arm.

The front door had been locked for years, and now the wood was so swollen with the damp that it couldn't open even if anybody had tried it. Hector and Viola crossed the garden to the little gate opening into the yard, and at a solemn, funeral pace they circled the house.

.   .   .   .   .

Clare sat on the paddock rail and Charming blew down the back of her neck.

'No more sugar, old chap, no more till to-morrow.'

She saw an indistinguishable head darken the window of her father's study.

Lunch missed, tea missed; what was it all about? That funny person—not clutching and hungry like that other one. . . .

Clare wanted to see him again. The loft was always dark . . . she had scarcely dared look. . . . Nobody had been in her father's study—no stranger—since the Vicar came, years and years ago. . . . Everything was changing, happening so quickly, and she couldn't control it. The whole pattern of life was getting wildly jumbled suddenly. She had been depressed, alarmed, and sometimes nearly desperate these last days . . . things happened too quickly. What was it all about? Now there was a new sensation—it was so new that she had no name for the trembling, nervous pulse of excitement that beat in her blood. . . . She must fetch Viola; it was late. Where was Hector? Oh, she'd let them alone too long.

She jumped down from the rail as Hector and Viola came round the corner of the house.

Slowly they came towards Clare, leaning upon each other, their eyes dazed and unseeing—the blind leading the blind. They looked quite lost.

Clare had a feeling that in one moment they would walk straight through her. They didn't seem to see her —it was as if she weren't there at all.

.   .   .   .   .

Mrs. Humble unloaded the supper-tray on to the sitting-room table. There was cold bacon, cold potatoes, bread, butter, half a cold rice-pudding and some baked apples. She counted out the plates, the knives, and the forks.

'D'yer think yer father's going to 'ave something to-night to keep body and soul together?'

'I'll call him if he doesn't come,' said Clare thoughtfully.

'Shall I lay a hextra?'

'Yes.'

'Company?' asked Viola brightly. She was already sitting in her place at the table with her book laid open on her plate. Her eyes were fixed on Clare's face with a wistful and inquiring expression that made her look less incongruously pinched and more childlike than usual.

Hector leaning against the open window, turned round, and stared at Clare too.

She leant over the table and lit the oil lamp hanging on its brass chain. She knew that they were watching her as if they expected a green or a red signal lamp to flash an answer to their inquiry. She turned the wick up higher, and as she watched it spread and settle to a steady flame her brain worked rapidly.

Did they think one of those others would soon walk into the room? The room was quite still, but she fancied she heard a faint humming—like the vibration of a taut wire stretching to breaking point. Fear came to her suddenly, so that she had to press the palms of her hands down on the table for support. Fear from which she must shield them, against which she had till then pre-vailed. . . . In Hector's eyes, in Viola's it spurted up in tiny points of flame, a fire that would not quite lie down, would not be put out though one crushed the spark again and again. . . . It fed upon something inflammable, explosive, dangerous—but it burnt a pretty flame. They loved it though they feared—not knowing why they loved or feared, not knowing the danger but enthralled by this new sensation. Clare looked at the spent match curling smokily between her fingers. 'If only I could follow them,' she thought. 'If only I were not afraid too— afraid for them. But of what? Why?' It was only that her heart beat in jerks every now and then. The music of their world was out of tune. The humming in her ears and the flame dancing a sudden wild uncontrolled flicker across their faces.

This stranger in the study would be before them in a minute. They might turn from those others; from the vision that made Hector run wildly to and fro without purpose, racked by uncontrolled and madly rotating machinery; and made Viola sit, listless and unoccupied, by day and rise shrieking from nightmares at night.

A pink flamingo crossing the sky, an elephant or a fire-engine trundling down the lane—anything unusual appearing for the first time in their sheltered life *might* have had the same effect upon them. . . . But no, it wasn't the same, for the objects of their helpless, enthralled attention were human. Animals and trees and flowers returned you loyalty or beauty in even balance for your love. . . . Humanity was blind, relentless, and destructive. . . . She knew now what it was that she had guarded them from—what it was they must not suffer—born with heart-strings tuned so that any careless breeze could pluck a note in passing. The note twanged in her ears, changed to a cry: 'They follow and we are not well hidden!'

Mrs. Humble dumped a milk-jug down on the table.

'Father has a friend in the study,' Clare said, looking up. 'He's a sailor and he's very nice.' The green light had winked its signal of reassurance, and Viola bent once more to her book and Hector dragged his chair up to the table.

Sherbet pushed the door open with his paw and came trotting in. He never looked for Clare with his eyes; the blood of a sporting ancestor made him trot right round the room with his nose snuffling along the floor until he came to Clare's feet, and then he wagged his tail and lay down quite contented.

The door of William's study opened and Clare could hear him speaking.

'My dear boy, I do apologize. I've robbed you of two meals, and the best bed I can offer is my sofa——'

Steps crossed the passage and the door of the sitting-room was pushed wide open.

Hector and Viola both looked up, and Clare watched them. Their eyes stared for a moment, and then they turned away, indifferent and quite unmoved. Clare looked at the door and saw the smiling, bronzed giant beside her father; he filled the doorway, crowding William before him. She felt her heart-beats even down to a steady, peaceful throb. That was what the stranger had done to her before—the ground became solid under her feet; she felt safe and almost happy. She turned her head and looked again at Hector and Viola, but they seemed scarcely aware of the foreign presence—one quick glance and then indifference.

Clare locked her fingers together under the table. Why couldn't they feel as she did? They did not seem to know their danger or give any name to their distress, and all help was overlooked.

William sat silently, eating little. Every now and again he would glance at Max and then turn to one or other of the children and smile.

Max did all the talking and he ate enormously. Without any signs of shyness he often addressed remarks to Hector and Viola, and when they did not answer him he spoke to the ceiling before he tried again—and again, until with extraordinary cunning he had managed at last, by heaping story upon story, to gain their fleeting attention. To Clare he threw a dozen dazzling smiles, as if to say: '*We* are friends; we don't have to make any effort for each other.'

Mrs. Humble, who usually supped in the kitchen with the door left open so that she might supervise the meal, was drawn from her rocking-chair and pot of stewed tea. She stood against the doorway with her mouth open and one hand spread in mock horror across her face. Every now and again some phrase of Max's would be too much for her. A cackle of laughter spurted from behind the outspread hand.

'Well, I never did,' she would murmur, shake her head, pat her open mouth, and, still unable to find anything more expressive to say in spite of the shakings, the pattings, and the tut-tuttings, she would repeat, entranced: 'Well —I never did.'

'The colour of the water inshore,' said Max, gulping down the last mouthful of cold rice-pudding, 'is like mother o' pearl . . . no, I'm wrong, there are more colours in it than that; deeper and richer ones amongst the soft, liquid shades. It's the sea-weed and the coral that make the water like that. There are marine trees, too, the topmost foliage lies along the surface of the water. You can dive down, down as long as your lungs hold out, and then you swing up from branch to branch, right up to the air again. It's just like climbing on dry land only easier because you're bobbing upward like a cork anyway —no effort.'

'Well, I never did,' came hoarsely from the kitchen door.

'There's a haze round the hills sometimes in the evening that looks like smoke; purple, cloudy—looks like part of the sky if you see it when you're coming in from the sea. The only thing one small bit like it is that glowing bloom that hovers over heathered moors in the evening . . .'

Viola pushed back her empty plate and looked up.

'Have you ever been on the moors of the West Riding of Yorkshire?' she asked loudly.

'Yes,' Max answered, turning his head sharply in her direction. 'Yes, indeed I have. Have you?'

'I'm staying there at present,' said Viola carelessly, drawing her book towards her. She opened it, but did

123

not begin to read until Max (he had accepted the statement of her domicile without a sign of surprise) began to describe a waterfall that fell a hundred feet, bringing down in its foam and spray so much sand and so many fallen leaves that it looked like a torrent of sparkling green-gold wine.

'Very outlandish,' Viola pronounced, and ducked her head to the open page. She read aloud to herself in an insistent and sibilant whisper; it was the only method by which she could protect herself against the distraction of the conversation around her.

'I cut my hand once,' said Max in happy concert with Viola's snake-like hissing. 'A wide gash, right across the palm, and I dipped it into the cold spray of the waterfall to try to check the bleeding. In less than five seconds the sides of the wound drew together—not a scar, see.' He spread out his immense brown hand.

Three members of Max's audience did not miss a word of his story. One of them open-mouthed by the kitchen door; another dreamy-eyed and enchanted at the end of the table; and the third, opposite Max, like a mirror held before his face, reflected every change of expression; light and shade flowed across Clare's face.

'Housekeeping is easy,' said Max, winking at Mrs. Humble. 'All the fruit and vegetables you want planted by a thoughtful Providence at your own back door. No potatoes or mangel-wurzels, or lemons or oranges—just wild things, all edible and more delicious than anything you ever tasted. The wonder to me is how they got there —no birds to carry seeds or——'

'No birds?'

Max looked around, trying to find the owner of the soft, soprano voice that had asked the question. Hector, who had been sitting in his usual place by the window, with his hands hanging limply between his knees and his pale eyes set upon vacancy, was now standing up and looking at Max.

'No, no birds or beasts—yet.'

Hector's lip trembled; he jerked his head from side to side like somebody searching for a way of escape. He looked desperately lost and miserable, and his eyes flickered from face to face, to the window, to the door—and then very quietly he tiptoed out of the room and Clare heard the pat-pat of his feet running past the window.

Viola closed her book with a snap and rose to go to her bedroom. At the door she paused as if she had suddenly remembered that there were certain politenesses demanded of a hostess.

'With whom, sir, will you sleep?'

Max jumped to his feet, clicked his heels, and bowed.

'Mr. Peacock has been kind enough to offer me his sofa; I am to sleep alone.'

'Good,' said Viola, and departed slowly bearing her book and candle.

William seeing that his guest was thoroughly at home, or (which was more likely) seeing nothing at all, crept away to his study to sit alone bemused with happiness.

Clare helped Mrs. Humble clear the table, and Max immediately took the pile of dishes from her and carried them into the kitchen.

A minute later Clare heard sputters of shrill laughter above the clatter of plates and swish of water. She glanced through the door as she passed and saw Max by the sink, a dish-cloth strained to bursting point around his middle, helping Mrs. Humble wash-up.

Clare went out of the house and perched in her favourite place on the paddock rail.

It was a dark, still night. The stars were hidden and, looking down to the river, the only light was a tiny shining pin-point at the end of the pier. Clare felt a sudden lightening of her spirits—a soothed, comforted feeling as though trouble were but slight and transitory and the true substance of life was this secure, unquestioning happiness.

Perhaps the passing shadow had been no more than a vision of her imagination? There was security around her again. There would be security for them all. Max had spoken of a life that embellished her own creation a thousandfold—it was no idle dream; there were such places on earth. He felt about his island as she felt about Prince's Acre, only all that she had woven around her paradise seemed more real in his. His was impregnable, whilst hers, at times, was not well hidden. Her dream could be penetrated whilst his reality had a safety beyond the wildest hopes and the most far-seeking vision.

But in the midst of all these calming thoughts the muscles of her throat suddenly tightened with a smothered sob as she remembered Hector's face after he had said 'No birds?' Viola had been indifferent. . . .

Clare's eyes filled with tears, and as they slipped from

under her eyelids she raised her hand to feel them on her cheek.

She had known fear, despair, and anxiety, she had known simple happiness and pleasure in a life where the few problems were familiar and the rewards and satisfactions all, and more, than she ever asked. But the tears upon her face were shed in a new and strange emotion—they fell in pity for the helpless. But even that tremor which she could not analyse was overwhelmed and blotted out by a flood of half-peaceful, half-ecstatic wonder and excitement that made her lazy and inclined to drift.

What she did not see was that she, with her greater vitality and clearer vision, was also enchained as much as her brother and sister by a force hitherto unknown. She feared for them but not for herself, and therefore she supposed that her emotional experiences had no relationship to the thing that possessed their helpless souls and bodies.

A figure came softly from the darkness and stood beside her.

'Tired, Hector?'

He leant his head against her shoulder like a dumb, imploring dog, and she passed her hand lightly across his hair.

'It's bedtime,' she murmured sleepily, and then, feeling his body stiffen, she turned her head towards where, a lighter shadow in the darkness, the river lay. The faint, regular throb of a motor hummed on the still air and a green and a red light advancing stabbed the night. The engine stuttered into silence, the two lights went out and another, like a pale star, sailed upward a little way to guard the mooring. The splash of oars came across the field and the distant murmur of voices.

Max came out of the house and leant beside them on the rail. He lit a cigarette and smoked in silence.

Clare felt Hector melt from beneath her caressing hand, and saw his figure silhouetted for a moment in the doorway before he disappeared down the passage to the staircase.

The bright point of the cigarette glowed towards her, and she knew that Max was looking at her.

'Come with me,' he said.

'You see, I—we—can't,' she answered, knowing that somehow he saw and understood all that she could not explain.

'Yes, I see—little saint.' His voice was quite grave, but it turned quickly to the light, friendly bantering tone again.

'Will you, on your small island, sometimes think of me on mine?'

She slipped from the paddock rail and stood a moment, not knowing what to answer.

'Yes,' she whispered at last. 'Yes,' and the tears suddenly came again as she ran across the yard and into the house to look for pillows and blankets for Max's sofa-bed.

.　　　.　　　.　　　.　　　.

The night air was so very still that a church clock striking two miles away, beyond the wood, could be heard. Three faint mellow chimes sailing across the tree-tops.

Viola sat up in bed and listened.

From the lane came the restless footfalls—more faintly and then more loudly as they passed and repassed. . . .

And thus, as always, fulfilment followed swift upon the heels of prophecy. She had read again, that very evening, deaf to the petty discord around her:

'Gimmerton chapel bells were still ringing; and the full, mellow flow of the beck in the valley came soothingly on the ear. It was a sweet substitute for the yet absent murmur of the summer foliage which drowned that music about the Grange when the trees were in leaf. At Wuthering Heights it always sounded on quiet days following a great thaw or a season of steady rain.'

Viola's memory never failed her. She knew it all. 'He's in the garden by this time, and impatient to know what answer I shall bring.'

Yes, she had waited, she had listened with the 'vague, distant look I mentioned before, which expressed no recognition of material things. . . .' She knew her happy doom, her ecstatic fate. . . . The patient, sentinel footstep drew nearer, grew louder once more.

Viola struggled to the edge of her bed, preparing for the inevitable sequence. . . . And then—and then. 'The minute after a step traversed the hall; the open house was too tempting for Heathcliff to resist walking in. . . .' Viola rehearsed the scene that followed in a rapid whisper: '. . . in a stride or two was at her side, and had her grasped in his arms.'

Viola held out her arms and her fingers clutched at

the empty darkness. . . . The steps were retreating again—faintly and ever more faintly along the lane; and then—silence.

Tiny bubbles and clots of foam appeared at the corners of Viola's lips, she tore at the thin folds of her night-dress and began to whimper. A plaintive, animal whimpering, rising and falling in the soft crescendo of some wild creature's throaty howl, captured and caged in the spring-time and crying, crying to get out to the world where everything was bursting into blossom.

Candle-light reflected twin flames in Viola's glassy and unseeing eyes. Clare drew the torn night-gown across her sister's heaving breast, and pulled the bed-clothes over her as she laid her back upon the pillow.

'Hush, hush, my precious. . . .'

Another candle joined the first. An incongruous figure crossed the floor; crowned by a bristling diadem of curl-papers, pink flannelette ruffling at throat and wrists.

Mrs. Humble, never to be baulked, loosened Viola's clenched teeth with the handle of a tooth-brush and quelled the cries by pouring the sleeping-draught down the strangling throat.

Mrs. Humble looked at Clare, sniffed sharply, and then, grasping her candle, she took her leave.

Clare tiptoed to the open window, stood listening a moment, and then closed it softly.

Viola slept with her wizened face crumpled and furrowed with distress, and one cold hand was held in Clare's warm one until the candle was spent and dawn whitened the window-pane.

CHAPTER VII

Two months of exile had passed and Roger's poems were not edited, and neither were the dates and circumstances of his life and death, nor the brief tale of his ambitions committed to paper. Paul had not been idle, but the chief task of his exile, still unaccomplished, weighed heavily upon his spirit. He had organized his life at Prince's Acre into a flawless routine that made that life bearable. If it had been unbearable he knew perfectly well that he could return to London- but pride, mixed with a certain consciousness that some decision as to future conduct and circumstances had to be made, caused Paul to make quite a creditable effort to transform the unbearable into the bearable.

The sentimental reason for this self-imposed exile was merely a superficial covering for a dozen more pressing and insistent reasons. He had told Theodora and his friends that he was retiring into the country—Roger's country—to write Roger's life and obituary. He imagined that it was a reason that they would accept as rational and in character. He thought himself screened from unsympathetic criticism by its flimsy protection. The primitive creature in him was withdrawing into solitude to nurse his wounds, but the civilized man held his head high, hid his wounds, and declared: 'I go of my own free will.'

When Paul said that his nerves were shot to pieces he

only spoke the truth, but what he could not understand was that a person with a shattered nervous system was not acceptable as a mate or a companion to people of more equable temperaments and undamaged susceptibilities. In their failure to understand and accept him as he was, they also failed in humanity and understanding of a world-wide suffering of which he was a small part and yet a personification. He and the world had suffered a sea change, not into something rich but certainly into something strange. And it was not that he would not, but that he could not become accustomed to the change. It had reaped a cruel harvest; robbed him of friends, of hope; and it had ruined his marriage. If that ruin was partly of his own doing it was because he had been sadly altered by circumstances of which he was not the author. Paul had his pride, he could not face defeat, and Theodora, to whom he clung as the last hope in a ravished world, had turned her face away from him. She admired self-sufficiency, courage, and independence. He would show her that he possessed all those qualities. Apparently her sympathy and patience had limits, even her unquestioning love could go no farther than the span measured by unsympathetic humanity. Failure of heart in others could be faced; one bitter cry and then they were discarded; but with Theodora (limited and cruel as them all, Theodora without whom he could not face this altered life), he must find some adjustment.

Many times had she left him, with all the self-sufficiency and independence she admired in others triumphantly preserved in her own soul. She returned as many times to find him temporarily penitent, lonely, dependent—but unchanged. And so they muddled on.

But she always returned. That was Theodora all over. She had an unshakable sense of duty and a belief in convention that was strangely at variance with a good deal of her behaviour. Victorianism in conflict with the modern age, a kind of puritanical chain upon the lawless, Godless present. Paul knew that by that chain he could always hold her, but he was sensitive and he had his pride. Their mutual love had once had another form and given a sweeter promise.

All round him at Prince's Acre there was the indestructible serenity and peace for which he longed in his own life; but it remained outside of him, withdrawn from him with callous brutality. He was never one who could accept the gift left carelessly for acceptance by any who desired to make it their own. It was all too impersonal for Paul. Public presentation, deeds signed and witnessed—something very personal and definite was more in his line.

Life at Prince's Acre was so slipshod and unorganized. The weeds, the unfruitful orchard trees, the broken road and obsolete pier were all blots upon law and order. The tangled, unmapped wilderness encouraged unpunctuality, laziness, and careless thinking. The place was a positive harpy for weak natures. Paul steeled himself against the siren's song and organized his home and his days.

Jackson, as he had done in the days when he had been Paul's batman, stood to attention after breakfast and waited for orders.

The same amount of time was spent each day in the completion of routine. Breakfast cooked, beds made, cottage swept and polished, and at ten o'clock Jackson, stiff as a ramrod, standing before Paul's writing-table in the parlour.

A journey to the nearest town for necessary stores was undertaken by Jackson in the car.

The *Theodora* was treated as if she were a prize animal needing regular exercise. The yacht ploughed down the estuary to the sea every day that was fine. Tony refused to accompany his friend upon these expeditions, averring that even paddling made him sea-sick.

Paul took the same interest in all his possessions and took pleasure in them provided that they conducted themselves perfectly. They were cared for, and in return the boat as well as the car must run smoothly, the boiler must yield hot water for his bath, the well-paid Jackson must cook, polish, refuel, and steer. From himself Paul expected a like smooth-running and well-organized result. He dealt with voluminous correspondence punctually, he wrote articles for the various literary publications that employed him, he kept appointments, he wound his watch, he took aspirin when he felt a cold threatening; and yet in that apparently flawless mechanism there hid some injurious discord—he couldn't keep his wife and he couldn't write the simple story of a friend's life, and work, and death.

Theodora would return to London in the late summer, and for once she would not find him waiting penitent and solitary, and remembering (word perfect to the last uttered insult), the quarrel that had parted them. He would be gone, definitely and bravely removed, to concentrate in glorious independence upon a noble and inspiring task. Theodora would be amazed . . . perhaps just admiration would tinge amazement. A miracle might be performed?

The days, well-ordered, passed, and the nights, chaotic, were spent secretly (or so he thought) in dreadful company of dead memories, dead hopes, and one dead, accusing friend. Deep, dreamless sleep had vanished. He was accustomed to bouts of insomnia and sudden rending nightmares—Theodora had proved herself more kindly at those times, and a tender voice and a warm shoulder had soothed him. But the nervous crises were infrequent and certainly with her beside him they had seemed to fade and decrease in violence and quantity.

But now, when the lamps were lit, when Tony had yawned his happy way to bed and Jackson had gone back to his bunk on the *Theodora*, Paul sat listlessly wondering how to pass the night hours through which provision was made only for those who could sleep. Day passed in a succession of realities, but night followed with a horde of ghosts better forgotten.

The tangled, silent wilderness got the better of him at night. To lie down in bed was suicidal, only in action could he find a little respite. Up and down the tiny room until he feared his uneasy tread would be noticed even by the perpetually sleep-drugged Tony; and then out to the dark orchard and the lane. At dawn, when the birth of light seemed to rob the shadows of their terror and give to the abnormal a more normal and less twisted shape, he slept a little—a relaxation in exhaustion, and a sickening oblivion of the mind. But it was not rest; it left him twitching, taut, and more than ever dependent upon a completely untroubled daylight order and programme.

One black, starless night he had paced to and fro in the lane, the unlit way so familiar to him now that he trod with unfaltering step. There was a little comfort in the utter darkness, for moonlight, and even starlight, could lend the trees and shadows nightmare shapes. Backwards and forwards he went repeating, like some prayer for exorcizing fiends, any lines of poetry that came into his head. His spirit had seemed a little comforted that night, lulled by the idiot gabbling of any rhyming words or rhythmical cadence. And then, suddenly, out of the silence came a distant wailing cry, half-animal, half-human, it rose and fell, and rose again—the cry of some abandoned creature, mortally hurt and crying out for aid.

Paul began to run, blind with terror, he missed his way and could not find the gap in the hedge between the lane and the orchard. He stumbled into the ditch and felt the damp mud-plastered bank before him. He cowered down with his hands pressed against his ears, but sound would not be blotted out. As each cry faded a new one, with another voice, took its place. Words came and, taking solid shape, they beat around his ears like mobbing birds. They cried for 'Water'; 'Pity'; for the 'Mercy of God'; and one cried 'Mother, Mother,' in an impatient, fractious tone. He dropped his hands and heard again that first wordless howling, and with an almost pitiful resignation Paul stood against the bank with arms outstretched and let the nightmare take its course.

At his side crouched a shadow; familiar patience and familiar voice. A sort of tuneless murmur, half-complaining, half-grumbling. A shadow and an echo of old Sergeant Withers who had tried to watch over Roger and the other young ones.

'It's no good,' murmured the shape, hunched under the muddy shelter by his side. 'They're finished . . . can't get to 'em . . . do no good if you did. . . . They'll stop in time . . . nearly through. . . . Don't let the youngsters see you've noticed . . . make 'em windy . . . can't do any good.' A sigh, a soft laugh: 'Poor blighters. . . . I envy them. . . .'

'I envy them,' Paul whispered. 'I envy them. . . .'

Pale streaks of light threaded the sky. A steamy mist, greenish as poisoned gas, wreathed from the wet earth. Figures moved, they passed him silently, enveloped in the mist. Some paused a moment, drew near, bent over him where he stood crucified against the bank; and then they too passed on. 'Poor blighter. . . . I envy him. . . .'

The sun was up and the mist flew to it, dissolving on its breath. The trees and hedges stood out sparkling and dripping with moisture. House and wall, leaf and branch rose up distinctly, and the mounting sun swallowing the shadows and disclosing the serene aspect of the quiet, green country seemed like some malevolent spirit crying: 'See what a joke I've played upon you!'

.   .   .   .   .   .

137

At breakfast that morning Tony noticed for the first time that all was not well with Paul. He was used to his friend's irritability—the fractiousness that might at any moment turn to equally annoying high spirits. He knew Paul slept badly—he had heard his nocturnal amblings. But Paul had been like that as long as Tony had known him; he took it for granted along with the fact that Theodora was a subject for sympathy.

Paul and Tony had got along tolerably well during their weeks of solitary confinement. Tony would fall in with any plans provided that he didn't have to make them. He wandered, shadow-like, across Paul's orderly schedule. It didn't make him brisker or smarter—he succumbed to certain rules of punctuality where laxness would have been noticeable; he was prepared to listen and to argue to a certain extent in a lazy, good-natured way that always left a doubt as to his real opinions. But an occasional fiery burst of theoretical soundness displayed the Tony who had walked twenty miles on a burning road in Greece. It also displayed a character that, had it been consistent, might have had some influence upon the minds of other men. But the bursts were rare and of short duration; they withered at the first signs of impatience in Paul. Tony really didn't care about anything except the material comforts of life, and the conduct of his days and nights gave him an appearance of great frailty which belied the well-preserved mental and physical vitality which, seldom used, stored up within him like a well-charged battery, gave every promise of a Methuselah span of years to come.

Paul as a rule started the day with a spate of conversation at breakfast. Surprised by unusual silence this particular morning, Tony observed Paul from the corner of a sleepy eye.

Paul sat very straight in his chair and his movements were mechanical. A reflex action of habit lifted the coffee cup, spread butter and marmalade, and opened letters. His face had a strained, mask-like immobility that was frightening. The face of a dead man and the gestures of a machine.

'Oh, God,' thought Tony, 'I wish Theodora were here; the old idiot is going to explode. . . .'

His sympathy for the absent wife changed into annoyance. (It was her job to deal with Paul if he were going to be ill.) Tony fled from responsibility as a bird flies before the storm.

He rose cautiously from the breakfast-table and, gathering up painting materials and the second unhinged cupboard door, he crept out of the cottage.

Paul still sat expressionless and silent and his hands moved in jerks amongst his pile of correspondence.

Tony arranged himself on the top of the wall of Prince's Acre. Two feet away, in a basket-chair under the walnut-tree, sat Viola Peacock. She gave him one swift, searching glance and then, ignoring him entirely, became absorbed in a book. Her face displayed a furrowed concentration.

'Slightly malevolent,' thought Tony, settling to his task, 'like all cripples. . . . A nightmare imp, but lovely crooked lines. Divinely out of drawing.'

Only once was he troubled by a thought of Paul. He

glanced over his shoulder at the quiet orchard and shrugged his shoulders.

Was the old ass still sitting there? Looked pretty queer . . . those fishy eyes and jerky movements. . . . Perhaps he was stuck in that chair for—no, not for life (he looked dead already), but for eternity. A mechanical corpse; the Almighty's sole example of perpetual motion. . . . Well, he did look quite ghastly. . . . If Theodora didn't lend a hand or show a leg, or something, pretty soon. . . . (The cold and dusty studio where he had existed on neat whisky and an occasional boiled egg appeared before Tony.)

His model suddenly began to show signs of animation, and Tony, following the direction of her lively glance, saw Paul walking slowly down the lane towards the river.

.   .   .   .   .

Even the slight expenditure of energy needful to get him from the cottage to the gates of the pier exhausted Paul. His knees bent weakly as he leant against the rusty bars and for a moment he closed his eyes, thinking as he did so that never again would the weighted lids lift from his aching eyeballs. But, at last, the scene reassembled before him and the sparkle of early sunshine on the dancing water made such an unbearable blaze that tears ran down his cheeks. Through the mist he saw that something unusual was happening.

A bright green dinghy was floating, empty, in the middle of the stream, and a little way from it a fountain of churned water sprayed up from the flaying feet of a

man who was swimming on his back. Paul knew that
the gilded head and muscular arms curving from the
water belonged to no person usually seen at Prince's
Acre. The only other boat of any size comparable to the
Theodora was moored farther up the stream and the owner
lodged in the distant village. Paul knew him well by
sight; a stunted, grizzled man who always looked at the
Theodora with envious contempt and ignored Paul's
greetings. No, this splashing man who braved the cold
spring tide must be a stranger.

He had pulled himself up into the little dinghy and was
standing, completely naked, towelling himself vigorously
and singing lustily in a quivering bass with an undertone
of chattering teeth and exclamations against the cold.

He put on a pair of trousers and folding the towel
around his throat rowed the dinghy to shore and beached
it on the mud beside the pier where Paul was standing.

'Water is still pretty cold, isn't it?' Paul asked, gazing
with mingled surprise and admiration at the gigantic
bronzed Siegfried whose arms were so padded with
muscles that they hung stiffly away from his sides.

'Icy,' answered the man, smiling. 'It's never really
warm anywhere in England; positively death-dealing
after tropical seas.' He laughed and beat his arms against
his broad chest. He seemed miraculously anxious to talk
and be friendly and he accepted the cigarette that Paul
offered.

'Got a boat near here?' Paul asked.

'No, I'm staying up there.' The golden head was
jerked in the direction of the farm-house.

'Oh——' Paul was a little startled. 'You know the Peacocks?'

'They're my best friends,' Max answered simply.

Paul smoked in silence for a few minutes and tried to adjust himself to this new light thrown upon the family at the farm.

People with friends. . . . Quite ordinary folk after all. . . . Week-end visitors, just like other people who lived in the country. . . . Perhaps this man was the dark girl's fiancee? . . . Uncouth, but not bad to look at in a plebeian way; and quite an educated voice. . . .

But it was queer, suddenly, thinking of those unapproachable people with ordinary friends. Two of them were a terrible blot upon the landscape and ought to be shut up. It was ghastly letting that overgrown, half-witted boy run about the countryside by day and night without any keeper—he looked like a criminal. And the crippled child always sitting in the garden and watching every movement at the cottage. . . . The lovely dark girl didn't appear to have any control over them. It was rough luck on her having to waste her youth and beauty caring for two creatures that would be far happier in an institution where their misfortunes would be understood, and hidden. It was funny to think of this man chatting to the dark girl. . . . Paul could hardly get a word out of her; and he worried about her a good deal—lovely, wasted girl. . . . And the old man was a disappointment too. . . .

'Very talented man, William Peacock,' said Paul cautiously.

'Exceptional,' Max answered.

'I used to read him a lot. Sorry he doesn't write any more.'

Max preserved an acquiescent silence, for he realized he was out of his depth. He had been struck by the look on the face of the man beside him. He had seen that expression before. . . . Quite a few men he had seen just after the War had that bewildered look, as if their minds and actions had no connexion—a pathetic effort to 'join in' and play a game that had not been explained to them; going through the actions, trundling along with everybody else; but they lived in another world. In dreams he had seen those stunned, disconnected souls and bodies flocking to his standard to be transported to the island to be healed and comforted. . . . But they, curiously enough, were the greatest unbelievers of all.

'He had a great influence on me when I first started scribbling,' said Paul. Somewhere at the back of his mind he hoped his praise would be passed on to the unapproachable 'master', for it would be nice to talk to William Peacock and to make him feel less cut off. Poor devil, no wonder he hid from mankind when he was burdened with a family of idiots. . . . Any man would be sensitive—feel responsibility. Paul longed to show the once great man that there were those who could judge him by his past intellectual deeds and not by his present misfortunes, even if the latter were fruits of his own sowing.

'Are you a writer!' asked Max politely.

'I scratch a bit. I——'

143

'So do I,' Max interrupted with a twinkle in his eyes.

'Anything recent?' Paul tried valiantly not to look surprised.

'Have you read *Come With Me*?' Max watched the other's face with amused expectation. He was not disappointed. Flashes of amazement, incredulity, annoyance, crossed Paul's face.

'You didn't write that?'

'Why not?'

'Well——' Paul floundered badly, but managed to suppress a direct denial of the possibility. 'You—er—look too active.' Max looked puzzled.

'One has to be, banging around in boats.'

Paul was silent for several minutes. He was assailed with the suspicion that this young man was trying on the old schoolboy joke of pretending to be somebody important so as to lead people on and make fools of them.

'Exquisite little fantasy,' he murmured at last.

'Fantasy?'

'Yes.'

'I assure you, sir, that that book is no fantasy. It is a bald statement of facts.'

'Oh, stick to your joke,' said Paul, a little ruffled. 'I reviewed it, you know, for the *Weekly Revision*.'

'So that was you, was it?'

'Well, pretty good—wasn't it?'

'Yes, excellent. I thank you.'

Max smiled so warmly that Paul experienced an immediate change of heart and found himself beginning to like Max Ralston very much. Perhaps, after all, he had written the book and was shy at being thought a poet; hence this pose of being a practical, unimaginative sort of fellow.

Paul had been a little envious of the genius that had produced *Come With Me*, but now that he was faced with this raw, handsome pugilist he decided that the book, if Max had written it, was probably a rare fluke. It wasn't likely that any more poetic fancies would come out of that hard head.

'I only wish that there were such a place as your island,' he said, smiling back.

'Would you go?' Max asked sharply.

'I'm a married man and my work keeps me in this country.' Paul chuckled happily and decided to enter into the joke. 'How did you fake those photographs?'

'Just a trick,' Max answered sadly.

'Do you think the *Theodora* could get there?' Paul pointed to his yacht and burst out laughing when Max shook his head.

'Not stout enough,' said Max, squinting across the water under cupped palms. 'My boat is in America now, the one on the frontispiece of the book.'

'Writing another?' Paul asked.

'No,' Max looked surprised.

'Oh, but you should. Follow this one up quickly— that's the method. Makes your publisher and your public happy. When you sailor-men take to literature you always run us professional pen-pushers out of business.'

'I couldn't write any more,' said Max earnestly.

'Ah!' Paul was quite recovered and he was enjoying this encounter more than he could ever have hoped. 'Inspiration sometimes only comes once in a lifetime——'

'It isn't that,' Max interrupted. 'I've said all there is to say about the place, and if people won't recognize it, as I do, as the last chance for civilization, well, then I've done my best, haven't I?'

'Oh, all right, have it your own way. Stick to your story. You're too modest by half, but if you don't wish to be caught in the act of committing good literature I won't give you away.' Paul laughed again and Max shrugged his shoulders.

'Going to settle down in this part of the world, Mr. Ralston?'

'Lord, no. I'm going back this year.'

'Back?' Paul raised mocking eyebrows.

'Yes, back to the island, for ever.'

Paul, looking thoughtfully at Max's serious countenance decided that the pose should be humoured within limits, but that sooner or later, by astute questioning, the trap would fall upon this solemn buccaneer and the truth about the origin and authorship of that sensitive masterpiece, *Come With Me*, should be discovered.

Paul had come across colossal liars before. People who fashioned intricate webs of fantasy around themselves were not, as a rule, his chosen companions. But the trouble with Max Ralston was that he was so intensely likeable. He might be able to put this silly fabrication across on William Peacock but he shouldn't get away with the idea that other literary men were as gullible. It was a

pity, it should be squashed and then they could all get
together (Ralston, the Peacock girl, Tony and himself)
and it might be a lovely holiday after all.

. . . . .

Tony came down to the river to make his twentieth
attempt to paint a view that changed continually and
entrancingly.

When he saw the two men standing by the pier he stood
quite motionless for a moment, and then murmuring. 'Oh,
superb creature! Oh, lovely vision!' he stepped forward,
with an unusually lively speed, to the blissful introduction.

. . . . .

Hector, hidden amongst the flowers, had watched,
sick with horror, the operation being performed upon the
indifferent 'H.H.' Conflicting loyalties battled in his
breast. He thought, at first, he should cry out to her, to
warn her that her image was to be stolen from her and
that ever after, when the wizard had carried away his
trophy on the green-blue door, no pool or mirror could
reflect her face.

Hector had not dared to lean his head over still water
since his experience of the previous evening. He knew
that how ever much he might peer, even with his lips
almost touching the water's surface, only cloud and blue
sky would be reflected. He was in the wizard's keeping,
his spirit taken from him whilst his empty body still
roved in confusion across the fields and garden.

But love made him silent; the greater love he bore

147

this man demanded even the sacrifice of his darling sister. Crouched amongst the budding lupins and columbines he could not turn his eyes away. He watched until Tony had left the wall and returned to the cottage to get his tripod and canvas, and then Hector stole silently from his hiding-place and took the short-cut across the paddock to the river's edge.

His speed slackened when he saw the two men by the pier, and hesitating and troubled he stood, drooping, on the margin of the mud by the path. He saw Tony approach. . . . He saw their hands meet. . . . The wizard and the guest drew close to one another; they spoke, they laughed, and then all three men sauntered slowly up the green path.

Hector turned from the river in despair, his arms rose in a wild gesture, then he came back again and crouched in the mud. With feverish fingers he scooped and patted, and as he built his little image the warm air dried it into firm clay. His nails were filled with black mud as he scraped and smoothed and muttered softly to himself in broken whispers.

Rough in form, crudely fashioned, the baked-mud effigy of a man, six inches high—but displaying, even in miniature proportions, a bull-like breadth of shoulders and a muscle-knotted anatomy—stood on the margin of the incoming tide. The river would soon rise and swallow him. . . .

Crying softly, Hector ran to the woods.

Small blue butterflies fluttered amongst the grasses and the marguerites. A foal in the shade at the edge of the wood, startled by the pounding feet, trotted away to join its dam. Young birds, glossy-feathered and plump with slugs and flies flew low across the glade with a whirr of untutored wing-beats. As yet they had not acquired the soaring, darting swiftness of their elders far above them in the tree-tops. They were voluble on branch and bush, chirping hysterically in the maze of leaves.

Here at all seasons Hector, a most privileged person, had been allowed to see the self-sufficiency and sagacity of the wild animals that lodged there. He had watched the mole at work, and overheard the most private and intimate bickerings and murmurings amongst the trees. Creatures that worked from instincts of self-preservation; burrowing, building, protecting themselves with startling ingenuity against nameless enemies and dangers. Nature led them by the nose, the little sillies—they knew not why they did these things. But they were always busy; and brimming over with joy when the sun shone.

Hector leant against a tree and the slow tears ran down his face, and he knew not why he wept.

A sparrow carrying a may-fly, the insect's wings springing from his beak like the arms of a tiny propeller, flitted from the shadow to the light of the field. Hector watched him sadly, skimming out of sight towards the garden.

But nature, for the first time, could not comfort him.

.   .   .   .   .

Viola was very silent. She had seen the three men come up the lane and go into the cottage. What was the 'guest' about, thrusting himself forward in this unpleasant manner? Traversing each quiet scene with gross insensitiveness; capturing Clare's attention with his endless chatter; striding about the house and garden as if it belonged to him; waylaying Heathcliff and interfering with the course of the story.

Viola was troubled, for she did not know what would happen next. Everything was held up by this noisy guest. However, one must be courteous to visitors from foreign lands—they were only birds of passage; but, but . . .

'Hateful,' muttered Viola, clenching her fists.

Clare, digging up weeds in the border, talked idly to her sister—trying to attract her attention and disperse the furrow from her brow.

The garden was very green; it was the colour that predominated. Between the time of lilac and the time of roses there so often seems to be that rich green pause before the summer gathers her largest armful of flowers to scatter over the English countryside. The fruit blossom is all fallen and on every tree and shrub the leaf takes the place of the petal. The grass springs green and juicy and the shadows of growing things lengthen on the grass in the long evenings. Then, as July passes, the colours come, from the strident scarlet of poppies to the solemn, thoughtful blues of delphiniums; and as the brighter colours flow, so the green begins to fade or turn to burning tints as if ignited by the flaming tide round it.

Clare pulled up straggling sprays of shepherd's purse and unwound the bindweed from its strangle-hold.

'The garden is going to be lovelier than ever, "H.H."

I wonder if there'll be any walnuts this year—that tree is so old.'

'So old,' repeated Viola woodenly.

'Tired, "H.H."?'

Viola shook her head.

'Got a pain?'

Viola didn't answer. She was tired, tired to death, and her whole body ached and ached, within and without with strange, unfamiliar pains.

'Take a turn around the garden; It'll ease the cramp. You've been sitting so still, ever since breakfast-time.' Clare helped her sister to her feet and held her arm as they moved slowly along the border.

Occasionally, on better days in early childhood, Viola had run across this garden; even, with aid, scaled the low wall as actively as a cat. Years ago she had once walked as far as the river or the creek in the hazel copse below the paddock. But her feet moved more slowly nowadays and with greater effort, as if the natural decay of time were spreading more swiftly than the years she added to her age.

But as her body weakened her inner, visionary, life grew more strongly till the spirit ruled the body and the days of animal activity were almost forgotten and never regretted. She dwelt in perfect peace in the worlds of the books she read, a soundless world that passed before her eyes, the colour of dreams—shadowy, indefinite, and comforting in its vague outlines, and never troubled by the discords and solid shapes of reality. But during the last few weeks Viola had become startlingly aware of reality. It had stirred her emotionally and scattered unusual pictures in her mind, and she had woven it into the fabric of her present dream and made it into one gorgeous pageant of secret passion and romance. All would have been well if the guest had not arrived and disrupted the vision by an all too concrete intrusion into a scene where no part was written for him. His bulk and glowing features spread across the Yorkshire moors and lent a harsh radiance to the pale luminosity of the heathered heights. The brightness dazzled Viola and dimmed her vision. His sounding, brassy voice stilled the murmur of phantom bees amongst the harebells on the heath and topped the gentle grieving of the wuthering breeze. Viola hated noise, it plucked at her like red-hot pincers and confused her. Her secret passion, tender and unprotected, was in danger. She disengaged Clare's arm and sat down again under the tree. She must not cease to watch. . . . That dark-browed, misunderstood soul must be guarded from the discords.

'Have you nearly finished your book?' Clare asked, patting the cushions and lingering sadly near her sister.

'I read it again and again,' said Viola, opening a page at random. 'It doesn't matter where I start, or end. . . .'

'Are you sure you haven't got any pain, "H.H."?'

Viola shook her head and then suddenly lifting her head she darted a sharp, angry glance at her sister.

'Traitress! Traitress!' she murmured inaudibly, and then leaned back, closing her eyes, and straightway forgot her anger and its object. She was tired, hungry, and impatiently eager for her lunch.

·   ·   ·   ·   ·

Paul had suggested, had in fact commanded, a picnic. A cruise along the coast on the *Theodora* was counted out as Tony wouldn't venture upon the waters, and, miraculously he energetically and positively desired to be included in the outing.

Max, good-naturedly, didn't care what arrangements were made. He was willing to go anywhere and do anything provided that everybody was gay and did as they pleased. Paul bade him invite all those capable of enjoyment at the farm to join the party.

Jackson cut sandwiches, sliced cake, and filled the gleaming super-thermos flasks.

Viola, of course, could not go. She wished the guest would stop laughing and shouting, 'Picnic! Picnic!' She retired to her bedroom to rest, and later in the afternoon she fell asleep and dreamed she lay with Heathcliff beneath the heath and harebells, and one above them, a dark-haired, smooth-faced traitress, stood and 'wondered how any one could ever imagine unquiet slumbers for the sleepers in that quiet earth.'

Hector had not returned since morning, so that Max was not able, for the sake of politeness, to pass on the invitation.

William, in a softer key, murmured, 'Picnic? Picnic?' and retired to his study to pore over a packet of photographs that Max had lent to him.

If Max had not been present Clare would have felt that the invitation was a brutal assault. The spirit that animated the outing meant nothing to her who had dwelt the greater part of her life amongst the marshes and woods

153

where visitors sometimes feasted out of paper bags. 'Going down to the sea' and 'tea in the woods' were hollow phrases when the country and the water were always there, ever-changing in beauty but constant in spirit, at the door.

It is probably a pretty general fact that people who live their whole lives beside a sea don't bathe every day or lunch on the beach; and many people who live in London have never visited the Tower or the stables of Buckingham Palace. It is the unfamiliar that arouses curiosity and holidays (for those who take them regularly) are scattered with outings, sightseeings, and uncomfortable open-air feastings that puzzle the natives of the place.

But Clare's sole thought was that under Max's kindly shelter she could study her enemy and examine the danger that she hoped was imaginary. It took immense courage to attend that picnic.

Paul went because he loved to be the centre of a company. Tony went because Max would be there, and Max was a sight for sore eyes. Clare went for the reasons previously stated, and, because Clare went, so did Sherbet. They all talked as they wended their way through the green, sunlit woods, all but Clare, and she was not familiar with the art of *making conversation*.

'Not too bright,' thought Paul, but he bombarded her with questions and observations. Her beauty excited him and made him anxious for her attention; there was such promise of deep sensual content in her whole person; shelter in the brooding darkness of her clear eyes, safety in the soft moulding of her shoulders and breast—she seemed the personification of rest and peace. Again and

again his eyes returned to her thinking that with these
furtive glances he could read all that this silent person
kept unuttered. He knew the type. . . . No brains; no
need of intellect when a beautiful body was a still symbol
of blind, unself-conscious abandon—and, oh, the ecstasy,
the peace, the oblivion to follow. . . . Paul had one of
his rare poetic visions when he looked at Clare; it was
something half-felt, half-seen. A feeling of warmth—sun-
soaked and golden to the very core of his being—a complete relaxation of the nerves and sinews so that the body
could sink and sink in languorous release. . . . And a
picture of tired limbs entwined and still in liquid summer
shade.

Haunted nights of insomnia had given him an unusual
and exaggerated sensitiveness. As a rule he was cold,
calculating and suspicious of spontaneous emotion. But
now, for a time, he was young again—a boy; taut with
smooth muscles and tingling with a healthy glow, eager
to be off and away for sheer good spirits. But the mood
fed upon him like hungry flame, it took all his nervous
energy, and beneath lay a shaking fabric of tired bones.
He longed for peace, the peace that this silent, stupid
she-animal withheld behind the curtains of her brooding
eyes. Tear down the curtains! He couldn't leave Clare
alone.

She walked timidly through the wood in Max's shadow,
and that shadow was her narrow margin of security.
Enclosed in bands of steel, heaped over by cold marble,
locked up against the terror around her. Paul's words
beat about her in her fortress, beckoned to her, pleaded

with her to come out. . . . Impossible to resist another's need. She ventured forth a little way, turned her eyes in his direction, spoke softly and then beheld the trap that had been laid. He was upon her, that spirit of destruction, and back she fled to her fortress—walking softly, eyes lowered, heart beating, beating, in Max's kind shadow.

Tony, bearing the smallest of the baskets, dawdled in the van. Every now and again he called to them, but he didn't expect an answer; he had his own thoughts and dreams; his sore eyes were being soothed and, on the whole, he was quite content.

'Oh, Mr. Ralston, you comely man, you walk too fast for me. You sweep across the oceans in one wing-beat whilst I barely crush a daisy in an hour of plodding!' He might almost have found a rhyme, made a poem, but it was hot straggling along under the beech trees. Silly old Paul with his plots and plans and picnics. Fêting the sailor novelist! So like Paul. But the sailor was worth this dismal plodding and sandwich eating. . . . A golden, romantic presence, reminiscent of old fairy-tales and saints and heroes—a child's hero, a Galahad, a Siegfried. Tony sighed and tilted his floppy hat on to the back of his head. The fellow was really to impersonal and sure of himself; if he noticed any one it was that cow-like female from the farm. A funny world.

On they wandered under the branches glistening with young leaves, amongst the scented ferns and red-stemmed brambles.

Paul pointed out the beauties, describing them elaborately and sketching in the air with outstretched finger and thumb. They all looked obediently when he cried: 'See those beeches, like the flying buttresses of a cathedral! Oh, the sublime architecture of Nature!' They tried to see as he saw out of an uncomfortable feeling that courtesy was needed, but they felt depressed because of the passing thought, a vague suspicion, that Paul saw nothing.

Each member of the strangely assorted party had his own shadowy thought, his vision; and yet they would not have expressed it or dared to violate another's secret mind. But Paul had other methods, he was possessed by a frenzy for attention. On he went, a capering Cook's guide, jealous of the forest—flinging himself across the landscape before their dreaming eyes; voluble, dramatic, desperate, and seeing *nothing*.

The host arranged the guests in a circle and courteously invited the lady to spread the cloth and unpack the baskets.

Clare was utterly bewildered by this pilgrimage into the heart of her dearly familiar wood. The ceremony seemed a little bit incongruous to her; but for Viola's and Hector's sakes she must discover the nature of these two strange beings. Max helped her arrange the cups and plates. Remembering a dim yesterday she wondered how many years it might be that she had known and loved this person.

Paul teased the author of *Come With Me* unmercifully. Max let him rattle on.

'Are the native maidens of undreamt-of beauty?' Paul asked, munching cake and chortling with good humour.

'There are no natives, of either sex,' said Max solemnly.

'But, my dear fellow, wasn't that rather remiss of you? Very aesthetic and highbrow and all that. I quite see your point as an artist, but you're writing for a public of less refined tastes. No wonder your little joke miscarried. . . . no rush for the early doors, no chance for you to cry *rien ne va plus* to all the elderly gentlemen and unsatisfied wives. Even the Creator, in the beginning, saw the wisdom of putting one of each kind in Eden.'

'There'll be a pair there yet,' said Max, and Tony sighed.

Clare gazed from Paul to Max in bewilderment.

This badinage was beyond her. Max's sacred island! This man didn't believe in it! Max didn't mind! If any one attempted to defile *her* perfect world it would have killed her. She caught Max's eye and he winked, ever so gently—the mere quiver of an eyelid. It was reassuring; they shared a joke; it was suddenly delightfully exciting and very funny. She laughed softly and Paul glancing at her bent head thought:

'A giggler—of course. Beautiful, stupid, and therefore a giggler.' He felt suddenly sad and shifted his gaze to the sunflecked mosaic of leaves and sky above his head. At that moment, with a sickening misery, he thought of Theodora. His gaiety evaporated like a cloud of steam and he scarcely spoke at all on the homeward way.

Clare noticed the sudden transformation, and ever moved by helplessness and sorrow she ventured from her marble fortress and offered this strange man, no longer dangerous and destructive, a long look of loving pity.

Because he was too tired and sad to do otherwise Paul accepted the gift.

Sherbet panted at their heels, more exhausted by the curb his natural good manners put upon his usual exuberance than if he had been hunting at full gallop for several hours. To sit upon his haunches, patient, polite, chained by loyalty, for two hours whilst the breeze wafted a sequence of delicious smells in tempting samples past his twitching muzzle, had put a great strain upon Sherbet. His heavy head hung low as he snuffled along in the grass and his pink-rimmed eyes gazed at Clare's heels with just the faintest look of disapproval.

'Look in for a drink—any time,' said Paul to Max, as the party reached the wall of Prince's Acre. He was quite distrait now, and his face bore the inward-looking, mask-like immobility of a man whose unspoken thoughts are wholly engrossing. His imagination, usually so limited, had played him an alarming trick. He supposed he might be ill . . . lack of sleep . . . the ghastly, inexplicable experience of the previous night . . . any excuse. But the sudden bodily hunger he had felt in Clare's proximity had sent him blindly to the verge of a great mental unfaithfulness. He had thought of Theodora, to whom in thought and deed he would always be constant, however great the temptation to be otherwise. Such a code, alas, would not keep *her* eternally faithful (and his favourite form of self-persecution was suspicion of her trueness); but he, if the final breach should ever come, should have nothing with which to reproach himself.

But the air seemed suddenly suffocating and dusty when he turned his face from this despicable lust. Had Theodora been there (she who had always accepted his urgent, swiftly-passing, selfish caresses with the cold passivity of an over-civilized animal), she would have reaped the harvest of that seed suddenly springing and flowering in his blood. There would have been no moral need to chill its boiling tide; the right of law that made them man and wife would have released his passion, and though her acceptance might still be cold he, once returned to his normal code of calculated behaviour, would have had nothing with which to reproach himself. But Theodora was far away—an icy, self-sufficient, secret woman. How could he know for certain that that cold body and veiled mind were not vulnerable to the same lust that his had experienced. The memory of her habitual armour of sexual indifference, at this moment of bitter dissatisfaction and deprivation, seemed to make her doubly guilty of secret excesses.

Paul went silently back to the cottage and wrote to Theodora on the Mediterranean coast. The letter was slightly petulant, faintly accusing, and violently bitter; but it ended with a flourish of trumpets—a faked fanfare for independence:

'. . . I'm so settled here that I don't see how I can ever uproot myself from this peaceful soil. A perfect place for work. There are plenty of amusing companions too. The author of *Come With Me* (that best seller I sent you in the parcel to Brindisi) is here; an utterly humourless and open-air sort of chap (the book

is obviously one of those flukes that occasionally startle
and then, in the author's unprolific future, disappoint
the literary world), but he is good company and has
a certain knowledge of sailing-vessels, which last, of
course, is very sympathetic to me.

'There is also another writer, one William Peacock
(before your time, but a great hero once of Roger's and
mine). So you see that even in this lonely spot I am still
in the "thick of it", as you call it.

'I believe you said in your letter, *six weeks ago*, that
you would be back in August. The servants have
orders to be ready for you at any date you care to
specify, and if you want to let me know your plans
write to me here direct, as I don't expect to move from
this charming place for a long while. . . .'

.   .   .   .   .

There had been one other attendance at Paul's picnic.
High up above them in a beech tree, stretched along a
branch, hidden from their view by foliage, Hector
watched them without being seen. After the first shock
of horror at this invasion to which his beloved sister was
evidently a party, Hector's eyes never left the nodding
brim of the floppy hat straw. The continual jerking of
the covered head in the direction of the giant guest did
not escape Hector. So sad and perplexed was he at this
sight that after the picnickers had packed up and straggled
home through the fading light Hector remained crouched
on his dizzy branch too sad and beaten to think at all,
and too lost in spirit to contemplate descending and taking

the familiar track (known only to him and a few rabbits) under the bracken and tunnels of burrowed-through bramble bushes.

It was dark upon the floor of the wood, though still light with a pale grey and violet radiance above the meshed ceiling of the branches, when he swung down from his perch. There was a brief scuffle from where some startled creature sprang away as he bent his body to enter the undergrowth; but the silence returned at once. Hector was well known in the tree-tops and under the ferns.

A bell tinkled faintly across the meadow. . . . Humble shaking the little handbell for him when he had been too long away. . . . He shook himself free of the last, long, clinging tentacle of bramble and jogged across the twilit meadow to the yard.

Just as he was about to cross the yard to the house he noticed a tiny glow of light across the garden near the walnut-tree. He paused uncertainly until his eyes made out the dark shape in the shadows by the garden wall. Hector swerved to his right and trotted towards the tiny gold beacon of the cigarette.

Tony was leaning on the wall and gazing dreamily at the lovely, uneven lines of the roof and chimneys against the luminous evening sky when Hector rose up from the flower border beneath him.

'Hullo, Nep, how you made me jump. Where have you been all the day, Rendell, my son? I missed your silent company.'

Hector stood so close to the wall that Tony, on the farther side, could see the glitter of his eyes.

'Do you know, Nep, you're my true affinity—no effort, no wearing of the emotions like some people. I get all my fun in life through my eyes, but some sights are too much of a good thing, Nep. . . . A spot too stimulating for my limited emotions. But you're a true comforter, Nep. . . . But you shouldn't be too much of a slave; people like me take advantage of it, you know. . . . It might become as nearly harrowing as the devotion of a dog if one stopped to think.' Tony paused a moment and watched the minute golden arc made by the cigarette he flung across the lane. He was talking more to himself than to his companion, for it had become a habit during those one-sided conversations by the waterside, but he was suddenly aware that Hector was unusually attentive to his thoughtless discourse, and it gave him the feeling that the dog to which he had likened this dumb, unquestioning boy was sitting up patiently, concentrated on the expectation of some tit-bit.

'Tell you what,' said Tony with mock seriousness, 'we're too sensitive for this world and its course mortals; we ought to emigrate, you and I, Nep, to some out-of-the-way island where nobody has been before. . . . Just been hearing about the very place for us, Nep; lots of lovely things to look at, but not *too* exciting or disturbing . . . People are so disappointing; don't you agree? I bet you do. All in a groove; same thoughts, same qualities and vices till you don't know good from bad. Same old sport between the sexes. . . .

How weary, stale, flat, and unprofitable
Seems to me all the uses of the world!

163

I believe I could stand a sea-voyage if there were any place to sail to that was really different. . . . You'll come, won't you, Nep?'

Hector hadn't moved, but Tony could see that he was listening to every word, listening but, like a dog (Tony thought) not understanding the words or the real meaning of the nonsense.

'We'll take old Paul's boat one of these days, Nep, and sail away—steer straight for the sun—one of these days, you and I.' Tony yawned and then began to hum softly.

At that moment Hector stretched out his hands and laid them on Tony's chest, a gesture that seemed to have some primitive significance.

'I swear,' said Tony in a dramatic whisper.

Hector turned from the wall and ran towards the house and was lost under the falling night.

'Funny old misery,' Tony murmured as he wandered sleepily down the lane and across the orchard towards the cottage and his dinner.

.   .   .   .   .

Clare sat in her usual place on the paddock rail. It was a warm night and so still that occasionally she could hear, across the field, the faint chuckle of the flooding tide rippling around the wooden piles under the pier, and the regular 'chump chump' of Charming's teeth wrenching at the grass. He slept out in the warm weather, but Clare still roused him from his grassy bed in the mornings as his rheumatism persisted in all seasons.

The lamps in the kitchen and sitting-room made a pool of light half-way across the yard.

William's study curtains were drawn, and he and Max were chatting lazily over after-supper cigarettes. It was years since William had talked so much, and probably years since Max had listened for so long in contented and interested silence. But there was a deep sympathy between these men, so widely different in appearance and character, and yet not so widely separated in age. When Max said 'sir' and William said 'my boy' they merely designated the difference between the father of a family and a bachelor without domestic responsibilities.

Viola had gone to bed after sitting through supper without eating or speaking. Clare had gone up to the bedroom and holding up a lighted candle had seen that she lay with her face to the wall—apparently asleep.

Hector, for once, had remained indoors, crouched over the table under the lamp, studying the photographs in Max's book.

The distant church clock struck ten and Clare saw Max come out of the house and cross the pool of light spilling into the yard. He had an odd, rolling walk. He scarcely seemed to bend his knee-joints, swinging his long legs forward and rocking from foot to foot as if he balanced on heaving ground. He came to the rail and scrambled up beside Clare.

'Funny day, hasn't it been?'

'Yes,' said Clare, whispering in deference to the quiet night. 'What's wrong with that man?'

'Who?'

'Mr. Millard.'

'Nothing,' said Max laughing. 'He's quite ordinary. What did you think was wrong?'

'I don't know—only he seems. . . . Perhaps he's ill. I've never met anybody quite like that,' and she added quickly, 'but I don't know many people.'

'If *knowing* means *understanding*, I think you know more people than I do. In all my years of knocking round the world and hundreds of chance meetings I never get farther than the surface of a man's forehead—if you see what I mean?'

'Yes,' Clare repeated.

Of course she saw what he meant. Max, who had no need of people—that happy, independent, roving spirit skimming the surface of the world and passing, ever forward, immune from shackling relationships and arrogantly joyous of his life. She who had only known the dependent, the helpless, and the weak in spirit looked for the first time at another prospect and experienced a conflict between a duty (performed for love and her own need) and a wish (desired for an even greater but entirely selfish need). She who had always remembered to walk softly and look backwards to the safety of her faltering followers treading in the footholds she had marked for them, now looked forward and saw herself outstripped and left behind.

'I find it very hard to leave,' said Max. 'I feel I've known you for so many years; the only person I shall be sorry to leave behind and never see again.'

She wanted to cry out: 'Don't go! Stay with me!' and

chain him to her slow steps at the head of her crippled company. But she closed her lips firmly on the cry, seeing him, in her mind, already a long way away in his ever forward-going, self-sufficient progress.

'I'll go to-morrow morning. I've got a lot of things to attend to, and then I can sail before the end of the year; nothing to wait for now. I've told your father.

'Clare, I long to be back in that place; I can't explain to you what it does to me—what it could do to anybody. One's emotions, thoughts—one's whole outlook changes so that one couldn't ever feel depressed, or worried, or sad; just happiness endlessly lapping over happiness like little waves.'

'But won't you be lonely—Max?' she asked softly.

'Lonely?' His voice, that had been gentle and almost personal as it always seemed to be when he spoke to her, rose to it's more usual concert pitch. 'Why I couldn't be lonely; not even if I had to die there alone. One's not human there; none of the ordinary emotions; one is superhuman!'

'Father will be sorry you have to leave so soon. . . .

'Yes, I'm sorry; but it's the others—they don't like me. I bother them, that's what made me decide it was time to pack up—mustn't bother them. . . .'

'Oh, Max, do you really think that? I hoped . . .' Clare stopped speaking and looked miserably at him through the darkness. She could see the dark shape of his head bent thoughtfully forward.

'Yes,' said Max gruffly. 'I usually overestimate my own value. I wouldn't hurt them—not for anything.

. . . I've seen them look at me.' He turned a little and put his large hand lightly on Clare's. 'I expect they are very wise; they know I'd like to take their sister away from them.'

They sat in silence for a while, and he kept his hand upon her trembling one, and then, without another word, she slipped from the rail and went indoors. As she passed she glanced into the sitting-room at Hector crouched under the lamp; paused for a moment, listening, at William's study door; and as she got slowly into bed she gazed a long time at Viola's turned shoulder on the neighbouring bed.

That night, thinking how much she loved them, with an aching heart, she cried herself to sleep.

CHAPTER I

PAUL was disappointed when he discovered that Max had left Prince's Acre. They had not met again, and Paul felt slightly injured that his advances had met with so little success. When he questioned the Peacock girl about Max's sudden departure she had answered: 'He's gone,' and had turned her back very rudely as if she thought the inquiry was an impertinence.

It was really too bad, because Paul had liked Max Ralston and had hoped to have his friendly presence on the *Theodora* and in the cottage during long evenings when it is pleasant to sit smoking and talking around a lamp with the darkness shut out.

At times Paul regretted the acquisition of Tony and fretted that the latter was making no use of his country visit. They had both agreed to work, and the cottage was too far from London (to say nothing of the lack of accommodation) to allow for week-end visitors.

There was absolutely nothing to do but work. Yet Tony splashed good paint on worthless kitchen furniture like a child bedaubing everything within reach with its first box of colours. He sauntered about with the same old canvas, scraping out every half-finished picture and never accomplished anything. He was probably misleading the idiot Peacock boy, who was for ever trotting after him like a half-starved puppy. No, Tony was not worth helping, he had no sense, no stamina; lazy, wasteful, unmoral; burning his brief candle in the pathway of the sun. If only Max had stayed they could have got to like each other. Even if he were a terrific fraud, with his ideal health colony, he was worth ten of Tony, and his companionship would have done Paul a world of good. He felt so lonely and exhausted. There was no place for him in life. No help, no understanding, and no background. Max was an opportunity lost of making a pleasant contact with Prince's Acre.

And from that point his mind wandered, questing, to Clare. (What was there between her and Max? Some understanding. Some kind of relationship.) And so, from Clare, to Theodora and his empty world.

But now, at the end of June, he found himself in a state of monotonous mental exhaustion. No change had taken place in his circumstances and no manifest result of his perpetual worrying, so that now when he started on a chain of thought—about Roger, Theodora, or his life in general—instead of the long conflict ending in a practically insane state of mind, he found that thought slipped away and became vague, unimportant, and a blankness took its place.

Now, when he thought of Theodora and their relationship, he stepped into a world of fantasy. They would come together at last, without effort, one day soon, and start again perfectly atuned. That was what he longed for, and that, if he were to live at all, was going to happen—somehow, some day.

And what of conscience and Roger's book? That, too, was going to be quite simple, for he knew well how to compile the ordinary kind of popular biography: born on this date; died on that. Education, early influences, hopes. (What had the patient Roger hoped? Was it not apparent in those outspoken, slashing war poems that Roger hoped he would not die in vain?)

Roger had known that the voice of poetry had but a limited hearing, and he had often said that poetry was accepted as a stupendous emotional untruthfulness, an evasion and an anaesthetic, and was therefore an impotent vehicle for propaganda. The subject didn't interest people one bit, only the treatment.

'Paul, you must popularize poetry; write prose translations for the simple-minded,' Roger had said, and he had yelled with laughter, as he always did, at his own obscure jokes.

What a legacy to leave a friend!

Paul had meant, long before he came to Prince's Acre, to write an epitaph and a protest to lay upon the graves of Roger and all those others. Roger's poems would have been his most powerful weapon, for behind the carefully chosen words and beautiful cadences lay the truth, the naked, hideous truth, about human slaughter.

But now his rage had withered, his purpose was obscured, and he began to long to live in peace without the mental conflict which was so much more painful and personal than a world war. And it was only in rage that he could have written anything of Roger's message, and he knew now, in exhaustion and defeat, that anger and hate were vehicles that carried no weight. Nobody wanted to listen to unpleasant truths screamed out by a man with a grievance.

> Let us alone. What pleasure can we have
> To war with evil? Is there any peace
> In ever climbing up the climbing wave?

'There we are,' thought Paul, 'in a nutshell.'

It was a night in late June after Tony had gone to bed and Paul had begun to sort papers for the biography. At one moment he had thrust the papers and notes aside and, taking a fresh sheet, he had amused himself by composing a burlesque of his former state of mind.

'It is we, the living,' he wrote, 'who romanticize the dead. How blameless and pure that wasted youth appears to us. Was there ever their like? In comparison the youth of to-day is tawdry, perverted, and unambitious. The divine spark that leapt to a flame only to be extinguished a few years ago seems to have been the perfect manhood, not of a generation, but of a century of centuries of generations. They proved their exceptional worth by laying down their lives at the command of old men, arm-chair ridden, hysterical women, persuasive posters and martial music.

'No matter what they died for; they were made of too fine a stuff to question their right to live when the pride of a nation was at stake! Their murderers (ever just) shall sing their praise.

'But wait, ponder a little while as you mourn ecstatically upon this blood-soaked earth. If these of to-day (these small souls) were swept from your sight by a like calamity, would not a garden blossom in that dusty waste and a million stars make celestial music in that once dark night? Youth has that quality. When it is destroyed at the moment of its intellectual and physical blossoming on each cold brow we see the mark of a poet, a saint, or a hero lost to the world.

'But the survivors had their spring. The youths of to-day have theirs, passing, unnoticed, to a fruitful or an unfruitful season.

'By glorifying the sacrifice of those brighter spirits can we undo the waste or wipe out the pain? A million prayers rise on the smoke of smouldering sacrificial altars and dissolve in the indifferent sunlight of a new day.

'Let the dead bury their dead, and ye, who sing the praises of the youth that is no more, have pity on the living!'

Here Paul stopped, and having studied the flowery page he tore it up and let the flakes of paper flutter into the basket beside him. One would soon go dippy, like those Peacocks, if one continued in that style for long. Purple journalism wasn't in his line, and it gave the truth an unpalatable flavour. But it was healthy to be able to laugh at one's past emotions. Farewell to ghosts—ghosts whom he had once longed to join, turning his back upon the present.

But now there was Theodora, and she must return to him and give him the future. The torn sheet in the waste-paper basket was the gesture of thumbing one's nose at the past. Perhaps now the midnight hours would pass untroubled and the mind would be at rest. It was useless to pull against the tide; the crew was dead and one could not battle with the elements with a boat-load of corpses. What was the use, anyway, of trying to alter humanity when one's own house was not set in order, when even two people couldn't understand each other? Why couldn't Theodora love him—as he loved her? Nothing else mattered. Perhaps now things would alter, if he could forget . . . if he could forget.

'I wonder if she'd change her feelings about me if I got popped off defending the Union Jack?' he thought, and he smiled at the shadowed ceiling. Perhaps, after all, the truth was lying in the waste-paper basket. Oh, safe and happy dead, unconscious of the mockery of their sacrifice. One must no longer make oneself the living and sensitive butt of a world who had forgotten them. Yes, forgot them, their faces, their spoken thought, their written word.

> No longer mourn for me when I am dead
>   Than you shall hear the surly sullen bell
> Give warning to the world that I am fled
>   From this vile world, with vilest worms to dwell:
> Nay, if you read this line, remember not
>   The hand that writ it; for I love you so
> That I in your sweet thoughts would be forgot,
>   If thinking on me then should make you woe.
> Oh, if, I say, you look upon this verse
>   When I perhaps compounded am with clay,
> Do not so much as my poor name rehearse,
>   But let your love even with my life decay;
> Lest the wise world should look into your moan
> And mock you with me after I am gone.

He was very near to tears, and could not tell if it was

Shakespeare, himself, or the compound of the two that caused the emotion.

The lamp on the table began to make a stuttering sound as the last drop of oil was absorbed into the wick, and Paul looked at his watch and saw that it was three o'clock.

Well, it passed the night just letting a pen run across paper. To-morrow he would begin the damn book, and it would probably lie undefiled and uncut upon a few country-house bedside tables.

But let your love even with my life decay.

He raised his head suddenly as the lamp winked out and left the room in darkness.

A tendril of creeper tapped softly against the closed window-pane. The sealed room was stifling and Paul fumbled his way through the furniture and opened the window.

He leant against the sill and closed his eyes. It would soon be day.

The soft wind heralding the dawn cooled his face and as he leant there, too weary to make any movement, he felt as if something were going out of him. Through the wind, across the silence it went; beyond sight and beyond thought until it was no longer his. Somewhere it would mingle in the air around Theodora's lovely head and then blow on out of the world, for ever out of his keeping with all that he had lost. Roger, his mother, his hopes, beliefs, and ambition. Farewell to ghosts this dawning day.

He didn't often think of his mother. She had died

before he realized how much she meant to him. She had been a person of mental and physical beauty and she had never made any claims upon him; never grasping him to her in one of those complex mother and son relationships. She had always been something of an alien to him and to his dull, successful father. She had slipped through his early years leaving a fragrance and a bloom. Only now that she was gone did he realize that the happiness of those first years of life had been her doing.

The descendant of Persian princes, a creature of ice and flame, and yet always veiled in patience as if she knew that her strange nature could never be understood and must for ever be concealed. (Paul wondered if that was how he had got the idea that beautiful women were stupid: reposing languorous and acquiescent behind their physical perfection. . . .) No, she hadn't been a stupid woman. She had possessed some secret integrity.

It was from her that he inherited his love of music and all his intellectual values. She had once said that every artist should have a little Jewish blood. He could hear her now. She never spoke for long without straying into some other language—German, French, Italian, Russian—as if all her thoughts were universal and must be expressed in half a dozen tongues. . . . How she would have suffered had she lived to see the War.

'I wish Theodora had known my mother,' he thought irrelevantly.

He lit a candle, and as he held it up he noticed the cupboard standing against the wall. In the centre of each door-panel was painted an elfin head.

'Not bad,' he murmured, smiling. 'But he'll never make a penny that way.'

He tidied the scattered papers, resolving to start next day on a tabulation of facts for the biography, and as he stacked up a pile of old letters one thin sheet of lined paper unfolded itself like a live thing and lay spread out under his eyes. Standing against the table, the candle held in his hand, he re-read the familiar sentences:

'I am a little warmed by the ardour of life I still hold within me. Eventually I shall be happy—I can't help it! With every nerve screaming in revolt and driving me like a wild, unwilling horse to the brink of the gulf that divides the bearable from the unbearable I still can draw rein and plod back to the realm where the spirit fights an equal battle with the body.

'A bit incoherent? But you know what I mean; you've been through it. I repeat it because now it is true, but *afterwards* (what is that?) we, together, will wonder what past truth is true that day when mind and body no longer flood with the emotion we once felt. If it is truth we died for to-day, to-morrow we'll be dead for a lie. So let's have no more of truth. The world's a cabbage patch—and it don't 'arf stink at times.

'But, you know, there are compensations in the Almighty's doubtful humour. When we are first dead we stir the living into feelings of distress and melancholy (and often quite creditable poetic fancies!). But let us lie a while and even the poet will turn away and hold his nose. But there is a corrective: an arch of bleached bones is a lovely sight; it gives one all the pleasant and unpleasant emotions in miniature: wonder, surprise (a spot of bravado wit) and just a breath of sadness. . . . And after that the centuries to lie forgotten dust. One corpse in its time plays many parts!

'If I die to-morrow and you live to so ripe an age that the reigning monarch telegraphs his congratulations—on that day remember me and one poor bloke will not have died in vain. I'd do the same for you!

'I'm obsessed by a finicky dislike of waste. Can't get used to it! I dream I've found a way of insuring life after death, but when I wake I can't remember the formula and have to soothe myself by feeding waste bacon-rind to the rats.

'Enjoy your leave and stuff a book or two into your pockets for me when you come back. Sergeant Withers sends his comps. and says he hopes *it* finds you in the pink, as it leaves him.

'They are coming over thick and fast and fragments of roof fall like a plague of locusts—I alternately blow and write. . . .'

Paul folded Roger's letter and tucked it under the others.

Roger's breath had fanned that dry paper; his bright eyes had followed the tracing of his steady hand. . . .

Forget him. Forget him. . . .

Paul yawned and tiptoed up the creaking stairs.

He lay staring at the grey window until the first beam

of the rising sun set a yellow diamond in the pane. And still he lay, sleepless and sad, feeling empty—empty.

.   .   .   .   .

July passed in days of intermittent rainfall and sunshine. The barley in Mr. Kay's biggest field was beaten down in places by a storm. The long stalks were flattened in thick, swirling heaps against the rubble, and these hollowed whirlpools amongst patches of standing crops looked like the resting-place of some great beast that had passed that way.

The hay was cut and stacked under tarpaulin roofs and amongst the brown, shorn grass, sharp as needle-points, a fresh green was springing in a fruitless effort to yield a second crop and re-clothe the country before the withering of a year.

Mr. Kay owned an acacia tree, and its long trunk reared above his house and the foaming blossoms, waving high against changing July skies, sprinkled a soft snow-fall of petals. Grey pigeons rose in sleek companies above the yellow mustard fields that stretched to the curve of the beech wood screening Prince's Acre.

Across the sea-marshes on the southern border-line flowed a lilac tide of sea-lavender and grey-blue thistles, all amongst the dry, silvery grass and sand.

A checkered ribbon on the periphery of the triangle: the mustard-fields and the beeches, the dunes and marshes, and the sea sometimes as purple-blue as the Mediterranean mingling with the river flowing green and transparent between its overhanging banks.

The weeks of the summer were advancing and Paul had written, in phrases dry as dust, a criticism of the poet's frugal yield of work. He emphasized the early promise and and the brief fulfilment; checked all dates carefully and wrote a business-like letter (begging childhood recollections) to Roger's sole relative, an aged aunt who lived in Wales. The work was done, but still he stayed at Prince's Acre, and the melancholy and the emptiness was all that remained to him. Waiting, waiting—for a voice to call, for a door to open, for day to follow night.

CHAPTER II

I T was a bright, hot afternoon and the heat shimmered from the roof of the barn. A hen pecked in the dusty yard and Charming drowsed with hanging head in a corner of the paddock, his tail waving the flies away from his twitching quarters. Sherbet was slumped against the rainwater-butt, lolling his tongue and snapping his jaws at passing bumble-bees. He had been out early with one of his brothers hunting rats along the river bank and he was hot, exhausted, and heavily booted with mud.

Clare came on to the kitchen step and looked across the paddock to the woods beyond the river. Her hair clung in damp curls round her forehead. She had made twelve pounds of raspberry jam and her finger-nails were stained red and she was sick with the smell of hot fruit and sugar.

Mrs. Humble leaned out of the sitting-room window and shook out a tablecloth. The solitary hen came running with neck outstretched and ridiculously striding gait to gather up the scattered crumbs.

'Them chickens never think of anything but their stummicks,' said Mrs. Humble leaning over the sill. 'Covered with feathers and running about as cool as cucumbers as if it was Christmas. Wot I always says is: nature protects 'erself. I once knew a lady (a friend of yer mother's) wot 'ad a pekingese that mewed like a cat— lifelike it was—even deceived the cats. And there was a young feller working at the opera 'ouse wot 'ad never worn any underclothes, covered in 'air from top to toe he wos. 'Is wife told me," she added primly.

Clare brushed away a fly and sighed.

'I wish I had a tail.'

'I think 'er 'ighness 'as got one all right,' said Mrs. Humble in a hoarse whisper from the window. 'She's regular possessed these days. Snapping my 'ead off when I tells 'er to eat 'er dinner and not waste good food. "Be quiet, Joseph!" she says to me the other day ("Joseph", if you please!) and went on mumbling about an "hindignant helder". *Now* wot's got into 'er? I harsks meself. All this book reading. . . . And 'Ector ain't much better——'

'They'll feel better when the warm weather is over,' said Clare sadly.

'Yus, and when the visitors go back to where they come from. . . . Showing hoff in front of strangers the 'ole time, that's wot those two children are doing. No knowledge of respectable be'aviour. Goodness gracious if I thought their goings-on were on account of bad 'ealth I'd harsk yer father to send for a doctor.'

'No, Humble!'

'Yus, I would. I don't believe in taking liberties with the good 'ealth the Lord gives us——'

'Humble, they're not ill.'

'No, I know it. Don't I see to it has you're hall kep' in good 'ealth. But there's something wrong with those two, and hI've a good mind to harsk a doctor to horder them a bottle.'

'But if they are not ill what good could it do?' Clare asked patiently.

'Give 'em a good fright,' said Mrs. Humble nodding an angry head.

Clare smiled and turned away. She knew her Humble —all bark, no bite.

'More trouble than a cartload o' monkeys.' The acid voice floated after Clare as she turned the corner of the house.

Clare walked slowly down the drive from the yard. Over the garden wall on her left she saw the top of Viola's fair head bent over a book. In the small kitchen-garden to her right William was wandering between the beds.

Since Max's visit William had begun to live a slightly more active life. He seemed to be taking a more practical interest in his property: making a bonfire of the weeds that Clare extracted from the border; hanging perilously out of windows tacking back the creeper that veiled the panes; prodding plantains out of the mossy lawn and walking every morning right round Prince's Acre with a greater alertness and an eye watchful for places where repairs could be made. But it was only a half-hearted effort. Prince's Acre had for too long gone its own wild, sweet way and William had neither the ability nor the desire to make a conventionally orderly estate out of the tangled pattern. His interest seemed to be animated by a wish to form some personal contact with his home, and, with eyes for once turned outward, behold the strength and beauty of his chosen exile.

He called to Clare as she passed and brought her a few

raspberries on a cabbage-leaf platter. Clare was nauseated by the taste, smell, and sight of raspberries, but she accepted the gift and even managed to hold one berry in her mouth.

'What beauties! Thank you, father.'

She walked on down to the lane holding the proud gardener's offering, and then, when she was out of William's sight, she dropped it into the ditch.

In the bank of the duck-pond under a bower of hazel and dog-rose was a little alcove where it was always shady and where the grass was moist and cool. There was a flat stone near the water's edge and here Clare sometimes sat in the afternoons now. Since Max had left she had found that more and more frequently she wanted to get away from her family for an occasional hour of solitary musing. It was impossible to think of Max when anybody was near; even covering her eyes didn't bring his face to mind, if there was any other person in the vicinity. She climbed to the loft when Mrs. Humble wasn't watching, or sat in the bower by the pond and gazed at the dark water, so filmed with vivid green slime and tiny weeds that there could be no reflection of sky or of her own face to distract her mind with visible pictures.

Her thoughts ran in a circle, beginning and end interlocking and continuing endlessly in a repetitive sequence: all that Max had said, every turn and gesture, every expression. Sometimes a particular movement that he had made and that seemed to bring him very close was held for a moment, a still photograph, that she lingered over before passing on and round again until the same picture of his head turned to her in the darkness by the paddock rail floated before her eyes once more. Only in solitude could she find Max; he had no place in the life she lived with her family. She gave her dreaming no imaginary future; only a few memories and then back to the ordinary round with a mind refreshed by this communion. It had become a necessary part of her life; a short space apart with something of her own. There was no longing, no false hope or desire to alter her lot. After that one blind turmoil of longing when Max had first come among them all, that wish to fit her brother and sister into a scheme which she believed now to have been wholly selfish and utterly impractical; she had seen the sober course of her life stretching on its way. It had to be, and from that precious and brief emotional upheaval she preserved one thing for herself alone: the right to remember that encounter.

Looking up, she saw that Paul Millard was coming across the field from the woods. In a minute he would be in the lane and he must pass the pond to reach the cottage. She sat very still and held her breath with the hope that complete immobility would make her invisible. Since the day of the picnic he often spoke to her when they met. She wasn't really frightened of him now, but she found him difficult to understand. He used unfamiliar phrases and seemed to expect replies.

He came down the lane slowly, fanning himself with his panama hat, and as he got abreast of the pond he stopped and smiled at her.

'I see you've found a cool spot.' He laughed suddenly.

'You look rather like a little water-hen tucked away in there. Is there room for me on the nest?'

Without waiting for an invitation he scrambled along the bank. At one place his foot slipped into the mud and he stood for a moment on one leg examining his splattered shoe.

Clare looking at him frowning at the muddy shoe thought how queer was the way in which he switched so suddenly from thought to thought. Each passing idea absorbed him completely. There he was concentrating on a splash of mud, his mind twisting and puzzling over some secret worry, and then, a second later smiling at her, devoting all his attention to her in a concentrated assault of sociability. He didn't sit down, but stood directly before her so that Max's face passed right through him and disappeared.

Clare sighed softly and blinked.

'Day-dreams?' asked Paul. ' "And the thoughts of youth are long, long thoughts." Am I right?'

He stood across the only path of escape, and short of leaping into the pond and wading a few yards to the lane there was no choice but to exchange a few tortuous amenities.

'We've been making jam,' she said quietly, smoothing out the crumples in her cotton frock. 'It was so hot indoors and there is very little shade in the garden until much later.'

'That little sister of yours is a regular salamander; sun or shade, there she sits basking by that hot wall all day.'

He spoke kindly, and Clare glanced up and smiled at him.

'She doesn't notice weather, nor does my brother. We've been brought up so much out of doors.'

'But you are different.'

He was looking at her with that penetrating intentness that always warned her that she had ventured too far in friendliness, and unless she could retreat from the dangerous ground he would involve her in some terrifying personal discussion. He was standing easily, one lifted arm hooked over a branch. It was a careless pose, but his eyes stared at her animatedly.

'Don't you ever think of leaving this place? Going out into the world and mixing with your—with your own kind?'

Paul thought, calmly and benevolently: 'I'm paying her a compliment really—telling her that her beauty and intelligence (comparative intelligence) is being wasted. . . . All girls of her age have dreams; she can't *want* to stay here for ever. . . . Must have natural desires, with that face and body. . . . She'll turn into something awful if she doesn't get out of this rut.'

Clare smoothed away at her frock and lowered her eyes.

'No,' she answered timidly, whilst a tremor of alarm ran through her.

'Now, look here, Miss Peacock,' said Paul, laughing good-naturedly. 'You ought to think of me as a friend, and you mustn't imagine I'm interfering and impertinent —I'm nearly old enough to be your father—and I have nothing but admiration for the selfless way in which you are dedicating all your youth and vigour to caring for others.' He paused a moment and looked down at her bent head. He was much stirred every time he looked at this beautiful creature and a good deal enraged when he thought of a selfish father making her the guardian of his idiot children and a prisoner in an unnatural solitude. Paul saw red when he contemplated the egoisms of relationships. It was criminal to cage this young animal— deny her the rightful experiences of life—so long and so successfully sequestered that she probably couldn't analyse even the less complicated of her natural instincts. Interference be blowed! Her silence and her bent head seemed to be acquiescent. . . . Poor little devil, why shouldn't she live a normal life?

'Your father was a very fine man, you know?' he continued earnestly. 'And you have a noble heritage.' She looked up then with such a look of pathetic bewilderment on her face that Paul, frowning and filled with righteousness, took a plunge.

'I believe in freedom, don't you?'

She nodded, her face clearing for a moment.

'And freedom can only be understood after education. Perhaps you have had nobody to help you, advise you. . . . Now I understand, better than you can know, how your father has suffered. He has a perfect right to retire from life. . . . But I, as your friend, know that you should have a different fate. You mustn't think, my dear, that it is your duty to remain here for ever. It is a false knowledge of values. With the education and chances offered to most girls you would realize that. It is *not* a duty. You are doing yourself a grievous wrong—through the highest motives, I know. Don't let yourself suffer unnecessarily. . . . Because nobody has had the common decency to explain to you——' He stopped and smoothed his hair with an agitated hand. He was so dizzy with his own oratory that he was beginning to lose the thread of his discourse. Never had he been so worked up before. Anti-vivisection campaigns, pacifist propaganda, sea-side holidays for slum children, employment preference for ex-soldiers—none of the causes for which he had battled with all the ardour of a convinced believer in justice, freedom, and fair rewards had ever so excited him as this unhappy girl robbed of even average enlightenment and held prisoner by so abnormal an existence. He cleared his throat and searched for phrases that would not only show her his overwhelming sympathy but also open to her (those lovely eyes were surely dreaming of the happier life denied her) the road to freedom.

Clare got to her feet and took a hurried step towards him; so near that their bodies almost touched and he felt a romantic and idiotic desire to sweep her up in his arms and carry her off, full gallop, away from Prince's Acre. Very gently he leant forward and rested his hand on her shoulder.

'My dear, you know there are very excellent places—schools and—and institutions—where your little sister and brother would be cared for. There are homes run by kindly people, trained to deal with such cases . . . they would be happier, and some kind of training, which is of course beyond you . . .' He stopped speaking as

Clare shrugged away from his trembling hand and stood pressed against the hedge. Her eyes searched his face and her lips were parted as she panted for breath.

Now, at last, she knew him. The man who had taken her mother. . . . The Vicar like a beast of prey hunting down Hector and Viola. . . . And now, this man trying to hold her down whilst he destroyed them; snatched them from their happy life and shut them up, hurt them, killed them! Clare had no knowledge of manners and modes, and she couldn't say haughtily, 'Please stand aside,' and sweep past him. To her he was not an impertinent person blithering with mistaken friendliness, but a figure of terror; he was Death himself. She jumped for the farther margin of the pond, and landing in the middle, struggled and splashed up to the lane and ran, covered in mud and slime, up the drive and into the garden.

Viola raised her head and gazed reprovingly at her hoydenish elder sister, who flung herself upon the ground beside her, panting and mud-soaked, with her arms outstretched, as if she tried to cover with her body some creature threatened by an uplifted sword.

.   .   .   .   .

For a moment Paul was very much embarrassed. It is always disconcerting to address a person in a normal manner and then discover, by his subsequent behaviour, that you are alone with a maniac. He was also troubled by the passing thought that somehow, without any evil motive, he had hurt her. She had not been offended certainly (how could she be when he was only urged by feelings of sympathy and kindness?), but in some way her uneducated mind had been outraged, she had behaved as if she thought he was making a sexual attack upon her! It was decidedly unpleasant, and he must really forget the whole incident and stop bothering himself about the fate of the beautiful Peacock girl. He had thought she was all right—going about with Max Ralston. And that truly beautiful face was misleading. . . . She didn't bear the physical signs of imbecility as did the other children, but there was no doubt about it: *she wasn't all there.*

He stepped carefully to the lane and scraped his muddy shoes in the grass. He wanted to go back to the cottage, but the two girls were sitting in the garden beyond the low wall and they would see him pass. He could see the tops of their heads from where he stood, and he felt that he could not command the necessary nonchalance to walk past them in full view and with proper dignity. It was a damn bore. He wanted to get back to write to Theodora before the postman called for the letters. Theodora was back in London. He had spoken to her on the telephone. It had been a nuisance having to walk all those miles through the woods to the village where the only telephone was—and an inefficient exchange at that. She had answered when he said 'Hullo' and had seemed quite pleased to hear his voice. (Ringing up the day she got home was the sort of courtesy and remembrance she appreciated.) She had joked about her trip, asked after his work with proper seriousness and interest and he had told her he was very busy (perhaps he had made too much of his work, insisted just a little too emphatically that he was happily and fully occupied). If she thought he was busy she might not suggest coming down to join him or, if she wanted him, beg him to come to her. She had her pride too . . . but he mustn't wail. She must be the one to weaken—this time. Not a word had she said about her future plans (he had only hinted—he hadn't asked), And then quite humorously he had quoted:

> From you have I been absent in the spring,
> When proud-pied April, dress'd in all his trim,
> Hath put a spirit of youth in everything,

and as he got to the end of the third line there was a buzzing and a humming and all the cursing and swearing of which he was capable could not move the operator to re-connect the call. He could write it to her, that little, borrowed lovemaking, for the last two lines were the important ones:

> Yet seemed it winter still, and, you away,
> As with your shadow I with these did play.

She'd be amused; she might be touched. . . . Of course she'd never guess how true it all was; how spoiled everything was without her; dull, colourless. . . .

> Nor did I wonder at the lily's white,
> Nor praise the deep vermilion in the rose;

he murmured softly as he scraped the side of his shoe along the grass.

'Damn those two girls,' he thought. 'They might have the decency to go indoors. . . . Can't walk past without saying something, and if I do they'll scream or have a fit.'

He looked around, searching for a way of escape, and saw William in the kitchen-garden above the bank to his left.

'Good afternoon, sir,' said Paul cheerily. ('No harm in talking to the poor old thing, even a common labourer accepts a greeting from a stranger in this part of the country.')

William tipped a barrow-load of weeds on to the smoking bonfire and then, straightening his thin back, he peered at Paul in the lane.

'Good afternoon,' he answered politely.

'That bonfire makes one realize that summer is nearly over. A truly autumn smell.'

William, seeing no need to converse about his bonfire and its seasonal portent plunged a long-handled fork amongst the weeds and disclosed the red-hot skeleton of the inner fabric.

'I'm sure this place must have a history,' said Paul, settling on the bank and lighting a cigarette. 'I asked Mr. Kay about it the other day, but he merely said he supposed it was "too old by far and past praying for".' Paul laughed. 'There's only one apple in his orchard of several dozen trees, so I expect that finishes his interest in history. Have you got any records of your place?'

'There's a date cut in the wall at the back of the study mantelpiece,' William answered, remembering that he was taking a new interest in his property. 'But a good deal of the house is probably much earlier. There are the remains of the original foundations under the turf in the paddock at the back—we can't plough the field

because of them, but I don't know how far they run. . . .
The coast has changed, I expect, in the last seven or
eight centuries . . . probably a castle on the sea once,
until the outer walls sank. . . .'

'You should write a history of Prince's Acre, sir.'

'But there is no history,' said William plaintively.
'There's no information to go on—the sea or the marshes,
or perhaps a great fire, destroyed everything.'

'Well, I expect our friend Ralston could supply a
history.'

'Ah,' sighed William, leaning on the fork and gazing
dreamily in front of him. 'He might discover——' He
paused and turned his head in Paul's direction. 'Oh,
I see what you mean. You—er—don't believe he really
did discover—anything?'

Paul waved his cigarette in the air and laughed.

'Well, you know, in spite of all his comic seriousness
I don't think he expected anybody to believe in a place
that is scientifically impossible. Those seas are pretty
well known, aren't they? What he has done is to play a
good joke on the public. Naturally they don't take the
island seriously, but the things he's written about
civilization and humanity in general have made 'em sit
up a bit; and where he is so clever is in realizing that
you can make people swallow any amount of home truths
provided you make 'em palatable and amusing. But of
course you know Ralston better than I do; he may be
a man of very high principles and he may write seriously
about world reform one of these days, or stand for
Parliament. My private opinion is that imaginative work

is not really in his line. He won't bring off another book like that; it was a pure fluke; personality (he's a born actor) plus the gift of story-telling—mind you he's not a bore; not the sort of chap who sends you to sleep with a yarn about the giant trout he caught or the height of the fence he cleared on horseback. Oh, no, his lies are good ones; worth a lot of money—provided he *admits* they are lies. After all, he is writing for an adult public, not for children who live in a world of fiction anyway.'

'And adults don't?' William was staring at Paul with an expression of bewilderment; and though he made one or two timid movements towards the bonfire he seemed almost paralysed by Paul's stream of words.

'Of course not,' said Paul. 'The appeal of that book is entirely intellectual; and that is why I am convinced that Ralston won't write another. The only thing he is really truthful about is that he wrote the book with the idea of making it a stirring adventure story: *Treasure Island* plus a bit of Munchausen. He's knocked about the world and he's probably had a good many unusual experiences, but so have a lot of people—you don't have to be a buccaneer or an explorer if you want to see the world in these days of simplified travel. And everybody can write a travel book if they want to; so our friend cooks up his experiences into a rare dish, and quite by chance it appeals to the intellect, and not to the spirit of adventure, of the average schoolchild. So, you see, if he were really the artist that that book makes him seem, he'd have to go on writing *that* kind of book for *that* kind of public. . . . But we've seen him and we know him; he hasn't got a spark of intellect, the book is a fluke, and the next lot of "experiences" he doles out will be a bloody bore.' Paul chuckled and wagged his head knowingly. 'I know the hall-mark of a charlatan.'

'I don't understand. . . .' said William faintly.

'Weren't you surprised, knowing him as you do, that he ever managed to write a book at all?'

'I didn't know him as a boy,' William whispered. 'I just met him the other day.'

Paul made a sound like a person who has swallowed a spoonful of boiling soup.

Just for the sake of argument and discussion, only because he had been starved of intelligent conversation, he had entered into this idle discussion of Max Ralston's merits as a writer. It wasn't as if he were jealous of the man or cared a hoot if he was a liar, or an idealist, or just a temporarily inspired idiot. . . . It just happened to be an easy subject to discuss with this old hermit. And quite by chance, what a hornet's nest of deception was being disclosed! Max had said the Peacocks were his best friends! A damned lie of course, for the old man had just admitted he had only met the fellow the other day.

Paul's mind was working at lightning speed.

Poor old William Peacock. He was just the kind of good-natured, dreamy person that a crook would get hold of . . . believe anything he was told. Ralston probably realized in a flash that he was easy game—a half-crazed old man with no worldly sense—just the type to get money out of.

Paul gave another hot-soup gasp.

'There's something wrong somewhere,' he said solemnly. 'I suspected there was something fishy about the fellow when I first set eyes on him. . . . Instinctive, I suppose. Anyway, I'm usually pretty quick at summing people up, and Ralston struck me as a particularly low type of intelligence: undeveloped, scapegrace, soldier of fortune. . . .' Paul stopped speaking for a moment as another and illuminating idea struck him. He was quite unconscious of William's horrified stare or of the terrible thought in William's brain.

'This poor man is insane,' William was thinking, and the mere thought of the affliction made his hands tremble and his tears flow.

'Good God!' shouted Paul. 'I've got it. He never wrote the book at all!' He spread out his hands in a vigorous gesture as if he had suddenly produced a conjurer's rabbit and wished the audience to see that there was absolutely no deception.

One day Paul was going to write an immense book on the literary history of the past fifty years. William Peacock, as the most brilliant critic since Leigh Hunt, already had a place in its pages. But Paul now saw how he would add, as the climax to William's brief career, that the man of letters in his last days was a prey to charlatans and blackguards, but that a friend who appreciated his simplicity had protected his interests in those last sad, shattered years.

Paul sighed happily, and then, looking up, he suddenly saw, with horror, that William Peacock was crying.

'I hope he didn't try to get anything out of you, sir,'

he said gently, looking away and pretending not to have noticed the embarrassing sight. 'Naturally if I heard that the man was trying to get money out of people to finance his impossible scheme I should make it my business to make investigations. But as nobody has taken the affair seriously I don't think we need worry. . . . Of course, sir, he will have made a tidy sum out of the book, and I am sure that we shall hear no more of him. As I see it now, his original idea was to collect subscriptions for establishing a health colony, or some such thing, and then abscond with the money. But he has managed to make a small fortune in a way he least expected, so there is no need for us to be philanthropic.'

Paul laughed carelessly and took a furtive glance to see if William had managed to pull himself together. It was horrible to think of that young blackguard trying to get money out of this defenceless creature. Paul hadn't worried about the affair at all until now. He had thought Max very stupid in the way he insisted that his island was a real place, and he had suspected that there was more in it than just a humorous pose. The fellow had been so alarmingly solemn about it all, and he did look (when one came to think of it) like the kind of person who would stick at nothing. . . . There was no knowing by what sinister means he had come by that manuscript. . . .

Paul, who had never been susceptible to flights of fancy before his tenancy at Prince's Acre, had the most exciting and grim thoughts. He pictured a murder! Some unknown poet exiled from home in a South Sea island had written the fantasy. . . . Perhaps he had met Max

Ralston and undoubtedly he had been swept off his feet by the man's charm. (Yes, there was no doubt he had charm: a dangerous, overwhelming and unscrupulous personality.) The poet had confided in the man whose physical presence alone encouraged confidence. . . . The precious manuscript had been read, and in the mind of the criminal, blind to the intellectual value of the work, grew this scheme for a colossal deception. The poet was murdered and Max Ralston was the unchallenged possessor of the weapon for extorting money from gullible beings—like William Peacock. . . .

Paul lit another cigarette and began to criticize the work of his imagination.

Perhaps murder was rather fantastic? Yes, it was going a bit too far.

He began again, and his final summing up was as reasonable a supposition as could be arrived at by a man who was perpetually concerned with the hidden and endlessly evil motives of humanity.

'He took the manuscript to England,' Paul muttered to himself. 'Promised to get it published and encouraged the exile with pictures of a large fortune and release from penury. He published the book as his own work, whilst the only person capable of contradicting him was chained by poverty in a distant land where the facts of the crime would never be heard.'

'Well, that's not impossible,' Paul said aloud. 'If you've lost anything by the business, sir, I'd be delighted to make a rare old stink. I'll get the Royal Geographical Society on to it (just for the sake of having all our facts correct) and they'd be able to prove (if we *need* any proof) that there is no such place, and then if I hear of him trying to get money out of people I'll——'

'Please, please,' William interrupted gently. 'You mustn't worry, you mustn't worry.' He produced an enormous cotton handkerchief and blew his nose.

The supper-bell sounded across the yard and William looked timidly at Paul.

'Have you far to go?'

Paul was startled by the question and didn't immediately grasp William's meaning.

'Far to go?' he asked, and then muttered to himself: 'And does the road wind upward all the way?'

'Are you far from home?' said William in the same dreamy voice.

'Home? Home?' muttered Paul, hardly conscious that William had spoken, and (by aid of the poets) trying to disentangle himself from the rights and wrongs of the Ralston case.

'Home? Home? . . . "From you have I been absent . . ." Oh, I'm sorry sir. . . . No, no way at all; I'm at Kay's cottage.'

'I'm glad you live here,' said William earnestly, and Paul's heart bounded with pleasure.

Here was real gratitude and appreciation. . . . The poor devil *was* lonely. He did want somebody to talk to. . . . Paul felt he had guessed right about William Peacock all the time. It was a desperately lonely man who had accepted Ralston, and had been deceived by him. . . . Paul clenched his fist.

'This is really a very fine man,' he thought. 'With the most direct simplicity he accepts my good feelings towards him. I will protect him and I will provide him with the companionship he has been denied.'

'I'm glad you live here,' William repeated with great tenderness, and Paul looked up at him and smiled.

'I'm very glad to be here, sir,' he said, and was only a little pompous because he was very much touched.

William stood hesitating a moment before turning towards the house, and then he said very firmly: 'My wife found great solace in this place and my children are very happy. . . . You will be happy here too.' And with bowed shoulders and shuffling steps he made his way towards the house.

'Poor old man,' murmured Paul lovingly, gazing after the retreating form of the shattered man of letters. 'He can't even keep his mind on one subject for a few minutes. Poor old man. . . . What a fate!'

He rose to his feet, and seeing that the two girls had left their strategic position in the garden he went home to write to Theodora.

.   .   .   .   .

Colour flowed back slowly into everything as the white-hot day with its bleaching glare faded.

Tony sitting on the cottage doorstep drowsed like a sleepy cat, and between his slitted eyelids he saw the grass grow green again and the light shadows of the fruit trees elongate like strokes left by a painter's brush.

Behind him, in the little parlour, Paul was busily writing to Theodora.

'Theodora's back in London,' Paul said, looking at Tony's head silhouetted in the sunny doorway.

'Oh! Did she have a good time?'

'Yes, not bad,' Paul answered carelessly.

'Coming down here?'

'Shouldn't be surprised.'

Tony sighed. Comfort and security never lasted. He had got on all right with Paul, but he knew that somehow he had failed. Perhaps Paul expected him to become famous over the summer. . . . Paint fifty landscapes; make a fortune—all the impossible things. It would be just like Paul to think that the light of his countenance was enough to make a man famous. 'England's premier artist,' Tony thought sourly, 'flood-lighted by Millard and all rights reserved. . . . And not one canvas filled! Well, Paul's backed another loser. . . . But we haven't quarrelled. . . . Wonder if he'd loan me fifty quid? Who wants to *make* money? So much better to borrow. . . . If Theodora comes (bet she doesn't though) I'll have to clear out. . . . Oh, dear, not one canvas. . . . Not one bean. . . . I wonder if Paul would loan me fifty? No, he hates lending—too much fuss and bother. I'd better get on to Theodora; she'd give one the coat off her back. . . . I'd like to give *her* something—start right, anyway; and then if Paul blows up there's always dear, lovely Theodora, and the back door of the flat when Paul's about. I wish I'd painted just one picture I could give her. . . . Can't paint here; not when I *see* it the whole time. . . . One day, when I've forgotten how it *looks* and only remember how it *feels*, then I'll paint it. . . .'

'What are you going to do this winter?' Paul said suddenly.

'Emigrate,' Tony answered yawning. 'Go to Russia.'

'Um—you might do worse.'

Tony looked over his shoulder and was entranced by the effect of strong evening light and shade in the little room. Paul, leaning over his desk, was wrapped in a deepwater obscurity and his face and hands and the mounts of two pictures on the wall behind him gleamed with greenish-white transparency.

'An old, old fish,' thought Tony smiling sleepily. 'An old fish, rather green about the gills. When he speaks tiny bubbles will sail up to the ceiling; and when he moves he'll ripple his spine and come floating out into the shaft of yellow light coming through this door— coming straight through me. . . . I'm impaled on a spear of sunlight. . . . A dead fish frying on a skewer.'

The light fell full upon the painted surface of the cupboard at the back of the room and the two faces on the doors glowed with soft colour. Two dream faces— twisted, fantastic features—reflected in blue glass.

I'll give that cupboard to Theodora, he thought; she'll be vastly amused. It is lovely, and old Paul hasn't noticed it.

'I say, Tony.'

'Yes?'

'I've discovered that that Ralston man is the most stupendous impostor and blackguard.'

'What a triumph,' Tony whispered inaudibly.

'I'm pretty sure he never wrote that book himself.'

'Tut-tut.'

'It's no joking matter; one can't be sure what is at the back of it.'

'Oh, I'm as solemn as an ape. Awful thing, imposing.'

'Didn't you think it was a bit fishy? That book—a fine piece of intellectual writing; the work of a scholar, of a man who thinks—and then Ralston, utterly un-educated. He couldn't write his own name on a cheque.'

'Perhaps he could write somebody else's.'

'There,' said Paul, ignoring Tony's wicked chuckle. 'You did think he looked like a criminal. He's been trying to get money out of poor old Peacock.'

'How do you know?'

'Peacock told me himself. He's absolutely miserable about it——' Paul stopped talking abruptly. Remem-bering the conversation of the afternoon, he couldn't quite recall how William had said he had been robbed, not in so many words. The poor devil had cried, the weak, ineffectual tears of a fading mind. . . . But he hadn't said anything—at least, nothing sensible or rele-vant. How on earth had he, Paul, arrived at these alarming conclusions? He stared, unseeing, at the golden doorway and tried to recapture that feeling of certainty that Max Ralston was a criminal; that conviction that William had asked for protection. Gently there slid before his eyes the picture of Max and Clare exchanging glances at the picnic. Two people sharing something; furtive, triumphant glances; shutting him out. The boys at school used to exchange glances like that; running off into corners and whispering . . . never sharing with him. He didn't want to know their dirty secrets, but it made him so lonely. . . . People always pairing off. . . .

Quite suddenly Max Ralston and all his works became intensely boring. Without speaking another word Paul finished his letter to Theodora.

CHAPTER III

THE air was very heavy. The sky suddenly grew dark; black from horizon to horizon, and the light beneath the clouds was lurid and outlined each separate object in the countryside with vivid clarity. It weighed on the head, drained vitality and shortened tempers, that dark overburdened air. But the rain did not come, and again and again the sky cleared and the sun poured down upon dusty lane, parched garden, and fields as brown as slices of toast.

At night intermittent lightning illumined the woods in a soft blue radiance. Frail, ghostly shapes, trees cut from thin paper, cardboard houses and the fine pencil-line of river and lane were disclosed by a flicker of blue light, and then cast back to solidity under the hot, dark night.

Sleep was elusive in such weather. One's body, soaked and filled with sunshine, generated electricity and would not relax. Even the light weight of a sheet was too much, and limbs, of their own perverse accord, fell into impossible positions, legs and arms spread out for a minute then twisted or bent into momentary postures. Heads turned on hot pillows, and turned again, searching for coolness, and sweat broke out on tense bodies and lay in dewy pools between the breasts and thighs of sleepless people.

Hector lay on the floor by his bedroom window and each swift stab of summer lightning bathed his naked

208

body in an eerie light and flickered a point of flame into his staring eyes.

Clare sighed and turned, snatching at tiny morsels of sleep, and ran her hands slowly down her body feeling the moisture on her palms. Towards morning she slept deeply; the sheet trailed upon the floor with her discarded night-gown; her legs were spread; her head turned sideways on the crumpled pillow and her hands cupped over her breasts.

Viola was unaffected by the trying weather and slept peacefully beneath her smooth counterpane. Not a sigh, not a sound disturbed her in her deep bowl of silence, and her waking visions invaded her sleep and the hushed, thundery air seemed only to increase the silence of her world.

Mrs. Humble muttered: 'Enough to try the patience of a saint,' and stirred unhappily in her shroud of suffocating flannelette. In the passage beyond the door she could hear Sherbet trample and turn uneasily on his square of carpet, and then whine in his sleep and beat his tail as he dreamt of glorious hunting days along the river.

William sat all the night through in his study and wrestled with reason.

The conversation he had had with the stranger in the kitchen-garden a short while ago returned to him frequently. He did not alter his opinion of the stranger's unhappy mental condition, but the memory of what had passed between them served to illumine some very dusty and neglected corners of his own mind.

For years he, alone amongst men, had realized the need

of some place on earth where civilization and progress had not penetrated. Miranda had known it and Prince's Acre had been a makeshift for a time, but it had not been well hidden, for circumstances had obliged him to sacrifice her to those very things: civilization, progress, and science.

He had continued his search, but somehow, on the way, reason had flown and fantasy and slovenly imaginative thought had possessed the mind of the scholar. He had created dream worlds and lost them again. It had become a pastime and a hobby, but never practical in so far as his and Miranda's children were concerned. Then Max had appeared, the dream had come true and William had realized that it was too late to be of any practical use. His children were content; Miranda, who should have been saved, was lost, and he knew now that he had wasted years of life dreaming of the place that could no longer benefit her. What he should have been searching for all that time was, not a concrete manifestation, but a state of mind. In hoping to discover some actual place on earth where life would be easier, more fair, and devoid of care, he had failed to realize that what he most needed was a state of mind incorporating those things: a philosophy, a complete mental integrity. In himself there must be Eden! In that way should Miranda's children be protected.

'It will be very difficult,' he murmured, 'but I must succeed. Max can't help me any more, and they can't help themselves. I must discover my own heaven, and there they shall all dwell.'

He stared across the room and through the window

into the night. His lips were closed lightly and his face glowed with serenity and hope.

No sound through the sleeping house, no breath of wind passing over the night-wrapped garden. Peace without—there should be peace within.

He rose and going to the bookcase took down Max's book. He fluttered the pages until he came to a photograph, taken from the sea, of a misty coast set in a collar of ruffling foam.

William smiled as he remembered a suggestion that the Royal Geographical Society should be questioned for proofs.

There was the island, on a quiet day, in a calm sea. His body trembled with longing as he gazed at it, and then he closed the book quickly and stood staring before him. Now it must be in the mind; a quiet place washed around by cool, placid thoughts, flowering with faith.

William spread his hand across his face to hide his sudden weakness from the empty room.

If once, only once, he might behold that fair place with his outward eyes!

CHAPTER IV

A<small>N</small> occasional shower during the last weeks of August did not clear the overcharged atmosphere. Thunder rolled threateningly at a great distance, but the heavens did not split asunder and release their explosive burden until September was advancing.

The solitary apple in Mr. Kay's orchard fell into the grass and was excavated by sleepy wasps.

Paul, peering into the looking-glass in his dark bedroom beneath the eaves, noticed that his hair was turning grey. He did all his work at night now and he was existing on the least possible amount of sleep. He wrote letters and articles and gathered notes for his *Fifty Years of Literary History*. The work was mechanical and left him no time to think. He had suddenly grown apprehensive without knowing what it was he feared.

At times, sitting in the little parlour, through the stuffy, electric summer nights, he would feel so hemmed in and overpowered that he gasped and struggled like a person being buried alive.

No word came from Theodora, and if she did not make a sign soon she might finally discover him petrified and lifeless, walled up in invisible masonry.

Again and again he told himself that he must get out of Prince's Acre. The fantasy of perfect married bliss was replaced by the idea that he could ignore Theodora, that he could live without her. He would return to the old life; he would be strong and self-sufficient; he would go his own way and she would go hers. He needed nobody—he could live alone. . . . But he did not move. His brain refused to contemplate such a future for long. His nervous resistance tightened and tightened, and he waited impotently for fate to make a decisive move, and with an aching head he worked mechanically and heard every tick of the clock. He told himself that he was being strong-minded. . . . That he was merely proving to himself that he was quite independent and therefore nothing could ever hurt him again. . . . And then, suddenly, he was too tired to bother any more.

One morning coming up the estuary with Jackson in the *Theodora* he discovered that the engine was missing badly. The broken rhythm hurt him physically and he waited impatiently, leaning on the rail and gazing across the shining water at Prince's Acre sunk amongst its trees, whilst Jackson tinkered ineffectually.

'Take her into Southampton after lunch,' said Paul. 'It's no good wasting time. Bring her back this evening if you can, otherwise stay there till it's finished'; and then he almost shouted: 'This can't go on!'

.   .   .   .   .

The carrier had called at 'The Load of Hay' and, with Mr. Vaux's help, the cupboard was carried up the lane to the van. Tony was as nervous as a cat. (If Paul came up from the river before the abduction was completed there would have to be silly explanations.) He breathed a sigh of relief when the van bumped away to the main road, bearing the gift for Theodora. Paul would not notice its absence. . . . He didn't appear to notice anything these days. . . . It was like living with a deaf mute.

Tony went into 'The Load of Hay' for a mug of beer.

During lunch Paul scarcely spoke at all. Once he shouted to Jackson: 'There's a storm coming, you'd better get off directly you've washed up,' and then he sat glowering around the room like a caged tiger.

Tony had pushed a chair and a small table into the corner recently vacated by the cupboard and he hoped that everything looked all right; but when Paul's eyes became fixed upon the denuded corner of the room so ineffectually screened, Tony rose quietly from the table and, bearing his coffee cup, he went out into the orchard. Not a sound came from the cottage and the silence seemed ominous.

Tony strolled on a little farther, sipping his coffee, and trying to look unhurried. As he got to the bank above the lane he saw that Viola Peacock was sitting across the way in her usual position as guardian of all local exits and entrances.

'Cerberus,' said Tony loudly, and Viola glanced up and frowned.

'Didn't mean to frighten you,' said Tony. He looked swiftly over his shoulder and then scrambled down and went over to the wall, where he placed his cup and saucer.

'I was thinking about my dog.' He smiled lazily and sighed. 'Stifling, isn't it?'

Viola huddled back into her chair and stared blankly at him.

'Not afraid of being caught in the storm?' he asked. 'It's going to pelt fire and brimstone. We might have to take to the roof, you know. . . . Might be the second flood.' He chuckled, visualizing an ark inhabited by himself, Paul, and the Peacock family. He looked up at the sky, but though there were heavy black clouds around the sun the glare was so intense that for a moment he saw nothing but whirling, scarlet catherine-wheels.

'The atmosphere tastes like a rusty nail. . . . Do you think that is the way the inside of a horse's mouth usually feels? Bit and bridle—you know——'

Viola's head seemed to sink farther into her shoulders and she raised her tiny bird-claw hands to her ears.

'Sorry, was I shouting?' He snatched another swift look behind him and saw Jackson disappearing down the lane towards the river.

'This creature is difficult to talk to,' he thought. 'Old Hector may not say much, but he's exceptionally responsive in his way.'

'I'm a bit on edge to-day,' he said. 'Storms brewing all around and I'm not so easy in my mind as I could wish. Ever feel that way? No criminal offence according to your own—er—civilized code, but a mortal sin in the eyes of the savage tribes of Israel. Thou shalt not steal—you know? Thou shalt not dispatch tokens to another man's wife, neither shalt thou curry favour by unlawful means.' Tony sighed and looked hopelessly at Viola's stony countenance. 'Think we could be discovered chatting gaily if old Paul came along?' he asked pathetically. 'Must be kind to old war wounds, though,' he continued. 'They cover a lot of sins—especially the scars you don't see'; he tapped his head. 'But he's got three holes in his leg.'

Viola suddenly straightened in her chair and looked interested. Tony twiddled his fingers, playing an imaginary tune.

'Expect he could play a tune on it. Piccolo in leg——' He groaned as he realized that Viola's attention was not for him, and, without turning his head, he knew that Paul was approaching.

'Tony, where's that cupboard?'

'What cupboard?'

'The one you painted, of course. It's been spirited away. It was there this morning, I could swear.'

'So could I,' thought Tony. 'Oh, observant fellow, how I wronged you!' He added aloud: 'I didn't know you'd noticed it.'

'What do you mean? I bought it, didn't I?'

'Yes, yes—just a few shillings. Of course—you told me. Didn't realize you'd noticed that I'd painted it.'

'Very charming. Where is it?'

'I've sent it away.'

There was a long pause and Tony smiled invitingly across the wall at Viola.

'Amazing likeness, wasn't it, Miss Peacock?' he said sociably.

'Shut up,' Paul said loudly, and leaning on the wall near Tony he knocked against the cup and saucer and they fell and broke on the stones in the lane and the sound seemed to ignite Paul's temper.

216

'Where have you sent it? First thing *I've* heard about it. Don't remember your asking me if you could take my furniture out of my cottage.'

'Oh, it's all right Paul—didn't want to bother you. Thought it might please somebody—pretty little thing like that. I've—er—given it to Theodora.'

Paul drew in his breath sharply and asked icily: 'At a price, I suppose?'

'Certainly not. I thought she'd appreciate——'

'Painting or no painting, it wasn't yours to give.'

'Oh, well, old boy, it's still in the family.'

'Sneaking behind my back,' Paul shouted wildly. 'Thought you might not get anything out of me. What? Making sure of Theodora behind my back. What?'

'Don't keep on saying "What?"' said Tony, as angry and flustered as a hen.

'I'll say what I damn well please, you dirty little thief!'

'I'll pay you for the blasted thing, you old Shylock.' Tony's voice rose to a scream.

'So that's the way you feel about it.' Paul lowered his voice and put his face close to Tony's. 'You think I care about the money?'

'Sounds like it,' Tony murmured, trying to curl his trembling lips into a careless sneer.

'Get out,' said Paul very quietly. 'Go on, get out.'

'By all means. How would you suggest——'

'With Jackson. You can get a train in Southampton. I presume you have your fare as you have just offered to pay me for your theft. I decline to accept payment—keep the few shillings for your journey.'

'Good afternoon, Miss Peacock,' said Tony faintly. He raised his degraded straw hat and walked off down the lane.

Paul closed his eyes and gripped the top of the wall until his knuckles turned white.

'I'm going mad,' he whispered. 'Oh, God! I'm going mad.'

A cold, soft touch on his hand made him shudder and look up. Viola had struggled to the wall and with open mouth and startled eyes she was studying his face. Bent and shrunken, panting and mewing like an animal with a broken back, she crawled nearer to him and her cold hands clutched at him. He jerked backwards with a cry of horror and ran blindly up the lane.

.   .   .   .   .

Tony stood on the deck of the *Theodora* holding his overcoat round him as if it were the draped folds of an evening-cloak. The sun was totally eclipsed by ponderously rolling black clouds. A sudden wind crimped the water and the air turned icily cold. Tony's stomach contracted uncomfortably and he groaned. By the gate of the pier he saw Hector standing but he felt too weak even to wave his hand. As the boat got under way he closed his eyes.

'Think you could lend me a quid, Jackson?'

'Certainly, sir.'

Tony tottered into Jackson's little cabin and stretched himself upon the bunk.

.   .   .   .   .

Hector stood staring at the *Theodora* until she disappeared around the bend of the river. With open mouth and limply hanging arms he stood planted on the bank, staring and staring. Then suddenly he gave a short, piercing cry and drummed his fists wildly against his forehead.

He had just come from the wood, and sauntering slowly along the river path looking for Tony, he had seen the yacht's dinghy putting out from the pier. Not until he noticed the tripod and canvases being unloaded did he become alarmed. Tony never put forth upon the waters—that great experience was being reserved for the day when he and Hector were to sail together. Hector had not forgotten the evening by the wall and the solemn promise they had made to each other.

The figure in the dark overcoat came to the rail and looked across the water to the pier and then, turning away abruptly, disappeared into the cabin. Hector was transfixed with horror and his mind was in such confusion that he could do nothing but stand staring helplessly until the yacht was nearly out of sight. Then he realized that he had failed his friend. The hour had struck and he had not been at hand. With that one wild cry and upflung hands he began to run along the bank towards the marshes. Beyond the bend the yellow, spongy grass sank beneath his feet. The yacht was far down the estuary, dipping delicately to the waves rolling in from the Channel. Hector's arms gestured like storm-tossed branches.

'Wait for me!' he screamed. 'Wait for me!' and the

rising wind drowned his voice. Panting and sobbing
he stumbled back to the pier and squelched through the
mud to his dinghy. He pushed it out until the water rose
above his waist, and then he scrambled aboard and
seized the oars. The rowlocks screeched as he swung
backwards and forwards digging at the water desperately.
His chest ached and his head lolled from side to side, and
once, flinging it up as he pulled, he saw the black sky,
the hill and the house outlined in the coppery glow, and
his sister Clare standing against the paddock rail waving
to him. He swung forwards, and back again, sobbing
for breath.

.   .   .   .   .

When Paul ran up the lane Viola had but one thought:
she must find Clare. All around her, in nightmare silence,
she saw walls crashing down. Without a sound the
ghostly masonry toppled over and an icy wind rushed in
and tore at her. She was frightened; she gasped like a
fish flung from its safe prison of water by an explosion.
Swinging her head from side to side she saw only foreign,
unfamiliar things. She tottered from the wall, trying to
run, completely lost in a strange and terrible world she
had never looked on before. Half-way across the garden
she fell and lay for a moment with her face against the
grass. She tried to call out for Clare, but no sound came.

A moment ago a ghastly discord of screaming and
shouting had pierced the silence—sounds she had never
heard before. Everything had gone black for a while
and then great shadows of trees had leapt up in a sudden

glow of light and swung swiftly back into darkness. . . .
Then she had gone quite deaf and her eyes beheld the
silent disintegration of the walls round her. She was lost!
She was unprotected! Where was Clare?

On hands and knees she struggled through the gate
and pawed blindly at objects which rose before her.
Like a wounded animal dragging paralysed legs she
crawled across the step and into the sitting-room. She
lay for a moment with her head against the sofa and the
clock ticked busily between each slow breath that she
snatched.

A red blind was half-drawn down on the window above
her head and it tapped in the wind.

'Tick—tick—tick,' went the clock in rapid rhythm.
'Tap—tap—tap,' the blind struck in with a slower beat.
And far behind, slower and slower, the gasp of laboured
breathing.

The thing against which she leant was floating away
and with a supreme effort she pulled herself on to it and
lay with her face turned to darkness. She opened her
lips once, trying to speak her sister's name, and then,
as if in answer to the unuttered cry, she heard steps
approaching. The silence broke once more, but this
time there was peace on the air and a soft voice said:
'Viola?' She was a long way away, and she did not turn
her head. She knew Clare would reach her. . . . A
gentle hand brushed against her cheek, then rested
lightly. She smiled happily as she floated onward with
Clare's hand upon her.

.   .   .   .   .

Clare had been in the loft when she heard the wind rise and the thunder roll nearer. 'The storm is coming,' she thought, 'I must get Viola.' She gathered up Sherbet and scrambled down the ladder. As she crossed the yard she looked towards the river and saw Hector in his boat and she ran to the rail and waved—pointing to the sky and calling to him against the wind.

'What's the matter with him?' she wondered in distress. It was unlike him to be stupid about weather. . . .

A peal of thunder echoed away above the woods and rolled back, gathering volume, and Clare ran swiftly to the garden. When she saw the empty chair she walked back to the house, supposing that Mrs. Humble had waked from her afternoon nap and fetched Viola. Perhaps they knew where Hector had gone.

As she entered the sitting-room she saw her sister lying on the sofa with her face buried in the cushions.

'Viola?' she said softly, and as there was no reply she tiptoed to the window and put a heavy book on the cord of the tapping blind. Gently she turned her sister's head to a comfortable position on the cushions and stroked her cheek.

Mrs. Humble opened the kitchen door and came in with the tea-tray.

'Oh, I was just going to get 'er 'ighness. It's going to rain cats and dogs.'

Clare put her finger to her lips.

'She must have come in by herself. She's worn out,' she whispered. 'Humble, Hector has gone down the river. . . .'

'Well, 'e'll catch it,' Mrs. Humble whispered back.

Clare frowned and stood thoughtfully stroking Viola's cheek.

'Humble . . . she's awfully cold. Don't you think we'd better light the fire?'

'Summer's hover,' said Mrs. Humble, taking a box of matches from her apron pocket. As she bent over the grate the thunder cracked above the house and soot came tumbling down the chimney. There was a rushing, crackling sound like large sheets of stiff paper being crumpled and down came the rain like a volley of spears. In a moment the gutters were gurgling musically.

'Hector——' whispered Clare, but Mrs. Humble interrupted impatiently:

''E's on the marshes by now, poking around. 'E'll come 'ome by land in double quick time——' she stopped speaking suddenly.

Sherbet had been pacing uneasily up and down the room, and just then he had slumped down against the wall. His fat white throat swelled and trembled; his silly mouth opened and a long howl shook the room as if it had been a belfry shuddering round a tolling bell. Mrs. Humble stared at him, straightened herself, and then turning her head she looked at the sofa. Sherbet's howl mounted again, and Mrs. Humble dashed across the room, slapped Clare's hand away, and bent over Viola.

'Go and fetch yer father,' she said in a funny, strident voice.

CHAPTER V

RAPID walking along the main road failed to cool Paul's temper. He would far rather have gone home and stormed within four walls, or rowed out to the yacht and given Jackson a talking to about the unsatisfactory condition of the *Theodora's* engine. But circumstances demanded his absence while the subjects of his wrath made good their rapid departure. He tramped dejectedly towards the village brooding over his manifold wrongs, until the terrific thunderclap, followed by the cloudburst, drove him into the shelter of the wood, and he turned back towards Prince's Acre at a run, forgetting his troubles in the present discomfort. The rain poured down through the branches, vivid flashes of lightning broke through the sudden darkness, and he realized that he was in considerable danger dodging amongst the swaying, storm-bent trees. He was soaked to the skin by the time he regained the lane and, splashing blindly over the flooded ruts, he collided with Mrs. Humble, who ran towards him with an old macintosh over her head.

'Oh, sir! sir!' she shouted above the wild drumming of the rain. 'We've nobody to send to the village—we must 'ave a doctor.'

'What's the matter?' he shouted back, dashing the rain from his eyes.

'Miss Viola, sir; she's gorn! Oh, please, sir, could

your man go for the doctor?' She repeated the request
several times as the rolling artillery above nearly drowned
her voice.

'Jackson's gone to Southampton on the boat—taken
my friend to the train. . . . I'll go to the village. . . .'

'Oh, Gawd!' screamed Mrs. Humble, clutching at the
flapping folds of the macintosh. 'That's what 'Ector was
after, going out in the storm. . . . It's the hend of the
world, sir.'

Completely bewildered, Paul struggled back up the
lane to 'The Load of Hay' to get the car.

'That child can't be dead,' he thought. 'I saw her in
the garden only an hour ago. . . . What was she yelling
about the boy? Is everybody going mad?'

Paul did a noble deed that afternoon. In the worst
storm that there had been for years he drove along the
flooded, tree-bordered road and brought a doctor on a
fruitless visit to Prince's Acre.

In the evening the thunder rolled away fainter and
fainter, tumbling and reverberating across the Channel,
but the rain sheeted down ceaselessly. When the men in
the cottages came home from work Paul waded along the
marshes with them, searching vainly for Hector or a
sight of his dinghy.

Late that night he splashed across the yard and stood
hesitating before the closed door of the farm. The
windows were curtained and no light shone anywhere.
The overflowing gutters bubbled and sang and the gusty
wind splashed rain in a deluge upon his face.

'Perhaps I'd better not go in,' he thought as he turned

miserably home. 'It is really a mercy. . . . Christ, what a day!'

Jackson had not returned and the cottage was in darkness. He sat huddled on the sofa, shivering and listening to the monotonous pounding of the rain.

'A place of death. A place of death again,' he repeated stupidly, and his teeth chattered.

'We are all being buried alive!' he suddenly shouted aloud, and sprang to his feet. He struggled up the narrow stairs and took off his soaking clothes. Still shivering he lay on the bed, staring into the darkness and listening to the muffled pounding of the rain upon the roof of his tomb.

.   .   .   .   .

Day came with limpid clearness. Small clouds floated across the blue sky and there were pearly colours in the mist wreathing from the soaked earth. The petals of the flowers in the garden were bent forward like parasols blown inside out and the air was full of the musical 'drip, drop' from all the trees. A fat thrush on a high branch of the walnut-tree began to trill and then was silent, turning its head from side to side in comic surprise at itself for such a strange outburst. It flitted softly to the lawn, and with head still jerking from side to side it pecked at a worm in the spongy moss.

Going down the lane towards the river Paul saw the sunlight sparkling on the window-panes at the silent farm.

The *Theodora*, like a phantom ship, came ruffling softly up the estuary through the pearly mist. She swung quietly to her moorings, and Jackson came to the rail and began to wave his arms at Paul leaning on the gate of the pier.

'What the hell is the matter with him?' Paul muttered furiously.

Jackson began to shout, and Paul's irritation increased for all he could hear across the water was: 'Ow, wow—wore wow.' And yet the voice was frightening, for, without knowing why, Paul wanted to run away—run from the news that silly, indistinct voice was trumpeting.

Perhaps he had picked the boy up.

But when he saw Jackson climbing alone into the yacht's dinghy and pulling for the shore Paul knew that there was never really any hope for the people of Prince's Acre. (He had not seen Clare or William the previous evening when he had waited in the car whilst the doctor made his brief examination, but the old woman had come to the door, still hooded in the ridiculous macintosh, and had shouted to him: 'We could bear it, sir, if we only knew that 'Ector was safe.')

Jackson fastened up under the pier and scrambled out holding something in his hand.

'Picked it up about a mile out,' he said excitedly as he came to the gate. 'Thought it belonged to the young gentleman from the farm. . . . The bright colour 'e'd painted it. . . . Not a sign of the boat, though I went in circles for about an hour. . . .'

Without a word Paul stretched his arm over the gate and took the bright green oar from Jackson's hand.

'He's been missing all night,' he said at last. 'Couldn't he have landed on the sand-bank?'

'Went right around the bank, sir. Not a sign of anything. 'Ailed two fishing boats too, sir. Big sea running last night, sir, and the rain was enough to swamp a small dinghy. I waited till morning on account of the bad weather, sir.'

Walking slowly with the oar across his shoulder Paul went up the hill to Prince's Acre.

> There is not one,
> No, no, not one
> But thee to comfort a poor lonely maid;
> Thou art her mother,
> And her brother,
> Her playmate, and her wooer in the shade,

Paul recited firmly, but the words brought him no comfort. As he went round the house to the back door he noticed that the red blinds were still drawn down on the sitting-room windows. Mechanically his features assumed a look that mingled pity with determination. The task before him was not a pleasant one, but he had never been the kind of man who shirked an unpleasant duty. He had served these unfortunate people disinterestedly and gallantly during the last few hours, and they could but be grateful in return. He was conventionally sympathetic and not a little oppressed by the heavy atmosphere of tragedy hanging over Prince's Acre, but the sequence of disasters was, in reality, merciful. His comfort to the bereaved would be to point out to them that this was so. . . . Suggest to William (not too seriously, of course) that he could return to an active life . . . leave this melancholy place—this accursed spot.

Paul knocked on the open back door and stood leaning, in deep thought, upon the oar.

When one came to look at the thing all round it was really nothing short of a miracle. No longer would one be irritated and depressed by the sight of those two unfortunates.

Paul straightened his shoulders and knocked again, but his determination was withering. The silent house seemed so forlorn and deserted.

Impatiently he strode down the passage and tapped softly on the closed door of the sitting-room. He remembered, quite suddenly, the first time he had entered this house and the shock of surprise he had felt on entering the room now closed against him. The three, strange faces that had turned to him that day.

Very gently he opened the door and took a step into the room. The sunlight coming through the lowered blinds filled it with a dull fiery glow. The hanging lamp was alight, burning an ineffectual, forgotten star of light under the shadowed ceiling. On the sofa, under the window, lay Viola's body. From where Paul stood he could only see the two sharp points of her small feet breaking the smoothness of the white sheet laid across her. In a semicircle near the sofa, on three straight-backed chairs, sat the father, the daughter, and the old servant. Quite silently they stared at Paul hesitating uncomfortably in the doorway. They did not appear to be sitting there in reverent vigil—their anguished eyes— the eyes of caged animals—seemed to be waiting for some manifestation from without: waiting for release from torment, expecting, perhaps, that invisible gates would open. And yet they sat motionless, crouched, hopeless.

Paul felt a quiver of irritation at their inaction. They had made no effort to search for the boy. They had allowed the men from the cottages to tramp the sodden marshes through the night without even displaying the feverish anxiety of people who hope for the return of the lost one. They had no hope, no will, no spirit; they just sat and waited for somebody else to do something decisive. 'Defeatism,' thought Paul, and cleared his throat, searching for the appropriate key in which to pitch his voice.

'My man picked this up about a mile out to sea,' he said softly, and leant the oar against the wall, turning his head away so that he might not see those three pairs of eyes. 'He asked the fishing-vessels to keep a look-out, but he made a thorough search. I'm afraid . . .'

With a shriek Mrs. Humble flung her apron over her head and tottered out of sight into the kitchen.

'I'm terribly sorry,' he said weakly. 'If there is any-thing more I can do . . .' The words faded away and he stood uncomfortably in the centre of the doorway, wondering miserably, like an inexperienced actor, what to do with his feet and hands, and how on earth to make a natural exit.

Mercifully William had turned his head away, but two eyes still held Paul prisoner.

'You've done enough. You've done enough,' a voice said evenly.

Paul made an ineffectual gesture and tried to speak,

but suddenly he beheld the face before him disintegrate in the most loathsome and frightening manner. The flesh seemed to crumple like crushed rose-petals and take on a blotched, bruised appearance—like the face of some person who has been weeping for days and nights. But there were no tears in the girl's eyes; they were abnormally bright and the welling passion in them seemed to overflow and engulf her distorted features until Paul could see nothing but the two great, dark eyes blazing at him. She rose quietly to her feet and stretching out her arms with the palms of her hands spread towards him she cried out sharply:

'Go back! Go back!'

Sweat lay on Paul's forehead and he tried (and failed) to shrug his shoulders. As he left the room he saw William Peacock put out his hand and draw Clare down on her chair—and there they sat again, two forlorn, witless, broken people.

He drew a deep breath as he got outside again.

'I'll have to leave this place,' he thought. 'I can't stand much more. . . .'

He went back to the cottage and ordered Jackson to pack, and then to take the *Theodora* back to Southampton and proceed to London. As he sorted papers and emptied the drawers of the writing-table he felt very determined. He frowned and his jaw stuck out pugnaciously. He was vaguely conscious that he hadn't really thought this decision out properly, and that if he paused for a moment, if he analysed his actions at all, some depressing and insurmountable obstacles would appear.

He ate his lunch hurriedly and then paced up and
down the room until Jackson had finished clearing
up.

'Shall I put the luggage in the car, sir?'

Paul turned and stood staring vacantly, and his breathing laboured as if he had been running.

'No,' he said sullenly.

'Shall I wait, sir?'

'No!' Paul repeated, shouting.

'Very good, sir.'

Jackson was trained to obey, unquestioning, the word
of command. Several years' service in the army and many
more as a personal servant had taught him not to think.
However peculiar the order, he automatically obeyed,
repeating mechanically:

'Very good, sir.'

As he surveyed the pile of luggage neatly stacked at
the door the automaton noted that nothing had been
forgotten and that everything was in its right place. But
as he went out of the cottage the human being beneath
the petrified mask of servitude showed itself for a moment.
He hesitated in the doorway and looked critically at
Paul's agitated face.

'Sure you'll be all right, sir?' he said faintly. He was
disturbed. . . . Things didn't seem somehow to be as
correct and shipshape as he could wish.

'Hurry up, Jackson, you'll miss the tide.'

Jackson, crossing the orchard, scratched his head and
grunted.

.   .   .   .   .

The afternoon advanced and the orchard was bathed in a humid golden light. The cottage door stood open and the orderly pile of expensive suit-cases still reposed on the mat. The quenched bonfire in the kitchen-garden at the farm had evidently been lit again, for the smoke floated over the hazel hedge and clung in the cool, still air amongst the apple trees. There wasn't a sound. Paul sat in the chair at his bare writing-table and stared into the golden mist through the doorway.

All of us have moments when life and the perpetual striving and conflict seem utterly useless. The centuries that have been, and those that will be when one is no more, stretch out endlessly and engulf the little present that is one's own. The brief moments of ecstasy that one has known dim before the knowledge of one's nothingness. One life is too brief and too unimportant to matter in the gigantic pattern of the universe. Why strive? Why suffer? Why moralize? Of what use is anything if it must ultimately be destroyed? The criminal and the saint, wrestling with their second of time in a world without end, are both turned to dust. And when this moment of melancholy does not pass people sometimes kill themselves and prove that they were right not to believe that life was a thing to cling to; for when it is gone from its possessor it no longer matters in the scheme of things.

Paul had reached the lowest depth of despair, and it affected him physically, so that he could not so much as raise a finger. Every thought (and now his brain revolved ceaselessly) had a mourning air. Every hope displayed its real character, its barrenness, and its frustration. And he who had cried out against war and destruction remembered days he had spent with Roger, in discomfort, in agony, and often in fear, as the best moments of his life. Then there had been something more than the unequal passion wrangled over by man and woman; something greater and more satisfying than this endless hope of the future—that was no hope, and no future. Then one had lived for the hour, fully, richly; sharing one's spirit with one's neighbour, welded together by a common fear and filled with the pure, uncomplex love of humanity that knows itself equal in all things. . . . But even that had gone from him; inequality had returned—they had died and he lived on.

Twilight filled the doorway and the ghosts drew nearer.

Paul sat shivering in the warm room and waited for the dead to materialize, to invade the room and claim him.

There was a rustle in the orchard; a twig snapped, and then another, and another louder and nearer. He felt the blood draining from his face and he was conscious of his numb, still body as if he stood outside it, looking at it.

A dark shape filled the doorway, blocking out the pale evening sky. It stood a moment and then moved towards him. . . . The pale sky and the netted branches; a star and the dark earth were framed once more in the doorway. The shadow stood at his elbow—he could not see it. A faint, familiar perfume filled his nostrils. He tried to speak, he tried to move, and, at last, with a moan he collapsed against Theodora's breast and felt her cool, strong hands imprison his aching head.

CHAPTER VI

Tony had reached London on Jackson's pound note, and there was very little change to spare. One small, battered suit-case, a tripod, and several canvases insecurely strapped together baffled him completely when he tried to mount a bus. He had but two hands and the conductor was abusive. Tony, sighing deeply (for he was thirsty) spent the remaining shillings on a taxi.

The noise of the traffic was deafening. He felt as if he had been living at Prince's Acre all these months with his ears stuffed with cotton-wool, and now that it was removed the sudden assault of sound distressed and exhausted him. He had taken an hour or two to recover from his sea-voyage, but as the train had drawn near the suburbs of London he had begun to see things more clearly, and he was able to relax his agonized concentration on keeping his stomach in its right place and turn his mind to more general problems. Bumping along through the traffic, he suddenly decided upon a course that had been till then no more than a vague 'Shall I?' or 'Shan't I?'

Tony had been worrying about Paul! All was not well in that quarter—he had realized that for some time past. A man didn't sit up all night, and every night, or jump at every sound, or fly off into wild rages about nothing at all unless his nerves were badly frayed. He couldn't banish the picture of Paul's twisted, angry face, or the

235

memory of the morning when Paul sat like a graven image
at the breakfast-table, gesturing like a mechanical doll—
looking as if one slight touch from a passing hand would
knock him over. Paul's corpse must not be found so
soon after his departure. It wouldn't look right. . . .
Theodora wouldn't like it, for she was funny about Paul.
She didn't like living with him, but she didn't allow other
people to hurt him. Paul's enemies were hers—a ridiculous kind of automatic loyalty. She never made secret
treaties. She said life was already too complicated for
her to side against Paul. Her feelings about him were her
own affair, but if anybody agreed with her treatment of
her husband, or even criticized him, she did not like it.
She had her own friends—people Paul didn't know—
and, as a side-line, Paul's friends were her friends—
until they became the common enemy. Without Theodora, who had always been kind in her admirable, cold
and impersonal manner, Tony felt that he would be in
a bad way. Undoubtedly Paul had finished with him,
but there might still be a method by which Theodora's
valuable patronage might be preserved.

Tony leaned out of the window and re-directed the
taxi-driver.

The lamps were alight and there was a thin autumn
fog. Tony felt the quiet melancholy that comes over
people returning from a long holiday enveloping him.
Indistinct memories of a silver river, a soft sky, and
evening light amongst apple branches returned to him.
He even felt a pang remembering the rich smell of the
breakfast coffee floating up the cottage stairs. The

illusive scents of country mornings and the feel of sun on his body, and the warm touch of sheets on waking, in silence, to days of luscious idleness. The noise enclosing him now was the voice of work and hurried living, and it pressed down on him, crushing him and making him feel rather forlorn and peevish. He told himself that it would pass when he got acclimatized, but he huddled into the corner of the musty taxi and shivered.

Reluctantly he handed his entire fortune to the driver. If Theodora had gone to a theatre or, worse still, was away on a visit he would be in the soup. He breathed a prayer as he soared, with all his worldly goods, up in the lift to Paul's super-luxury flat. He rang the bell—the prayer was answered, and the maid led the way into the sitting-room.

'There is not one thing in this room,' he thought, 'that I could pay for. Not a book, not a fire-iron, not even one single spray from that sheaf of madonna lilies in the great amber vase on the piano. . . .'

A door on the farther side of the room was open and a voice called sleepily:

'Who's that?'

'It's Tony,' he replied before the maid could cross the room. 'How are you, darling? Can I come in?'

'Is Paul here?'

'No, we're divorced.'

'Oh!' Her voice suddenly went flat and she added: 'What do you want?'

'Don't be rude. I want to see you. Are you in bed? Can't I come in?' He went in without being asked.

Theodora, in a grey-blue diaphanous *négligé*, was lying on a sofa standing at the foot of the bed and a supper-tray was on the table beside her. Light spilled softly from behind parchment shades, and she lay half in lilac shadow and half in amber light, her dark head turned on the pile of cushions and her sleepy, veiled eyes scrutinizing Tony as he stood with head on one side and his hands folded in front of him at the door.

'That is how women should always look,' thought Tony, narrowing his eyes and enjoying the delectable scene. (For a moment he quite forgot why he was standing there.) 'Women should always be beautiful; always rich; always lying down—just something to be looked at, dressed up, kept, admired. . . .' He turned his head slowly from side to side, peering first with one eye then with the other.

'Don't stand there like an inquisitive old crow,' said Theodora. 'I've got a headache. I'm going to Scotland to-morrow and I've taken a sleeping-draught and it's just beginning to work.'

The cold, unfriendly expression on Theodora's face must be banished. Tony decided to take the plunge at once and avoid further misunderstandings.

'Theodora, darling,' he said, padding around the room looking for a cigarette, 'Paul is not well——'

'In the jade box by my bed,' she interrupted acidly. 'Don't fidget. Sit down. Did Paul send you here?'

'Good Lord, no! We've had a row—about nothing. I'd sent you a bit of something I painted (it'll be here to-morrow) and he blew up——'

Theodora suddenly laughed.

'Oh, Tony, what a triumph. Was he jealous of *you*?'

'Be quiet! I'm by far your most ardent admirer—if you only knew. I don't believe he'd have cared a damn—ordinarily—but he hasn't been sleeping. He sits up all night and looks like something the cat brought in.'

'Why does he stay there if he's ill?' asked Theodora lightly. 'He said on the telephone that he was having a lovely time (I felt quite piqued!), and that he was working better than ever. Don't you think you are exaggerating, Tony? You know, it's not like Paul to do anything he doesn't want to do.'

'Well, he must have changed since your day,' said Tony bluntly, and Theodora flashed him a clear, open-eyed glance.

'I know quite well,' she said quietly, 'that he sometimes gets worked up when he's writing, and then, you know, he had a bad time in the War.'

'Oh, yes, but it is worse than ever before,' Tony sighed, and wished that Theodora were not quite so cautious. 'He's been absolutely obsessed with this book he'd got to write about that poet—but I don't know that he's done much about it. He's got something on his mind and it's eating into him. He hates the place and he won't leave it—never stops talking about what a loathsome hole it is.'

'And is it?'

'No, it's divine—only a bit queer.'

There was a short silence and Tony closed his eyes and saw Prince's Acre. He smiled and breathed slowly as if he were taking an anaesthetic, and then the vision and the sensation vanished as Theodora spoke.

'How, queer?'

Tony shrugged his shoulders and she looked keenly at him.

'What are you getting at, Tony?'

'Simply that I know he oughtn't to be alone. I got so on his nerves that it was worse than useless for *me* to stay,' said Tony, and added carelessly: 'I thought I'd better clear out of my own accord before he booted me out—or cracked me on the head. Honestly, Theodora, I'm miserable about old Paul.'

A smile flickered over her face and, quite suddenly, she changed the subject.

'Don't you want a drink? Go and help yourself in the next room—there's a decanter on the table by the piano.'

When Tony came back with a treble whisky Theodora was sitting at her dressing-table, her face supported between her hands and her heavy-lashed eyelids closed.

'Tired?' he asked, standing behind her and studying her reflection.

She lifted her eyelids slowly and looked at him in the mirror and smiled teasingly.

'Funny person,' she thought sleepily, 'No trouble whatsoever in a bedroom. . . .'

'What's the joke?'

Theodora shook her head and Tony moved away humming softly.

'This is the place for the cupboard,' he said.

'What cupboard?'

'The one I've painted for you. It's lovely.'

'Oh, Tony, how nice. Do you think it'll be very, very valuable one day?' Theodora was still smiling.

'Yes, very, very valuable—one day.'

'You shouldn't give it to me then.'

'I'd like you to have it,' he said with disarming simplicity. 'You can sell it for a fortune when you're a penniless old lady—good investment for you.'

'You might want to take it away from me, Tony, when you're a penniless old man. . . . I've got a much better idea. I shall give you something on account. Now don't protest——'

'I wouldn't dream of it,' Tony whispered.

'It'll be a sort of option, you see. You can't take it away without refunding then.' She opened a drawer and held out her hand to him, and he felt the joyous crispness of paper in his hand.

'You're a good business woman, Theodora.'

'Pretty good business woman yourself. Now kiss me good night—I'm drugged to death and I must sleep, and, much as I regret it, I have to add, in the master's absence you can *not* sleep here.'

Tony had been prodding the mattress of the bed thoughtfully and he turned away with a sigh.

'Lovely bed. . . .' He kissed the top of Theodora's sleek head. 'Going to Scotland to-morrow?'

'I usually keep my appointments,' she said crossly and, getting up, she pushed him towards the door. 'Oh, go away, you bird of ill-omen.'

Tony chuckled as he tiptoed away with a ten-pound note in his pocket.

.   .   .   .   .

Theodora lay in bed and struggled to resist the effect of the sleeping-draught.

All this had got to be thought out, and what made it so hard was that 'all this' had been thought out, over and over again, the whole summer—her holiday had been ruined. Perhaps a day would come when she would no longer be restless; when life, her own personal and inviolable life, wouldn't matter so much. One would just give in and be a good wife gracefully. She had seen that moment approaching many a time, and had ever experienced an emotional exaltation at the thought of sacrificing her individuality and forcing herself to like all the things that she disliked in the trying system of marriage.

Unfortunately for their joint peace of mind she rebelled at the last moment and flung away from him with no better excuse than that he irritated her and he would not alter. Tony said that Paul was changed. Theodora knew better. It was just an extreme example of the same old trouble. Paul suffered for a motive—he was drawing her back to him in the surest way. An unfair emotional attack upon the weakest joint in her armour. She loved him for his dependence, his weakness, his need of her as a background, a prop, and a reason for existence, and then she hated him because he would not own it, would not be honest with himself and submit to her power over him. He schemed and intrigued to win her, straying about as helpless as a two-year-old crying for its mother, and when she fell into the trap and flew to him he suddenly became arrogant, a law-maker, a dispenser of justice, and she was expected to play an inferior role.

She adored his need of her; it was bliss sometimes, and yet it wasn't love or marriage—all the cruelty, the misunderstandings, and truces.

Perhaps they should have married quite different people. . . .

Perhaps she ought to have a child and transfer her emotions to some one who would last her lifetime—if she lived no longer than the child's dependent infancy!

It was a ridiculously intricate and tangled web, but it was a universal muddle: everybody was in it, one way or another, and there were compensations.

Turning restlessly on her pillow, Theodora tried and, much to her disgust, failed to think, at that moment, of any compensations. Instead, she tortured herself by remembering a multitude of things that had irritated her. She knew that she must go to Paul, and that she wanted to go to him, but there must be no self-deception, no false hopes of a changed future. This time it would have to be for ever—good-bye to dissatisfaction and restlessness, for he would never alter. It was she who must change, discipline herself, submit—some kind of quiet happiness might follow.

Her head throbbed and she sat up amongst the pillows and lit a cigarette. The sleepiness had worn off, but she felt depressed and rather sorry for herself.

Just once more she would rehearse some of the things

that annoyed her most—feel all anger and impatience fully and completely so that she would be purged and incapable of ever reacting to them again. It was quite wrong that a person so fundamentally good as Paul could upset her so much and so often. It was petty of her, it crippled her love for him, and it must be crushed—for ever!

Theodora's eyes moved sadly round her lovely room and lingered on the glow of gold-backed hair-brushes and her discarded rings, passed on to the folds of the silky blanket, and her hands crossed lightly on the embroidered sheet, the lengthening ash of the cigarette—a dozen details of her surroundings.

She thought of Paul listening to music. He wasn't musical at all; it was a silly *snobisme* about people with Jewish blood understanding music. And yet he had the most uncanny memory for tunes. He said 'Tut, tut,' loudly when he thought somebody was singing out of tune; and going to a concert with him was bound to be embarrassing. He would be restless and superconscious of the other members of the audience as if he were the star turn of the evening. He always took seats in the front row of the stalls, and even after the music started he'd keep turning his head as if his collar rasped him. Actually he was trying to see the people behind him, and wondering (in the inconvenient darkness) if he knew them or (more important still!) if they knew him.

A seat in the front of the gallery with a pair of powerful night-glasses would have been better for his purpose—but Theodora had never dared suggest it.

Sometimes, after a violent twist of the tortured neck, he would espy an acquaintance and bow elaborately before settling down, in a pompous, satisfied way, to join in with unerring knowledge (so curious, considering his previous inattention) at the exact place the music had reached. He hummed tunelessly and waved his hand, beating time. Sometimes, when the orchestra was muted by the conductor, Paul's humming was the only sound heard in the hall as the waving of his beautiful hand exhorted the instrumentalists to disobey their leader.

But for all his apparent unself-consciousness he was immediately, vividly aware that he had made a mistake when he burst gaily into a bar that had never been written. He would clear his throat to expel the sounds that were issuing from it *malgré lui* and give his companion a shrewd glance of scarcely veiled dislike. And then, passing his hand over his face, pinching his nose with a delicate thumb and forefinger *en route*, he would gaze dramatically at the roof and murmur: 'Wonderful! Wonderful!'

Under cover of the next outbreak of music he would blow his nose several times very violently, and, leaning over, he would ask her if she felt the draught from the door.

By then at least ten rows of stalls would know that she was responsible for him.

The first time she had accompanied Paul to a concert she had laughed at him helplessly. He had raised his eyebrows and his face had twitched as he asked (in the tone one might use to an illbred, sniggering person who knows no better): 'And what is the joke?'

She had never laughed again, and only by great effort could she prevent herself from screaming. Chopin, Brahms, Beethoven—a hundred ghosts turned in their graves when Paul attended a concert.

There was Paul being jolly with waiters, making obscure jokes in three languages and embarrassing the poor devils, who felt the jokes were being made at their expense when they were not in a position to answer back.

There was Paul losing his temper with the same waiters (five minutes after the quips and humorous sallies) because the food was not to his liking.

Theodora had been obliged to eschew two of her favourite relaxations: concerts and meals in restaurants.

But, after all, these things were only characteristics, petty irritants that could be laughed off—she ought not to mind. . . . And then, suddenly, she remembered a day not long after their honeymoon when he had said something that had changed everything. Before that moment she had been in love, in love with love, and positively lightheaded and frivolous about the sanctity of marriage. It had been an emotion and yet a conviction: one loved a person and he you, so everything was bound to go well—blissfully. But Paul had brought her down to earth with a bang and, at the time, she had felt she would never forgive him.

She could remember now how he looked that night when he had talked to her in a wise (positively parental) voice. Poor, frightened Paul who was so afraid of life that he must always shift his responsibility. His face had borne an expression of patient suffering as he told her that, sexually speaking, she was a disappointment to him.

She had uttered no word, made no defence or complaint to her selfish, inexpert husband. He, with his posturings and temperaments and frequent passivity, demanding her to woo him, to cherish and protect him— he had criticized her femininity.

Theodora pushed back the blanket and stretched her arms wearily above her head.

Thunder rolled distantly—away in the country somewhere there had probably been a storm. . . .

She switched off the light and turning on her side drew the pillows more snugly under her head. She was a little apprehensive. He wasn't normal, he did get ill. It might as well be faced. She could not banish the picture of an ill, frightened Paul trying to be strong and brave in self-imposed solitude.

Did he believe that his misery would punish her? She tried to thrust the suspicion aside. . . . 'Think of the compensations,' she told herself repeatedly, but the balance weighed ever more heavily on the other side. . . .

'I'll think to-morrow,' she murmured before she fell into uneasy sleep.

. . . . . .

Theodora took a taxi when she left the train, and the journey along the country road seemed interminable— the chauffeur had to ask the way several times and it was twilight by the time she reached Prince's Acre. She

inquired for final directions at 'The Load of Hay', and
then picked her way, tottering on high heels, down the
lane and through the misty orchard. She hesitated a
moment when she saw the cottage. There were no
lights in any windows, no sound, no life; the door
stood open. She went on again and stepped over the
threshold and peered into the dim room—and caught her
breath.

There he sat, his face white in the gathering darkness,
his arms extended stiffly in front of him on the writing
table—he looked like a person dispensing justice to an
invisible assembly. He didn't stir or speak—he appeared
not to see her.

Swiftly she crossed the little room, and as she reached
his side he collapsed suddenly against her as if his spine
had snapped.

As she held his head against her breast and smoothed
his forehead Theodora, the imperfect woman, felt as
if her life blood were flowing from her. Willingly she
was giving her life that he might live.

.   .   .   .   .

Paul didn't speak until Theodora had steered the big
car on to the main road. She had dismissed the taxi,
loaded the car, single-handed, with the pile of luggage,
and exchanged her unpractical shoes for a pair of Paul's
and four pairs of his socks to keep the large shoes from
falling off.

Mr. Vaux had watched the departure from the doorstep
of 'The Load of Hay'. He did not offer to help because

he was so overcome with suspicion and curiosity that he remained spellbound and open-mouthed. With narrowed eyes he had watched Paul trotting obediently and silently behind the strange woman who tramped up and down the lane and swung suit-cases into place, and peered professionally under the car's bonnet by the light of a pocket-torch, and behaved like a female whirlwind, sweeping all before her.

'Sad times at the Acre,' Mr. Vaux had remarked affably. 'No sign o' Peacock's lad, they tell me.' He had got no reply, and so he sucked his teeth and watched until the zooming of the high-powered engine had faded away beyond the trees.

Thoroughly disgusted, Mr. Vaux slammed the door and retired to the empty bar and left Prince's Acre to its darkness and its silence.

The trees had slipped away behind the speeding car and the road, bordered by mist-filled meadows, stretched before in the white shafts from the head-lights. Paul suddenly wrenched around in his seat and looked back. The wood, like a solid rampart, stretched under the star-spattered sky.

'It's like a tomb,' he said, and, turning back abruptly, he huddled down beside Theodora and his hand lay heavily against her leg.

'I wish I didn't feel so weak and dizzy . . . must keep my mind on the driving,' thought Theodora as she pressed her clumsily-shod foot down on the accelerator.

PART IV
HAIL AND FAREWELL

CHAPTER I

Mr. KAY was by nature a very kindly man. He had offered one of his farm wagons to bear Viola's coffin up the lane to the motor-hearse waiting on the main road. Mr. Kay was the only mourner who had wept, and he was quite uncontrollably moved when he saw his clumsily gathered garden-bunch laid across a shop-made wreath of lilies sent mysteriously from London. He and three of his hands, all cottage dwellers from the waterside, had been the pall-bearers. . . . That coffin had been no weight at all.

The solemnity and pomp of the simple burial would have gratified 'Her Highness'. Flowers from her kingdom, a voice intoning a majestic farewell, and the muted tolling of a bell—a fit passing for a queen. She had been so unlike her brother who shunned display. He was more like a bird who feels his wings begin to fail and seeks its own burial in some deep, deserted wood where waves of green roll overhead.

It had been a prime tragedy, thought Mr. Kay.

Once launched upon a stream of sentimental thoughts he remembered Charming. The Prince's Acre pasture was baked dry as an oaten biscuit and, in all probability, after such a fine summer, it was in the nature of things to expect a severe winter—no weather for the rheumatic and the ailing.

Charming should have a warm stable and a dry feed for the hard times.

Mr. Kay sent word to Prince's Acre that he was calling for the veteran, and Miss Peacock would be relieved of her charge.

As Mr. Kay was definitely a kindly man he had, of course, no intention of being cruel.

.   .   .   .   .

Clare slipped a halter over Charming's venerable head and led him through the paddock gate into the yard. He buried his whiskered muzzle in a pail of water and sucked up a cooling draught. She leant her head against his dusty side, and for the first time she felt the tears sting behind her eyelids and roll down her cheeks.

No chick, no child—no more light burdens to be gladly borne. Empty days and empty nights. No care to occupy the long hours and lessen the increasing anguish in light and darkness. All gone. . . .

When Charming went plodding up the lane with the man from Kay's, Clare felt the heavy hoof-beats battering on her heart.

.   .   .   .   .

The swallows that had built beneath the eaves of Prince's Acre had that season raised two broods. The last family of five were fledged and flying by the beginning of October, when out of the sky swooped the elder five and gathered with their younger brethren on the ridge-pole of the farm.

Neat and shining, gay and debonair, and not the least bit worn by so much care and nursery life, the parents instructed the ten perched children upon the journey they were all to take. They were in no hurry, for, when the lesson had been given and hearkened to, they wheeled amongst the chimney-pots for a last bit of sport. Down and out in a flash as clean as a knife—a giddy gnat snapped up, and then, as if they had hit against some invisible object in the air, the swallows shot suddenly upwards. Away, away, all together—a last turn over the top of the woods, a dive across the river, and there, beneath them, was a chequered landscape. Prince's Acre did not looked screened or separate from a bird's-eye view. From that height it was simply an indistinguishable part of the rolling, autumn country.

One more dizzy whirl around the old chimney-stack, one more English gnat, and then—forward! Southward! Southward!

CHAPTER II

THE squirrels garnered the ripe fallen nuts. Larders were being stocked in hollow trunk, in overgrown bank, in stacked wood-pile. All the sagacious creatures who winter at home and spend so many cold, dark days wrapped warmly into themselves in sleep were busy as the first frosts of the dying year crisped their furry coats.

But Tony, with the blunted teeth, soft hands, and vulnerable body of a member of the civilized human colony, had no natural sagacity. With empty pockets he could not provide for himself against the approaching winter. He could sleep as well as any squirrel; curling his thin body into a tight snail-shell, ducking his head and wrapping his arms across his chest until his fingers touched his shoulder-blades—generating a little tepid comfort and clasping it into himself. But hunger woke him, and the cupboard was always bare. Theodora's money had not lasted very long: a meal a day for a week or two and a great many bottles of whisky. Whisky was so satisfactory. You drank three or four glasses and then you were no longer hungry, or cold, or even dragged down and enchained with sleep. Wide awake and glowing with vitality he worked at an enormous canvas. Giant shadow-forms emerging from foam, from fog, from a luminous nothingness—a depth unfathomed, going down, down for ever, so that as he weakened, as his stomach contracted, and as his eyes began to mist he had to totter to his tumbled, rickety bed to keep from falling into the depth that he had painted—to keep from falling, head over heels, spinning onward, downward; winded, deafened, throttled, and broken—first his neck and then his spine snapping like twigs in the tornado of air rushing past—limb parting from limb; fragments of his body twirling away like leaves in the endless descent into the bottomless grave he had fashioned for himself.

At last he took the canvas down unfinished and turned its face to the wall and saw only the blank, white back staring into the room.

'And that is all there is behind a picture,' murmured Tony, wrapping a tattered, champagne-coloured pyjama coat round his throat like a muffler as he curled up on his bed.

Tony had no friends. Occasionally he attached himself to people—watched them with amusement and pleasure, enjoyed their lives quite impersonally, but never got involved or really interested. He quite liked everybody—impartially. He understood them in a way; particularly women—he sympathized with women and knew, better than they did themselves, how women felt about men. But it all passed and left no mark, no yearning or regret. He borrowed money when he could and drifted on contentedly, outwardly solitary and inwardly entertained by the world inside his head.

It was only at times, after a bout of work, when he was underfed and whisky lost its magic, that he had a sudden

257

feeling of rage against the world. All kinds of wild notions about unfairness and injustice rose up, and he felt ill-treated, caged, tortured, and he began to remember days of childhood—days when he had been fairly comfortable and a woman, a half-forgotten shadow-woman, had cared for him. Her featureless wraith would drift into the dusty studio and lurk in corners just out of reach. Tony would shake his dizzy head, search once more through empty pockets, and wonder if Theodora would lend him a pound, or if the fat Italian woman at the little restaurant down the street would allow him just a little more credit?

He'd been down town twice to see if he could find Theodora in (and Paul out), but Jackson (a wise, a sympathetic, and a knowledgeable man beneath the expressionless military exterior) whispered through the half-open door: 'Mr. Millard is in, sir; he's sitting with Mrs. Millard,' and he hesitated politely, half-inviting the caller to enter, and then nodding solemnly as Tony murmured: 'Oh, I won't disturb them. Don't say I called. I'll write . . .' The first time too Jackson had recounted, standing on the door-mat, all that had happened at Prince's Acre after Tony had left. 'Reg'lar 'olocaust,' Jackson said at the end, and Tony said: 'Christ!'

And so he wrote and, for a week, there was no reply, until one evening, going down the stairs, stepping softly to avoid disturbing his landlady who nested in the basement like a bird of prey, he found a letter on the door-mat. He read it by the light of the street-lamp shining through the dusty transom.

'DEAR TONY,

'Ethel Coburg saw the cupboard the other day and she is frenzied and panting for you to transform all her old heirlooms and what-nots. She's got no sense, but she has a kind heart, a neurotic passion to be modern, and pots of money. I said you were rather expensive!! But she's set on it and is sending you a cartload of stuff to strip and re-clothe. Just a word from an old friend: don't ask her for a bit in advance. She was brought up in the best traditions of "Coburg and Gugenheim" and will pay on the nail for goods *delivered*—but not a penny on tick or speck!

'I enclose a morsel and you can refund when the ship comes home. I think it's in sight! Paul is working on a stupendous volume and I am putting on weight.

'God bless us all.

'THEODORA'

The morsel was a five-pound note. Tony closed the door behind him and walked jauntily down the street. Lights shone through the fog like blurred moons and people hurried by with lowered heads—feeling cold, thinking about the winter, clasping parcels, and going home to fires and meals. They had such strange faces. A Chinaman shuffled along near the wall, hugging a loaf of bread and looking miserable and ridiculous, like a dog dressed up, in his bowler hat and dirty tweed coat. A group of dark-haired children ran past, and one collided with Tony. It lifted enormous, dark Italian eyes to his face, frowned, and then screamed something cheeky at him before scampering away. Two dejected bay-trees stood on either side of the door of the little restaurant and light filled the frosted panes. Tony hesitated a moment, questioning his stomach. . . . He wasn't really hungry —only rather in pain and feeling a bit sick. . . . He decided against the restaurant. He owed more than five pounds, and they might expect the arrears to be paid if he produced the note for his dinner. . . . He felt he didn't really want a square meal—a snack would be the best thing to settle his stomach and smooth the way for a few drinks. He'd feel better then and to-morrow he could eat something really substantial before setting to work on the Coburg woman's furniture. He visualized himself sitting in the corner of some snug bar, drinking slowly and thinking out the new designs. Happiness was once more in sight.

He pushed through the swing-doors of a public-house a little farther down the street, and having procured a ham roll and a double whisky he sat down at an empty table near the generously blazing fire. He nibbled slowly at the ham roll, sipped his drink, and, after a time, he sighed with relief and lit a cigarette. For a moment as he inhaled the smoke his head felt thick and dizzy, and then it cleared, warmth trickled through his limbs, his fingers uncurled, and he stretched his legs out under the table.

He had been so occupied with the business of food, drink, and warmth that he had taken no particular notice of the other clients in the room, but now, beaming benevolently upon the world, his eyes turned to the bar, where a few men were leaning. One man in particular attracted Tony's roving eye. He was head and shoulders taller than the people near him, and as he leaned forward with rounded back, intent on a newspaper, Tony opened his mouth in an amazed gasp.

Tony tilted the last drop of whisky down his throat and crossed to the bar, shouldering his way between the tall man and a weedy cockney who was soaking his moustache in the foaming crest of a Guinness. Tony pushed his glass forward noisily and ducking his head to a level with the newspaper he murmured:

'Hallo. Remember me?'

Blue eyes, dull and heavy, turned to Tony.

'No—why—should I?'

'What'll you have, Mr. Ralston?'

'Same again. I'm stinking already.'

'Come over by the fire. . . .'

Max followed obediently and huddled down in the chair opposite Tony.

'How's business?' Tony asked brightly. He felt very nimble and gay.

Max closed his eyes and rocked his head between his hands as if it were a huge weight he was about to lift and hurl away.

'Wha' 's business?' he muttered crossly.

'The South Sea Bubble and all that.'

'Here, who are you?' He held his eyelids up with his fingers and glared at Tony. 'I don't know you.'

'Oh, yes, you do,' said Tony, smiling. 'We met at

Prince's Acre.' He turned his head, offering his flawless profile with great archness.

For a moment Max's face cleared, and then it clouded again with an expression of pathetic despair.

'Been back there lately?' Tony asked.

'I can't.'

Tony, remembering Paul's story of William Peacock's money, nodded sympathetically.

'No, I suppose not.'

There was a long silence and then Max said suddenly: 'Ever been in love?'

'I'm always in love,' Tony answered lightly.

'You drink that,' said Max, pushing his glass across the table. 'I've had enough, and it doesn't do any good.' He turned his head away and stared at the fire.

Tony studied the profile before him. The features were almost perfect, but all vitality seemed to have deserted the man. It had been his terrific, blazing energy and liveness that had made him stand out as an unusual person, but now there was something dull, heavy, shrunken about him, and his face looked vacant and a little stupid. It was not the vacancy of intoxication that Tony saw before him so much as a complete transition from sunshine to shadow, or, perhaps, from youth to middle age. Tony suffered a change of heart, and whilst once he had thought Max beautiful and had gazed upon him spellbound he now felt amused and patronizing.

'Well, I expect you made a packet,' he said comfortingly. 'What's the next move?'

Max was silent for some time, and then he turned his

head and looking sharply at Tony smiled in a manner that, for a moment, brought back the ghost of the golden, vital person that Tony remembered.

'You don't look well,' he said quietly. 'Had a bad time?'

Tony was startled, and he shrugged his shoulders.

'Mind if I sit here a bit?' Max continued, still smiling.

'Good Lord, no. As long as you like. . . .'

'I believe I'd like to talk . . .' Max paused a moment, pinning Tony down with his penetrating scrutiny; and then he blinked and rubbed his hands over his face. 'Order what you like. . . . I've been boring myself for weeks.' He laughed quietly. 'I'll bore you for a change.'

He went on for a moment scrubbing at his face and knuckling his eyes, and then, shaking his head like a dog emerging from water, he began to talk—a monotonous, hurried monologue. People drifted in and out of the bar-room; voices were raised in argument. A woman going out with a man burst into irrepressible cackles of laughter, and her voice, rising and cracking into tuneless song, faded away down the street. The cigarette ends piled up on the ash-tray between Tony and Max, and the room was blue with smoke as they sat in that crowded place as engrossed and removed from the life around them as if they had been on a mountain-top.

'I fell in love,' said Max. 'It had never really happened to me before. I suppose I've always been too interested in myself, always going on to other things; no time for women—in a serious way. I hate being tied down, and always thought I'd be hopelessly tied down if I got married. It made me feel quite crippled—the idea of being faithful to one woman. . . . Thought they were all alike so that it was silly to ruin one's life sticking to one when there were plenty of the species scattered about the world if one wanted to go to them. . . .'

Tony wriggled in his chair and felt a mild glow of pleasure as he murmured inaudibly: 'Coarse fellow. Coarse, coarse fellow.'

'And here I am,' said Max, with a little more animation, 'crippled, devilled, drunk as a clown because I've just realized there is one woman different from all the rest— the only one I've ever cared about. . . . And she won't look at me, and I can't pass on this time—nobody could ever be the same. . . . You know, women are extra-ordinary creatures. I never realized before what extra-ordinary, wonderful, valuable creatures they were.'

Tony, sipping his third double, wagged a solemn head.

'I've had a lot of big ideas in my time,' Max went on, 'I thought of 'em, carried 'em out—only myself to blame or praise. The biggest thing of all was this island.'

Tony's head wagged more violently and he let out a snigger that was intended for a jolly laugh, but Max continued speaking unperturbed.

'It's been my religion. I saw myself leading the chosen few out of the wilderness; starting a new world, a new life, on my lines, ruled over by me. . . . Doing good and gaining power all in one; see? I made it sound as attractive as possible of course. If you *believe* in a thing,' he said with sudden earnestness leaning across the table and tapping Tony's chest with a strong finger, 'you can make it into that thing, however poor your material. It's faith that counts—believe a thing to be good, and right, and necessary, and then it'll happen. But there it is—no good now, without her. All my big ideas gone up in smoke. Let humanity sink, let the island sink; I can't do anything without her. I don't want to lead people any more—I don't care what happens to anybody—I only want her.'

'Who?' Tony thrust the question in quickly whilst Max paused for breath.

'Clare Peacock,' said Max automatically, and then he repeated the name. 'Clare Peacock. Everything else can go to blazes. She's worth more than the whole world. She's done all the things I only hoped to do—and no wind and bluster about it either. She can make people happy, she can. . . . I'd like to help her, I'd like to take her away to that island and keep her safe for ever. The rest of the world can go to hell for all I care—it will too, and I shan't try to stop it; I don't care a tinker's curse now what happens to the ruddy old place.'

A pleasant sleepiness was creeping over Tony's senses. He nodded solemnly every now and again, drank steadily, and wondered vaguely what it was all about, and he sighed in regret for the vanished Siegfried. 'I wish he hadn't lost his looks,' he thought, 'Such a beefy, ordinary looking person. . . . Oh dear, nothing lasts. . . . He's not beautiful any more. How bored I am!' He added aloud: 'Where are you living?'

'Over a garage in the next street,' Max answered

mechanically. He was staring at the fire and his thoughts were sad—and very far away.

'Why don't you live at the Ritz?'

'Can't afford it,' said Max in the same dreary voice. 'I had to buy the island after all. Couldn't let anybody else have it . . . don't want it myself now. . . .'

'So somebody else discovered it?' Tony chuckled and blew three perfect smoke rings. 'It evidently does *exist* then?'

Paul had made a great to do about something or other connected with this man's book. . . . Tony felt more and more bored and sleepy as he tried to remember that flurry of excitement in the past summer. . . . Too far away now to bother. . . . There was an island after all! He supposed it was funny, but he was too weary to laugh. . . . It was old history now . . . he'd passed on. . . . Max was deadly boring, with the same old story, the same old worries—not a bit progressive. . . . Probably if Paul had known the truth last summer he'd have had something to say. . . . But they'd all moved on. . . . There was a new background now, a new atmosphere —things didn't taste the same in London. Life had changed . . . one *must* move on. . . . Old history—like Mary Queen of Scots being beheaded, and the Christian Martyrs in Rome. . . . One tried to take it all seriously and imagine how they felt . . . make it important . . . personally tragic. . . . But it was no good; it was over and gone and done with. Last summer was a century ago.

Max looked up and glared at Tony for a minute. 'Of course,' he said sharply, 'it's quite well known—in those parts. But I'm the only person who has been on it for the last fifty years——'

'Well?' said Tony placidly.

'It's an old native burial island.' Max stirred the cigarette ash in the tray with a spent match. 'The high-priests used to carry the corpses there in canoes . . . nobody else was allowed to land—holy ground. . . . They laid 'em out in rows—year after year. . . . Then quite suddenly, fifty years ago, they abandoned it— rumours of black magic, evil spirits—the high-priests who had been there died horrible deaths and the natives thought there was a curse on the place. Of course it was plague—all those corpses rotting in the sun. . . . All the animals and birds died too. . . . Anyway, the story got round and grew in horrible details. Everybody accepted it, and the white traders never troubled to find out the real reason—they just accepted the story and avoided the island. . . . "You can't go there," they'd say if you asked 'em why nobody settled on the island. . . . "You can't go there"—just like that—no explana-tions. Idiots! I went. . . . Not a bone left—things decay, *and* ripen, in double quick time in those seas. . . . The earth had been wonderfully fertilized and the air was purer than any I ever breathed; but the natives wouldn't come near me when I got back—thought I was going to blow up and die any minute. I didn't tell the white people, and I didn't die—I wrote the book. . . . Changed it a bit . . . cut out the corpses and the infec-tions . . . thought that once they got there and *saw* the place they wouldn't care what it had been. . . . But I expect there were evil spirits after all. . . . I can't go back. . . .'

'Why wouldn't Clare Peacock go?' Tony asked sleepily.

'Obvious reasons—her life's not her own. . . . Anyway, I didn't come first. . . . I couldn't even tell her I loved her——'

'You're talking through your hat—there's nothing to stop her now.'

'What do you mean?'

Tony stared and muttered: 'Good Lord, didn't you hear?' and he struggled to think clearly. As a rule there was nothing he liked better than knowing something nobody else knew. 'First with the news' was a blissful state, but he felt so sleepy and Max was so dull. . . . He longed for bed, but he struggled manfully to overcome his torpor.

'They all died,' he said, yawning. 'Hector and Viola—stone dead, weeks ago. . . . Fancy you not knowing ——'

'Say that again?' Max leant across the table and gripped Tony's shoulder.

'Can't repeat myself——'

'Poor kid, poor kid! . . . Here, pay for the drinks.' Max sprang to his feet and threw a handful of silver on the table.

'No trains to-night,' said Tony. 'No trains to-night.'

Max hesitated a moment, and Tony, looking up sleepily, was startled by his magnificence—vulgar magnificence—rather like the Albert Memorial. . . .

'One train a day,' he murmured, 'and then you ride or walk—or something. . . . I forget——'

268

'I'll send a telegram,' Max whispered ecstatically. 'She'll get it just before I get there. Then I'll walk all night—can't keep still now, I must move in the right direction—and hop on to the train when it comes along . . .'

Tony lifted his heavy eyelids in the sudden silence and saw that his companion had gone.

'You and your old cemetery,' he muttered to the startled barman as he paid the bill and pocketed the change.

Back again in his studio he lay down without undressing.

A gleam from the street-lamp sifted through the dirty window. Passing footsteps rang on the pavement—there was frost in the air. Just before he fell asleep Tony had a most startling thought:

'Paul and Theodora snug in a double-bed again. . . . The Sailor King hot-foot after his village fancy. . . . What made me do it? Organizing the world, ensuring posterity—loathsome thought! I must be God! Oh dear, oh dear, what a responsibility!'

He slept.

CHAPTER III

THE days in October dawned reluctantly. The sun seemed loath to dispel the clinging mists, and on the damp, heavy-limbed trees a few leaves twirled lazily on brittle stalks, colourless in the opaque half-light. A blurred woolly edge outlined each horizon and the clotted tree-tops were merged and indistinguishable from hills and clouds.

And then, morning advancing, the mists absorbed, the sun rising higher, warmer, and clearer in the heavens, colour, like the glowing reflection of a huge fire, spread over the countryside. All the richness of a fruitful year, boiled up, melted down, and poured over gardens, fields, and woods in a burnished flood of colour.

It seemed so strange that though the eyes fell upon such hot, pulsing, red-gold waves yet the scent distilled upon the still air was heavy with aromatic and deep-rooted decay.

Once more in the afternoon Prince's Acre shimmered in its net of gold. Brightness streamed across the western sky, licked like flames around low clouds and edged them with a copper glow; flickered, leapt higher, more fiery, and then faded slowly—slowly dying down to an ashy curtain drawn over everything. Vaporous wreaths curled lightly from the fields and orchards where the cremated body of the summer lay.

All day beneath the walnut-tree beside the wall the sunlight was clearest and the shade lightest—here was a space encircled by heaping colours and filled with still, watery purity. At nightfall it was the darkest corner of the garden. Under those spreading branches day met night, and as they passed each other their fingers met and the shadows drew in and gathered there.

.   .   .   .   .

A windy night descending, flinging a tattered banner of clouds across the curve of the young moon cradled on the tree-tops.

The swiftly flowing tide swelled up the estuary and clapped cold ripples on the swinging stern of the last boat left at anchor.

The oil lamp at the pier-head reflected a broken shaft of light in the dark water, and the few warm windows along the path from the river glowed a little while and then went out, showing cold, blind eyes to the empty track.

The young owls beyond the hazel copse hissed and wrangled in their swaying nursery and then fell silent.

A night-bird hidden in the branches cried once, sharply, and the sound was driven into the silence like a nail tapped smartly home.

Clare leant her forehead against the window of her unlighted bedroom and watched the moonlight steal over the garden like a creeping cat. The dahlias and the asters by the wall rose from the darkness like some nameless and moon-grown blossoms, and the dew veiled the grass in a spangled mist. Without opening the window she knew the smell of the garden when it bore that familiar aspect. The scent of Hector's flowers and the pungent perfume of the walnut-tree where Viola used to sit. . . . Under those branches the darkest shadows had gathered, still as sentinels and formed in almost human shape.

Another year was fading and the last chapter drew near its close. Once more she heard the steady pulse droning in her ears and her whole being yearned towards it until the beat of her own pulse submerged it and gathered it into the enclosed throbbing of her heart.

A cloud sailed across the moon and darkness poured in a sudden deluge, overflowing everything. The strange bird cried again in the distant copse and there was a patter of falling twigs.

Under the window-sill two sparrows rustled in the creeper and nestled closer to the wall under its heavy curtain of foliage.

Clare behind the cold window-pane heard no sound; in her hand, pressed beneath her breast, she held a folded sheet of thin paper.

She turned from the black and empty glass and felt her way across the room. Her outstretched palm stroked across the bottom rails of the two beds, closed round the handle of the door and turned it softly. From the shadowed height at the top of the staircase she gazed down into the glowing well of light below.

Slowly she descended, her feet barely pressing each stair as her ecstatic spirit piling up wave upon wave floated her downward.

Through the open door of the kitchen she could see

Mrs. Humble sitting in the rocker with her feet upon the hob of the range and her hands folded in her ample lap. She was just sitting, part of the quiet, but not noticing the hush.

Clare felt a stab of pain for this unbearable patience. It was many years ago that she had first looked at Mrs. Humble objectively. Then there had been a trim, bustling figure; shrill, commanding, energetic; some one ageless and a little to be feared though often loved in an undemonstrative and taken-for-granted kind of way. And now, with a sudden flash, a piercing vision, she had looked again upon this person who still bore the familiar name but had a different aspect and a different meaning. The neat knob of iron grey hair secured at the back of the nodding head by two jet-studded combs. The whalebone in the high net collar of the black blouse seemed built to keep the proud head from nodding in too pronounced and feeble a way.

Soon a clock would strike and release Mrs. Humble from that naked, agonizing idleness and some task made familiar by a million repetitions would claim the faithful automaton.

Unconscious of the watcher by the door, she sat and her whole quiet body cried out in mute appeal for charity, for care, for kindness.

Every harvest falls beneath the blade. The rose can no longer cleave to its last drooping petal. Time dripping down, down like fingered beads upon a rosary, and the years piled up behind. . . .

Clare brushed her eyes with the back of her hand.

'There shall be some reward on earth for all that endless giving.'

'You shall come with me,' she whispered and, as though in answer, there came a soft drumming from the shadows.

Sherbet, stretched beside the back door, flapped a guileless paw and beat his tail upon the mat.

'And you, old clown,' she whispered again, 'shall be the first beast in Eden.'

She tiptoed to the study door and turned the handle. William, bent across his writing-table, was scribbling, in his tiny, copperplate writing, marginal notes upon a book of travel. Dry, sarcastic remarks marked the border of a page upon which the author described the habits of a lost Arab tribe.

As Clare's eyes rested on the bent and silvery head there came again that flash, that sudden lifting of habitual obscurity. There once had been a golden head, a tuneful voice, and something rather vague and undependable. A person who had let himself be shouldered out into solitude. A presence rarely felt and never called for.

William raised his head and smiled, and the fingers he uncurled to receive her outstretched ones seemed to make a gesture that called for aid.

Clare laid her cool fingers on his upturned palm.

'Father, Max is coming.'

CHAPTER IV

IT was just before Christmas that Tony's painted furniture began to make bright corners in London drawing-rooms. It was very expensive and rapidly becoming prohibitive for all but the really wealthy. But it was new, it was gay, it was beautiful, and, above all, so fashionable. Drawing-rooms were being transformed. Antique cupboards, tables, and chairs were stripped and Tony, at a price, wrought miracles upon scraped surfaces.

Tony was rich and successful, and indirectly (but only so slightly out of the direct line) it was all Paul's doings.

A cupboard in Theodora's bedroom had started the ball rolling. Theodora's women friends coveted that cupboard painted in limpid greens and blues and decorated on the panels with the most fantastic, elfin heads of a boy and a girl. If cupboards, why not chairs, tables, mantelpieces, bed-heads, doors, bathroom walls, and lavatory ceilings?

Decorations by Tony were a wonderful investment. A house was let for twice its usual value if Tony's wizard hand had transformed it.

Paul was a good business man, and he remembered a few chairs, a tallboy, and a screen lying in danger of decay in an empty cottage. One shouldn't be careless about valuable and beautiful things. . . .

(Mr. Vaux received a letter and a key. He was bidden

to unlock the door and remove the treasure to the warmth of 'The Load of Hay', where it would be called for.)

Paul had intended to send Jackson with the car. The back seat was to be spread with clean sacks and padded with rugs, so that the sharp corners of furniture would not damage the upholstery. The latter part of the programme was carried out as first conceived, but on the cold December afternoon that the big car set out for Prince's Acre Paul sat beside Jackson in the driving-seat.

Theodora had spent several days in bed with a heavy cold, and Paul had thought the arrival of all those gay nicknacks from the cottage would surprise and enchant her.

He had been very tender and attentive while she was ill. Paul was wonderful with sick people. He petted, fussed, and made a great ado with doctors and medicine-bottles. He insisted on sleeping in a camp-bed put up at the foot of Theodora's, and she said not a word when the overpowering stench of eucalyptus rose from that lowly couch where the thoughtful and cautious Paul lay drenched in disinfectants.

He had an alarm clock, with a melodious and unalarming chime, set on his writing-table, so that he would know when the hour struck for the invalid's dose. However pressing the work he had before him he rose and went to administer it in person.

Theodora emptied the bottleful of loathsome fluid down the lavatory and replaced the doses with a little light burgundy of the same colour as the vanished prescription. Paul, all innocence, measured and ministered till the last drop was drunk.

In the evenings he broke all his engagements and sat reading to Theodora. He read her all his favourite poems and choice passages of prose. Theodora, languid and beautiful (though a little snuffling and hoarse), lay back among snowy banks of pillows and did not listen. She did not listen, but she loved him with a tender, and sacrificial love.

Paul, sitting muffled to the eyes in his car, thought about his lovely wife all the way to Winchester, where he suffered a puncture in a front tyre and his mind was at once occupied with torment and rage. The jack stuck, the wheel jammed, and Paul, hunched in the ditch, surveyed the struggling Jackson.

Why had he come? Jackson could have managed the furniture alone. . . . But he'd wanted to see the place again. Strange, incongruous longing for a place where he had been so unhappy! He wanted to see a face again —wanted to see it smooth, peaceful, and childlike as it had once been. He must know if that face had returned to glow serene and tranquil as the young moon in that green hollow. That blotched, staring, terrified mask that had taken its place was only part of the ghastly nightmare he had suffered, it must have faded now. All was well with him . . . all must then be well with her.

Jackson murmured that the wheel was fixed. Paul jerked his head impatiently and, seeing a star, he realized with fury that it was tea-time—time for Theodora's third dose and, already, nightfall.

The beam of the head-lights made a bright tunnel down the forest road—mile after mile, and then, with a creaking of sorely tried springs, they turned from the good metal road and drew up in front of 'The Load of Hay.'

The bar was deserted and smelt damp and rather beery. A discouraged fire smouldered in the grate and the oil lamp burnt a wan blue flame.

London, only a few hours back, had been bright with a frosty brilliance. It had been busy, live, and progressive. Here in this hollow there were a deathly stillness and a rotting immobility, and, as though there were no hurry, no fever or warm blood in life, Mr. Vaux came stumping slowly down the echoing passage.

Paul curbed his irritation, selected a bank-note, and sent Vaux and Jackson to load the furniture. There wasn't even a drinkable beverage in the place—nothing but stale, inferior beer. He shrugged his shoulders and made for the door.

There was just time for a surprise visit—a friendly greeting. The black mood was banished and he smiled as he stepped into the dark lane.

'They're all gorn,' shouted Mr. Vaux with fatal intuition. He stood silhouetted in the lighted doorway and peered into the night that had swallowed Paul.

'Left the Acre?' Paul stopped short as if a door had been slammed in his face.

'Ah,' said Mr. Vaux sucking his teeth with relish. 'Mister, miss, the old woman, and the dratted dog. All gorn to live amongst the cannibulls with that seafaring gent.'

Paul stumbled forward in the darkness.

What was the old imbecile jabbering about? 'Cannibulls!'

His eyes became a little accustomed to the light, and he saw a pale line where the gatepost leant drunkenly to the lane. He tapped with his foot, took a step or two and banged his knees against the wall. He lit a match, but it sputtered briefly and was blown out.

It seemed darker than ever here, he couldn't see a thing. There is nothing more hateful than that lost, blind feeling when one cannot find a way in the dark. His nerves had never been the same since . . .

His groping hand brushed against a tree-trunk. That was the great tree on the garden side of the wall . . . of course it was darker under those branches; he remembered how they spread. . . . He looked up and saw no canopy of leaves, only a skeleton tracery of bare branches tossing against the wind-blown stars.

He stumbled to one side, groped again, and found the open gateway.

Funny . . . it did seem lighter in the yard, although no windows showed a welcome radiance. . . . But it was at the back of the house that they lived. . . .

As he turned the corner, a sudden wind sweeping from the estuary sprang upon him—a cuff on each cheek, his hat nearly blown off, and the wind had gone leaving an invisible and swinging branch tapping against a window-pane. A gutter dripped in a hopeless rhythm and not one window glowed. He reached upward on his toes and pressed his forehead against the pane and stared and stared. But all the longing and all the staring in the world could not light or fill that black, empty room.

He stood a moment with his head hanging and his cold

hands thrust into the pockets of his overcoat. He tried to think, but it was too dark and cold for thought. He raised his head and listened. The branch tapped, invisible, and the gutter dripped. . . .

Back to the lane he went and paused a moment by the gate. Something had stirred. . . . Or was it only fancy?

He turned his head towards that deeper night, then, frowning, he started forward again, when, just beside him, a voice said softly:

'Good night.'

Paul jumped. His heart swelled to his throat and, without answering, he went stumbling, plunging over ruts and furrows, up the lane.

.   .   .   .   .

The car roared on. The million lights of London glowed on the sky ahead.

Paul straightened in his seat. He had been half-asleep, but as he jerked awake a thought that had hovered beneath the surface of his mind leapt like a flame and presented itself in the forefront of his brain.

It couldn't have been one of the cottagers . . . not that kind of voice. It had seemed so extraordinarily familiar. . . . (Of course it would make anybody jump in the dark, being spoken to so . . .) Where? When? (Not like him to forget—anything.) But whose was the face and what was the name that belonged to the voice that had said softly: 'Good night?'

The first Virago Modern Classic was published in London in 1978, launching a list dedicated to the celebration of women writers and to the rediscovery and reprinting of their works. While the series is called "Modern Classics" it is not true that these works of fiction are universally and equally considered "great," although that is often the case. Published with new critical and biographical introductions, books appear in the series for different reasons: sometimes for their importance in literary history; sometimes because they illuminate particular aspects of women's lives, both personal and public. They may be classics of comedy or storytelling; their interest can be historical, feminist, political, or literary. In any case, in their variety and richness they promise to confuse forever the question of what women's fiction is about, while at the same time affirming a true female tradition in literature.

Initially, the Virago Modern Classics concentrated on English novels and short stories published in the early decades of the century. As the series has grown, it has broadened to include works of fiction from different centuries and from different countries, cultures, and literary traditions; there are books written by black women, by Catholic and Jewish women, by women of almost every English-speaking country, and there are several relevant novels by men.

Nearly 200 Virago Modern Classics will have been published in England by the end of 1985. During that same year, Penguin Books began to publish Virago Modern Classics in the United States, with the expectation of having some 40 titles from the series available by the end of 1986. Some of the earlier books in the series were published in the United States by The Dial Press.